U0009678

格列佛遊記
Gulliver's Travels

中英雙語典藏版

強納森·史威特——著

張惠凌——譯　黃郁菱——繪

晨星出版

小人國遊記

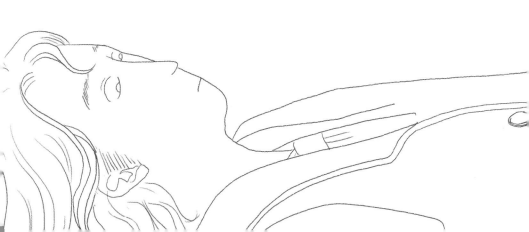

第1章

　　我叫格列佛，先後在兩艘船上當外科醫生，多次航行到東印度群島和西印度群島，我因此掙了不少錢。由於我在各處都能找到大量的書籍，閒暇時間裏我閱讀了許多古今最優秀的作品。每次停船靠岸，我都去觀察當地人的風俗人情，也學學他們的語言。憑著我強大的記憶力，我學習得很好。

　　有一回，我接受了「羚羊號」船主威廉·普利查德船長的聘請，起初我們的航行一帆風順……

　　那天大霧瀰漫，船被強烈的暴風雨吹到撞上了礁石，船身立刻爆裂，我和五名船員將小船放到海裡，盡全力划離大船和礁石，大約划了十英里遠，我們力氣耗盡，無法再前進了，只好任憑海浪擺佈，忽然吹來一陣狂風把小船掀翻。

　　我不知道船上其他人後來怎麼了，我聽天由命地游著，任憑風浪將我往前推進，不時地以腳尖探尋，但是一直踩不到底，眼看就要完蛋了。再也無力掙扎時，突然腳踩到地了，暴風雨也已經大大減弱。

　　海底坡度很小，我差不多走了一英里才上岸，那時大約是晚上八點，我又繼續往前走將近半英里，但是沒有見到任何房屋或居民。我疲憊到了極點，非常想睡覺，於是在草地上躺了下來，草很短很軟，記憶中我從未睡得如此酣沉。

　　醒來時正好是黎明，想站起身來卻發現自己動彈不得，我仰躺著，手和腳分別被牢牢地綁在地上，頭髮也同樣被綁著，從腋下到大腿，身上全都被細繩子橫綁。我只能向上張望，太陽越來越大，陽光照得刺眼。

　　周圍響起一陣吵雜聲，可是我除了天空什麼也看不到。過了一會兒，感覺有什麼東西在我的左腿上蠕動，輕輕地向前移，越過我的胸脯，來到了我的下巴，我盡力往下看，發現周遭盡是身高不到六英吋、手持弓箭、背負箭袋的小人們，推測至少有四十個以上。

　　我驚訝萬分，大吼了一聲，他們嚇得落荒而逃。其中有幾個急著從我的腰部往下跳，結果受傷了。

　　但是不一會兒他們又回來了，而且其中一個還走到能看清我整個臉的地方，舉起雙手，抬起雙眼，一副驚訝的模樣，他用刺耳卻清晰的聲音高喊著一句我聽不懂的語言，其他人也跟著重複喊了幾次。

　　我努力掙扎著，扯斷了繩子，扯鬆了地樁，總算鬆開了

左手臂，我把手舉到眼前，看清楚他們綑綁我的方法，再用力一扯，雖然十分疼痛，但還是將綁住我左側頭髮的繩子扯鬆了一點，這樣我的頭大概可以轉動兩英吋。

他們在我伸手抓到他們之前又逃開了。此時我聽見其中一個人大喊一聲，像是一道命令，隨即有一百多支像針一樣的箭射中我的左臂；他們又向空中射了一陣——就像我們在歐洲投下炸彈一樣——我猜想有許多箭落到身上，雖然我並沒有感覺到；有些則落在臉上，我趕緊用左手去遮擋。

一陣箭雨過後，我痛得呻吟起來，掙扎著想脫身，他們便向我發射更多的箭，有幾個還試圖用矛來刺我的腰，幸虧我穿著一件牛皮背心，那些矛刺不進去。我想現在最好乖乖地躺著，就這樣等到夜晚，因為我的左手已經鬆綁，可以很輕鬆地逃脫。至於那些居民，如果他們都長得和我看到的一樣，那麼就算他們派來最強大的軍隊，也不會是我的對手。

但是命運卻不如我所預測。

當這些小人發現我安靜下來，就不再放箭了，不過人數增加了。我的右耳聽見大約四碼外傳來敲敲打打的聲音，持續了一個多小時，我盡可能地把頭朝那個方向轉去，看見一個離地面一英呎半高的平臺，旁邊還靠著兩、三道梯子用以攀登。平臺可以容納四個人，其中站著一個看起來身分地位很高的人，他發表了一長串演說，但是我一個字也聽不懂。

　　他看起來像個中年人，比跟在他旁邊的三個人都來得高，那三個人中有一個是侍從，身高似乎只比我的中指略長一些，正捧著那人拖在身後的衣襬；另外兩人則分別站在他的左右扶著他。他是個十足的演說家，我看得出來他用了許多威脅的語句，有時也提出承諾，並且說了一些表示同情與友好的話。

　　我態度極為恭順地答了幾句，並且舉起左手，雙眼注視著太陽，請它為我作證。從我離船到現在，已經有好幾個小時沒有吃東西了，由於極度飢餓，再也無法克制不耐煩的情緒，頻頻把手指放入嘴裡，表示我要吃東西。

　　他完全看懂了我要表達的意思，於是他 從臺上下來，命令在我的兩側放幾把梯子，接著便有一百多個人爬上來，將裝滿肉的籃子送到我的嘴邊。我看得出是好幾種動物的肉，但從味道上卻分辨不出其中的差別，有肩胛肉、腿肉和腰肉，從形狀上看起來都像羊肉，料理得很好，但是比雲雀的翅膀還要小。我一口吃下兩、三塊肉，而像步槍子彈般大的麵包一口就是三個，他們對我的體型和胃口驚訝萬分，儘速供應我食物。接著我又作手勢表示想喝水，他們從我吃東西的情形知道，少量的水是不夠的。他們熟練地吊起一個超大的桶子，讓它運轉到我手邊，再把桶蓋打開，我一飲而盡，因為裡面裝的酒還不到半品脫，酒的味道很像勃艮地葡萄酒，但是更為芳香。接著他們又送了一桶過來，我照樣一

格列佛遊記

口就喝乾，並表示還想要，但是他們已經沒有了。

我表演完這些奇技之後，他們高聲歡呼了好幾次，在我的胸脯上跳起舞來。

我得承認，當他們在我身上來回走動時，我很想一把抓住最靠近我的四、五十個人，把他們摔到地上去。可是想起剛才所受的苦，也許那還不是他們最厲害的手段，而且我也承諾過要尊重他們，所以就打消了這個念頭。再說，他們如此大費周章地款待，原則上我也應該以禮相待。然而，我對這些小人的大膽行徑頗為驚訝，因為我的一隻手已經可以自由活動，他們竟敢爬到我身上走來走去，面對我這個龐然大物，他們連抖都不抖一下。

過了一會兒，皇帝指派的高官和十幾個隨從跟著他從我的右小腿爬上來，一直走到臉前。他拿出蓋有王室徽章的證件，遞到我眼前，然後大約講了十分鐘的話，他的臉上沒有怒容，不過口氣很堅決，而且不時地把手指向前方。後來我才明白，他指的是半英哩外的京城；經過研議，皇帝決定把我運到城裡，我回答了幾句話，但是沒有什麼作用；我又用鬆綁的左手，掠過大臣的頭頂——以防傷到他和他的隨從，指著右手，接著再指向頭和身體，示意他們鬆綁我。

但是大臣搖搖頭拒絕，然後作了個手勢告訴我，他們必須把我當成俘虜運走，不過他又另外作了一些手勢，讓我知

道他們會供應足夠的肉和酒善待我。

　　這使我又興起了掙脫束縛的念頭，但是想到臉上和手上起水泡的箭傷，疼痛不已，許多箭頭還扎在裡面，而且敵人的數量又增加了，我只好妥協，表示我同意他們的要求。隨後大臣和他的隨從寒暄過後便帶著滿意的神情撤離了。

　　不久，我聽到一陣叫喊聲，然後有一群人鬆開我左邊的繩子，如此我才能把身子轉向右邊稍微放鬆一下。他們也在我的臉和雙手塗了一種藥膏，味道聞起來很舒服，幾分鐘後，箭傷所引起的疼痛都消失了。因為這些緣故，再加上剛剛吃了許多美味的餐點，我不知不覺陷入沉睡。後來有人告訴我，我大約睡了八個小時；這一點都不奇怪，因為醫生們遵從皇帝的命令，在大酒桶裡摻了安眠藥。

　　原來我上岸後昏睡在地上時，就有人立刻通報皇帝，所以他早就知道了這件事，他在議會 上決定趁我睡著的時候

把我綁起來，同時提供大量的酒和肉，並且準備一架機器把我運到京城。

在皇帝支持學術研究的獎勵之下，數學家們在機械學方面也達到完美的境界。這個皇帝擁有好幾台裝有輪子的機器，用來運送樹木和一些重物，他常在森林裡建造大軍艦，有的長達九英呎，然後再用那些裝有輪子的機器把軍艦運到三、四百碼外的海上。這次為了把我運進城裡，五百名木匠與工程師立刻建造了他們空前最大的機器，那是一座高三英吋、長約七英呎、寬約四英呎、裝有二十二個輪子的木架。我剛才聽到的那陣歡呼聲就是因為這架機器運到了，好像是我上岸後四小時他們就出發了，他們把機器推來與我的身體平行放著，不過最困難的是怎麼把我抬起來放上去，為此他們豎起了八十根一英呎長的柱子，工人在我的全身上下纏滿繃帶，然後用非常堅固的粗繩，一頭綁住鉤子鉤住繃帶，再藉著木柱頂端的滑車，由九百名壯漢一起拉著粗繩，不到三個小時我就被吊起來放到車上了，最後動用一千五百匹高大的御馬，每匹約有四英吋半高，將我拖往半哩外的京城。不過整個過程中，我都因為酒裡的安眠藥而睡得酣沉。

那天我們走了很長的路，夜晚休息時，我的兩側各有五百名衛兵，一半手持火把，一半拿著弓箭，只要我動一下，他們立刻放箭。第二天黎明，我們又繼續趕路，大約中午時分就抵達離城門不到兩百碼的地方，皇帝和所有官員都出來迎接

我們，但是他的大臣們堅決不讓皇帝冒險爬上我的身子。

他們決定讓我住在一幢曾是宮廟的建築物裡，大門朝北，大約四呎高、兩呎寬，我可以爬進爬出；大門的兩側各有一扇離地不到六吋的小窗，皇帝的鐵匠從左側的窗戶拉進九十一條鏈子，看起來很像歐洲婦女用的錶鏈，再用三十六把掛鎖把我的左腿鎖在鏈子上。在大馬路另一邊二十呎外的地方，有一座約五呎高的塔樓，皇帝和他的大官員們登上那座塔樓觀看我的模樣。估計有十萬以上的居民出城觀看，而且，我身旁雖然有衛兵守著，但是至少有一萬個人由梯子爬上我的身體。不久皇帝便頒布公告，嚴禁這種行為，違者處以死刑。

工人們覺得我無法逃脫，便將捆綁我的繩索全部割斷，於是我站立起來感到前所未有的沮喪。當那些小人看到我站起來走動時，那種驚恐和喧鬧的情形實在難以形容。鎖在我左腿上的鏈條約有兩碼長，而且鏈條拴在離大門不到四吋的地方，所以我可以在半徑兩碼的半圓內自由地活動，也可以爬進廟裡伸直身體躺著。

第 2 章

我站起身來，往四周看了看，我必須承認自己從未見過如此令人心曠神怡的景色。四周田野像是一片綿延不絕的花園，圈圍的田地每塊約有四十呎見方，像是許許多多的花床。這些田地間夾雜著一片片占地約八分之一英畝的樹林，最高的樹大約七呎高。我望向左方邊的城鎮，看起來就像劇場裡的繪圖佈景。

此時，皇帝已經走下塔樓，正騎著馬朝我而來，看起來有些狼狽，因為那匹馬雖然受過良好的訓練，但看到我在地面前動來動去，仍然嚇得前蹄騰空躍起。幸好皇帝是位騎馬好手，依舊穩穩地坐在馬背上，直到隨從跑過來勒住韁繩，他才從馬背上下來。

皇帝下馬之後，用讚歎的眼神繞著我端詳了一遍，不過始終保持在鏈子長度以外的範圍。他下令廚子和管家把準備好的酒菜送過來給我，食物放在輪車上，我接過這些輪車，很快就把上面的東西全部吃光：二十輛裝著肉的車，每車只

夠我吃兩、三大口；另外，還有十輛載著酒的車，每輛車上有十個陶瓶，我一口就能喝完一瓶。

皇帝的身高比任何一個朝臣都高，大約高出我的一個指甲寬，光是這一點就足已使旁人對他肅然起敬，他的容貌堅毅，充滿陽剛之氣，有張奧地利人的嘴唇，鷹鉤鼻，橄欖色皮膚，身體和四肢很相稱，舉止文雅，態度莊嚴。當時他二十八歲又九個月，統治這個國家大約七年，大致上國運昌隆，人民幸福安康。

他站在離我三碼遠的地方，服裝很簡樸，樣式看起來介於亞洲和歐洲之間，不過頭上戴了一頂鑲滿珠寶的金冠，冠頂還插著一根羽毛。他拔劍出鞘，以防我掙脫束縛時可以用來防身，那把劍約有三吋長，劍柄和劍鞘都是金的，上面鑲滿了鑽石。他的聲音很尖銳，不過清晰宏亮，所以我就算站起來也可以聽得很清楚。

朝臣和貴夫人們都穿得非常華麗，他們站在那裡，看起來好像一條繡上金色和銀色人像圖案的裙子鋪在地上。

皇帝不時跟我說話，我也回答他，但是彼此都

聽不懂對方的話。在場的還有幾個祭司和律師，他們奉命跟我對話，我用幾種略微會說的語言和他們對談，其中包括德語、荷蘭語、拉丁語、法語、西班牙語、義大利語和通行於地中海一帶的混合語，但是毫無效果。

過了大約兩個小時，所有宮廷的人都離去了，只留下一支強大的衛隊，以防止暴民對我無禮或進行惡意攻擊。那些暴民急欲往我周圍推擠，並且盡可能地靠近，當我坐在門口的地上，有幾個人甚至對我放箭，其中一支還差點射中我的左眼。衛隊上校下令逮捕六個罪魁禍首，他覺得最適當的懲罰方法就是把他們綁起來送到我手中。於是，幾名衛兵用矛柄把他們推到我搆得到的地方，我用右手一把抓起他們，五個放入上衣口袋，然後對第六個做出要活吃他的表情。那可憐的傢伙嚇得高聲喊叫，上校和衛兵們的表情痛苦萬分，尤其當他們看見我拿出小刀的時候，但是我露出和善的目光，用小刀割斷他身上的繩子，然後輕輕放到地上，他立刻拔腿就跑。我用同樣的方法對待其他五個，一一將他們從口袋裡掏出來放走，我發現士兵和群眾對於我的寬厚都十分感激，後來這件事也讓我在宮廷 的處境變得十分有利。

天快黑的時候，我好不容易才爬進屋子裡躺下來休息，這情形持續了大約兩個星期。在這期間，皇帝下令為我準備一張床，於是車子運來了六百張小床舖，他們將一百五十張小床被 在一起，組成一張長寬適合我的床，然後再將四張

格列佛遊記

疊在一起，接著又為我準備床單、毯子和被子，但是我覺得睡在床上跟睡在平滑的硬石板上根本沒有差別。然而，對於一個歷盡苦難的人來說，這一切已經算相當不錯了。

我來到這裡的消息傳遍整個王國，引起無數富人、閒人和好奇的人們前來圍觀，以致於許多村落都唱空城計，若不是皇帝頒布了幾道公告加以制止，一定會發生無人耕種、無人理家務的情況。皇帝下令那些已經看過我的人立刻回家，如果沒有宮廷的許可——國務大臣因此獲得一筆數量可觀的收入——任何人不得靠近我的房子五十碼以內的地方。

同時，皇帝召開了多次會議，討論處置我的方法。後來，一位地位很高的朋友告訴我，宮廷因此面臨了許多難題，他們擔心我會掙脫鐵鍊，也擔心我的食量過大，會消耗太多食物而引起饑荒。他們一度決定將我餓死或乾脆用毒箭射殺，不過他們又考慮到，這麼一具龐大的屍體所發出的惡臭，可能會在京城引起瘟疫，而且說不定會擴散到整個王國。

正當他們討論這些事情的時候，幾名軍官來到會議廳門口，其中兩名獲得召見，把先前我處置六名罪犯的情形報告一番。皇帝對我留下非常好的印象，所有朝臣也都替我辯護，皇帝隨即頒布詔書，下令京城周圍九百碼內的所有村落，每天早上必須送上六頭牛、四十隻羊以及相當數量的麵包和酒，作為我的食物，所有費用由國庫支出。皇帝主要靠

第 2 章

自己的領地收入為生,除非有重大事件,否則不會向百姓徵稅,不過一旦發生戰爭,百姓則須主動跟隨皇帝出戰。

皇帝還下令組成一個六百人的編制,做為我的僕役,發給他們膳食費,並在我的大門兩側搭帳篷供他們居住。

此外,皇帝還命令三百個裁縫做了一套本國樣式的衣服給我,並且雇用了六名最優秀的學者教我他們的語言。最後,皇帝還規定,不論是御馬或貴族、衛隊的馬,都必須經常在我面前操練,藉此訓練膽量。

所有命令都確實執行,大約三個星期後,我已經學會說一些他們的語言。在這段期間,皇帝經常來探望,而且很樂意協助我學習,我們已經稍微可以對談,而我學會的第一句話,就是希望他可以還我自由。我每天都跪在他面前重複這句話,然而他的回答,據我所理解是:這需要一些時間,而且必須開會決議;前提是,我必須發誓與他以及他的人民和平相處。相對的,他承諾會善待我,還勸我保持耐心、謹慎行事,以此取得他和臣民的好感。

他又說,假設他命令幾個官員進行搜身,希望我不要見怪,因為我很有可能攜帶武器,若是這麼一個龐然大物持有武器,那一定非常危險。

我對皇帝表示,他大可放心,因為我已經準備脫下衣

服，翻出口袋讓他檢查；我一邊說，一邊用手勢表達。

他回答說，根據法律，我必須經過兩位官員的搜查，他也知道，要是沒有經過我的同意和協助，這是件不可能的事；他對我的寬宏大度與正直給予極高評價，因此放心地把他的官員交給我。他還說，無論他們從我身上拿走什麼，當我要離開這個國家時，一定會將物品歸還，或是依照估價賠償。

於是我抓起那兩名官員，先把他們放入上衣口袋，接著又換到身上其他口袋，除了兩個裝錶的口袋和一個祕密口袋以外。密袋裡只有一些瑣碎的必需品，對他們來說沒有什麼意義，所以我覺得沒有搜查的必要；兩個錶袋中，一個放著一隻銀錶，另一個則放著裝有少量金幣的錢包。

這兩位先生隨身帶著筆、墨和紙，把看到的每件東西列成一份詳細的清單，他們搜查完之後，要求我把他們放回地上，以便把清單呈給皇帝。我後來把這份清單逐字翻譯出來：

　　經過嚴密的搜查，巨人 上衣右邊的口袋裡，只發現了一大塊粗布，大小足以做為陛下大殿的地毯。左邊口袋裡，有一只大銀箱，但根本提不起來，於是請巨人打開箱蓋，我們其中一人跨進箱裡，結果發現有某種灰塵深及小腿肚，一些灰塵撲到我們臉上，使得我們打了好幾個噴嚏。

　　巨人背心的右口袋裡，有一大捆白色薄

薄的東西，層層疊在一起，約有三個人這麼大，用一條堅固的繩索綑綁著，上面有黑色的符號，我們猜想那是他寫的文字，每個字母幾乎有我們半個手掌那麼大。左口袋裡有一件工具，它的背面凸出二十根長柱子，很像陛下宮前的欄杆，推測那是巨人梳理頭髮的東西，不過我們並沒有問他，因為他很難理解我們說的話。

在他的馬褲右邊的大口袋裡，我們看見一根中空的鐵柱，大約有一個人高，固定在一塊比鐵柱還要大的硬木頭上，鐵柱的一端凸出幾塊形狀怪異的大鐵片，但是不知道用途為何。左邊的大口袋裡也有一部同樣的器械。在右邊較小的口袋裡，有幾塊大小不等的圓形金屬片，有白色和紅色的，其中白色的好像是銀子，又大又重，我們無法搬動。在左邊的小口袋裡，有兩根形狀不規則的黑色柱子，我們站在口袋底部，所以沒有辦法爬到柱子頂端，其中一根被東西包覆著；另一根的頂端有一個白色圓形的東西，大約有我的兩個頭大。這兩根柱子都嵌著一塊巨大的鋼板，我們擔心是危險的器械，所以請他抽出來給我們看。他告訴我們，在他的國家，他用其中一片鋼板來刮鬍子，另外一片則用來切肉。

除此之外，有兩個口袋我們進不去，他說那是錶袋，就在他的馬褲上端的兩個狹長的縫口裡面，因為他肚子的壓力，這兩個口袋被壓得緊緊的。

　　右邊錶袋外面懸著一條巨大的銀鏈，鏈尾繫著一部很神奇的機器。我們告訴他，不論鏈尾繫著什麼東西，都一定要拉出來，結果那是一個球狀物，一面是銀，一面是半透明的金屬。我們在半透明的一面看見一圈奇怪的符號，伸手想去摸一下，卻被那層透明的物體擋住。巨人把那部機器放到我們耳邊，只聽見它不停地發出像是水車轉動時的聲響。我們猜想，那個東西若不是某種不知名的動物，就是他所崇拜的神，不過我們比較傾向於第二種猜測，因為他告訴我們，無論做什麼事都要請教這個東西——他視它為神諭，生活中所有活動都由它來指定時間。

　　他從左邊的錶袋裡掏出一張大小足可供漁夫使用的網，不過像錢袋一樣可以開合，實際上他也把它當作錢袋使用。我們在那裡面找到幾塊又大又重的黃色金屬，如果這些是金塊的話，一定價值不斐。

　　遵奉陛下之命，我們徹底搜查過他身上所有的口袋之後，還發現他的腰間繫著一條用某種巨獸的皮製成的腰帶。腰帶的左邊掛了一把有五個人高的長刀，右邊吊有一只囊袋，裡面又分為兩個小袋，每個小袋都能裝下三個人。其中一袋裝了幾顆約有我們腦袋那麼大的金屬球，十分沉重，需要孔武有力的人才拿得動；另一袋裝有一堆黑色穀粒，體積不大，也不重，我們一把約可抓起五十粒。

　　以上就是我們在巨人身上搜查後所列的

詳細清單。他對我們非常有禮貌,以表達對
陛下授命的尊重之意。

簽名蓋章於陛下登基第八十九月又四日
克萊弗林‧弗瑞洛克、馬賽‧弗瑞洛克

當官員宣讀完這份清單之後,皇帝措辭委婉地要我把幾件物品交出來。

首先,他請我摘下彎刀,於是我連刀帶鞘一起交了出去。此時,他命令三千名精兵遠遠地將我圍住,手持弓箭隨時準備放箭;不過我並沒有注意到這件事,因為我的雙眼一直注視著皇帝。接著,他要我拔出彎刀,雖然浸泡過海水的刀有點生鏽,但大致上還是很明亮。一拔出彎刀,整個部隊立即發出驚恐的叫喊聲;此時正值烈日當空,我握著彎刀前後揮舞,刀面強烈的反射光使他們眼睛昏花。這位皇帝確實氣概不凡,他並沒有如我想像的那麼害怕;他命令我把彎刀插回刀鞘,並且盡可能輕輕地拋到離鏈尾約六呎遠的地方。

他要我交出的第二件東西,是其中一根中空的鐵柱,那是我的袖珍手槍。我把槍拔出來,並依照他的要求,盡可能清楚地向他說明槍的用途。我裝上火藥,幸好彈藥袋綁得很緊,火藥沒有被海水浸濕,並且事先警告皇帝不必害怕,然後朝空中開了一槍。

他們這次所受到的驚嚇,比剛才看到彎刀時大得多,上

024

百人倒在地上，彷彿被子彈擊中一樣，皇帝雖然站著沒倒下，卻也過了好一會兒才鎮定下來。就像拋出彎刀那樣，我也交出兩把手槍和彈藥袋，並且叮嚀他千萬不要讓火藥接近火，因為只要一丁點的火星就會引起爆炸，把他的皇宮炸毀。

然後，我把手錶也交了出去，皇帝看了非常好奇，命令兩個身材最高大的侍從用桿子扛到肩膀上，就像英格蘭的板車車夫搬運麥芽酒桶一樣。他對於錶連續發出的聲響和分針的走動大為驚奇，因為他們的視力遠比我們敏銳，所以很容易能看出走動的分針。他詢問身邊學者們的意見，雖然我並不完全了解他們說話的內容，卻可以看出他們的意見多麼分歧。

接著，我又交出了銀幣、銅幣、裝有九大塊和幾小塊金子的錢袋，還有小刀、剃刀、梳子、銀鼻煙盒、手帕和日記。我的彎刀、手槍和彈藥袋被車子送進了國庫，其他的物品則全部還給我。

先前我曾提到，有一個秘密口袋逃過了檢查，裡面有一副眼鏡、一架袖珍望遠鏡和幾件簡單的用具。那些東西對皇帝來說毫不重要，所以我覺得不必讓他們知道，如果冒險把這些東西交出去，還得擔心被弄丟或是被弄壞。

第 3 章

　　我和善彬彬有禮的舉止，到目前為止已經博得皇帝、宮中大臣以及軍隊和人民的好感，心想也許再過不久便可重獲自由。我用盡一切方法討好他們，當地人也就漸漸地不再那麼害怕了。有時候我會躺在地上，讓五、六個人在我的手上跳舞，甚至到最後，男孩和女孩都敢跑到我的頭髮裡面玩捉迷藏。語言方面，也有了很大的進步。有一天，皇帝突然招待我觀看當地的幾項表演，表演者熟練的技巧與華麗的裝扮，遠勝過我所知道的任何一個國家。其中我最喜歡的是走繩索特技，那是在一條長約兩呎、離地面十二吋高的白色細繩上所做的表演。

　　只有那些想要在宮廷做大官和獲得寵幸的人，才會學習這種技藝。這些人並非都是貴族出身或受過良好的教育，他們從小就接受訓練，每當有官員過世或是失寵而空出重要職缺——這種情況經常發生，就會有五、六個人呈請皇帝准許他們表演繩上舞蹈，以取悅皇帝和宮廷官員，跳得最高又不跌下來的人，就可以接任這個官職。大臣們也經常奉命表演

這種技藝，使皇帝相信他們並沒有喪失這項本領。財政大臣弗林奈普在細繩上跳躍的高度，比任何一位官員都要高出至少一吋。我曾看過他在一條固定於木板的繩索上一連翻了好幾個跟斗，而那繩索只有英國的一般打包繩那麼粗。如果沒有偏心的話，依我的看法，我的朋友內務大臣瑞爾德索的本領僅次於財政大臣，至於其他大臣則彼此不相上下。

這種娛樂時常伴隨著危險的意外事故，而且都被記錄在案，我曾親眼看到兩、三個候選人摔斷手腳。但是當大臣們奉命展現本領時，危險性就更高了，因為他們都希望跳得比以前好，也想要贏過同僚，所以都奮力表演，很少有不摔落的，有的人甚至會跌兩、三次。據說在我來到這裡的前一、兩年，弗林奈普就發生過意外，幸好當時皇帝的一塊墊子恰巧擺在地上，減弱了跌落時的力道，否則他的脖子早就摔斷了。

另外，還有一種娛樂活動是只在特殊節日專門表演給皇帝、皇后和首相看的。皇帝在桌上放三條六吋長的精美絲線，分別為藍色、紅色和綠色，這三條絲線是皇帝要頒發的獎勵品，不同顏色代表不同的恩寵。表演儀式在皇宮的大殿舉行，表演者必須展現出和前面完全不同的技藝。皇帝雙手握著一根棍棒，兩端與地面平行，演出者便一個一個地走上前去，他們有時跳過棍棒，有時在棍棒下反覆前後爬行，而往前或往後則視棍棒上提或下放而定。有時候，皇帝和首相各握著棍棒的一端，有時則由首相獨自拿著。表演得最敏

捷，跳躍和前後爬行的時間維持最久的人，就是第一名，獲頒藍色絲線，第二名獲頒紅色絲線，第三名則是綠色絲線，他們會把絲線繞兩圈纏在腰間，宮廷的大臣們幾乎都用這種腰帶來裝飾。

軍馬和御馬每天都被帶到我的跟前，所以現在看到我已經不再膽怯，即使走到我腳邊也不會受到驚嚇。我把手放在地下時，騎士們就會縱馬跳過，皇帝的一名獵人還曾經騎著高大的駿馬從我的鞋面一躍而過，確實令人驚訝。

有一天，很榮幸我有機會在皇帝面前表演一種非常特別的遊戲。我請他吩咐下人準備幾根兩呎長、普通手杖般粗細的棍棒。第二天清晨，六個伐木工人駕著八輛馬車把東西運來了，我挑選了九根棍棒，並把它們牢牢地豎立在地上，成為一個二點五平方呎的四方形；接著，我又拿了四根棍棒，分別橫綁在四個角落離地約兩呎高的地方，然後我把手帕綁在九根直立的木棍上，四面盡量拉緊直到像一面鼓，那四根與地面平行的棍棒高出手帕約五吋，作為四邊的欄杆。完成之後，我請皇帝讓一支由二十四人組成的騎兵到這平台上操演，皇帝贊成這項提議，於是我把這些馬一匹一匹地拿到手帕上，每匹馬上都已經坐著全副武裝的優秀軍官。他們排列整齊之後，立刻分成兩隊，進行小規模的演習，一時鈍箭齊發，刀劍出鞘，有的敗逃，有的追趕，有的進攻，有的撤退，總之表現出我所見過最嚴明的軍事訓練。因為有四根橫

木的保護，士兵和馬匹都沒有跌落下來，皇帝看了極為高興，他下令軍隊一連表演了好幾天，有一次還興奮得要我把他舉到平臺上發號施令，他甚至想盡辦法說服皇后，讓我把她連同坐椅舉到離平臺不到兩碼遠的高處，好讓她從那裡清楚地觀看表演。

很幸運地，幾次表演都沒發生意外。只有一次，一位隊長的座騎猛烈地用蹄子把手帕踹出了一個洞，馬腿一滑，人仰馬翻。所幸我立刻將人馬救起來，再以一手遮住洞，一手像原先送他上台那樣將人馬放回到地上。那匹馬扭傷了左肩胛，隊長則安然無恙，我儘量補好手帕，不過再也不敢用手帕進行這種危險的遊戲了。

為了恢復自由，我多次上呈請願書，皇帝終於在內閣會議上和全體政務委員會議上提出了這件事，除了斯開瑞奇‧博格蘭姆之外，沒有其他人反對。我跟這個人並沒有過節，但是他卻處處與我作對，這位大臣是當朝的海軍上將，深得皇帝信任，也熟諳國家政務，不過臉色陰沉、性情乖戾。幸好，全體閣員都表示贊同，皇帝也批准了我的請求。最後他還是被說服了，但堅持進行有條件的釋放，而且條件須由他親自起草，我必須宣誓信守那些條件。斯開瑞奇‧博格蘭姆在兩位次長和幾位顯要官員的陪同下，親自將宣誓文件交給我。宣讀完之後，他們要我先以自己國家的儀式，再按照他們法律所規定的方式宣誓履行。他們的方式是：用左手握住

右腳，再把右手中指按住頭頂，大拇指放在右耳尖上。我盡可能地把整份文件逐字翻譯出來，好讓大家看一下：

一、未持加蓋我國國璽的許可證，巨人不得擅自離境。

二、未得到指示，不准擅自進入首府；如經特許，應在兩小時前通知居民不得出門。

三、巨人只能在主要大道上行走，不得在草地上或麥田裡行走或臥躺。

四、巨人在大道上行走時必須極為小心，避免踩踏我國人民及其車馬；未經人民親口同意，不得將他們拿在手中。

五、如遇有特殊的緊急文件要傳遞，巨人必須將信差和馬匹裝進口袋，一個月一次、一次六日路程，如有必要，還須將該信差平安送返。

六、巨人必須和我國聯盟，一同對抗布列夫斯卡島的敵人，盡全力摧毀正準備侵略我們的敵軍艦隊。

七、巨人在閒暇的時候必須幫助我們的工匠搬運巨石，建造公園園牆和其他皇家建築。

八、巨人需在兩個月內，以沿著海岸線步行的方式，呈交一份我國領土周長精確測量報告。

最後，巨人如果鄭重宣誓遵守上述所有條款，他每天可獲得足以維持我國一千七百二十四位人民生活的飲食，並且可以自由地接近皇族成員，享有皇帝的其他恩賜。

頒布於皇帝登基以來第九十一月又十二日於貝爾法柏拉克宮殿

我高興地宣誓了條款，並且在上面簽字。雖然海軍上將斯開瑞奇·博格蘭姆故意刁難，有幾項條款不太合理，不過拴住我的鎖鏈立刻被解開，我自由了。皇帝親自蒞臨，我備感榮幸，於是跪伏在他的面前表示感恩，但是他命令我站起來，親切地和我說了許多話希望我可以成為他的忠誠僕人，不要辜負他過去或未來可能賞賜的恩典。

第4章

　　獲得自由後，我第一個請求就是希望參觀京城麥爾丹多，皇帝爽快地答應了，不過特別指示我不許傷害當地居民和房舍，居民也從公告中得知我要參訪京城的消息。京城四周有兩呎半高、十一吋厚的城牆環繞著，因此外圍可容許一輛馬車安全繞行。城牆四周每隔十呎就是一座堅固的塔樓，我跨過西側大門，輕緩地往裡走，側身穿過兩條主要道路，我只穿了件短背心，因為擔心上衣的下擺會損壞民房的屋頂和屋簷。雖然公告嚴禁任何人出門，以免發生危險，但我還是非常小心地行走，避免踩到任何在街上遊蕩的人。閣樓的窗前和房屋頂樓全都擠滿了看熱鬧的人，在我的旅行經驗中，從未見過像這樣人口稠密的地方。這座城市是正方形的，每一面城牆都是五百呎長，兩條五呎寬的大道在城中交叉，把全城分作四個部分，胡同與巷子只有十二到十八吋寬，我進不去，只能在路過時看一下。這座城市可容納五十萬人，城裡的房子有三層樓到五層樓高，商店和市場樣樣齊全。

　　皇宮坐落在全城的中心，正好在兩條主要大道的交會點

上。皇宮的四周環繞著兩呎高的圍牆，宮殿與圍牆之間有二十呎遠。皇帝允許我跨過圍牆，而圍牆與宮殿之間的距離很寬，可以很容易地看到宮殿的每一面。皇宮外院有四十呎見方，其中還有兩座宮院，最裡面的是皇家內院，我很渴望能參觀一下，不過非常困難，因為兩座宮院之間的大門只有十八吋高、七吋寬；外院的建築有五呎多高，雖然院牆由石塊砌成，厚達四吋，非常堅固，但是想要跨過去而不損害到建築物，實在不可能。

　　然而皇帝很希望我去參觀他那輝煌壯麗的宮殿，因此三天後我終於如願。在那三天裡，我在離城約一百碼遠的皇家公園裡用小刀砍倒了幾棵大樹，然後做了兩張凳子，每張約有三呎高，而且足以承受我的體重。市民們接到第二次公告後，我就拿著這兩張凳子再次進城前往皇宮。來到外院側邊後，我站到一張凳子上，然後把另一張凳子舉過屋頂，輕輕地放到兩座宮院之間約八呎寬的空地上。然後，我輕易地跨過了外院，站到另一張凳子上，再用帶鉤的手杖把第一張凳子鉤過來。藉由這樣的方法，我終於進入了皇家內院，接著我側著身子躺下來，把臉湊到那幾扇特地為我打開的窗子前，由此我看到了最富麗堂皇的內宮，看到了皇后和年輕的王子們在各自的寢宮裡，並有隨從侍奉在側，皇后帶著親切地微笑，又把一隻手伸出窗戶讓我親吻。

　　在恢復自由約兩個星期後的某天早上，內務大臣瑞爾德

格列佛遊記

烈索突然來到我的寓所，身旁只有一個隨從。他吩咐馬車在遠處等候，並要求我給他一個小時聽他說話。他的地位崇高、功績卓越，而且當初我向宮廷提出恢復自由的請求時，他幫了我不少忙，因此我立刻答應了他並表示願意躺下來讓他方便靠近我的耳朵，不過他卻希望我把他放在手裡交談。他首先祝賀我恢復自由，不過他又說，要不是因為宮廷目前的處境，我可能無法這麼快就重獲自由。

「因為……」他說，「在外國人看來，我們的國勢似乎很昌隆，但實際上卻深受兩大危機所苦：一是國內激烈的黨派鬥爭；一是國外強敵入侵的危險。關於第一個危機，你應該知道，七十多個月以來，國內一直存在著兩個敵對的黨派，一個黨叫做特拉麥克森，一個黨叫做斯拉麥克森，區別只在於他們鞋跟的高低。據說穿高鞋跟最符合古法，儘管如此，皇帝卻規定所有的政府官員只能任用穿低跟鞋的人，也只有穿低跟鞋的人才能獲得皇帝的恩寵，這一點你應該已經察覺到了，而且，皇帝的鞋跟比宮廷中任何一位官員的都還要低。這兩個黨派積怨頗深，從不和對方一起吃喝或談話，據我們估算，高鞋跟黨的人數比我們還多，但是權力卻完全落在我們手中。令人擔憂的是，皇帝的繼承人有高鞋跟黨的傾向，至少我們很清楚地看到他的一隻鞋跟高過於另一隻，走起路來一跛一跛的。

「然而，正當國內動盪不安的時候，我們又面臨布列夫

斯卡島敵人侵略的威脅。布列夫斯卡是一個大帝國，國土和軍力幾乎和我國不相上下。至於你說過世界上還有其他一些王國和國家，也住著像你一樣巨大的人類，但是我們的哲學家對此深表懷疑，他們寧願相信你是從月球或是某個星球掉下來的，因為只要有一百個像你這麼龐大的人，很快就會把王國內所有的果實及牲畜吃光。除此之外，在我國六千個月的歷史上，除了小人國和布列夫斯卡兩大帝國外，從來沒有提到過其他什麼地方。然而，這兩大強國已經苦戰了三十六個月。

「戰爭的原因是，自古以來，吃雞蛋的方法是打破雞蛋較大的一端，可是當今皇帝的祖父小時候按古法吃雞蛋時，有次不小心割傷了手指頭，因此他的父王就下了一道命令，要求全國人民吃雞蛋時必須打破較小的一端，違者重罰。人民非常痛恨這道命令，歷史上還因此發生過六次叛亂，導致其中一位皇帝丟了性命，另一位則喪失了王位。這些內亂經常都是受到布列夫斯卡君王的煽動所引起的，當叛亂平息後，流亡的人總會逃到那個帝國尋求庇護。據估計，先後曾有一萬一千人寧死也不願打破雞蛋較小的一端。針對這個爭論，曾經有數百本鉅著出版，但是大端派的書一直被禁止，法律上也規定這一派的人不得擔任官職。

「在這些紛亂的過程中，布列夫斯卡的君王經常派大使前來，指責我們製造宗教分裂，違背了偉大的先知拉斯陀格

在《布蘭德克爾》（他們的聖經）第五十四章中的基本教義。不過我們認爲那是他們曲解了經文，因爲原文是：『所有虔誠的信徒都應該從較方便的一端打破雞蛋。』依我個人淺見，哪一端是方便的一端，似乎只能留待各人的良知判斷，或是由主要行政長官來決定。大端派流亡者深得布列夫斯卡帝王的信任，又廣獲國內黨羽的秘密援助和慫恿，兩帝國之間便因此展開了血戰，三十六個月以來，雙方各有勝負。這段期間，我國損失了四十艘主要戰艦以及衆多的小船和三萬名精銳的海軍和陸軍。據估計，敵人所受的損失比我們還要嚴重。不過，他們現在又裝備了一支強大的艦隊，正準備向我們進攻，皇帝深信你的勇氣和力量，因此請我把這些事情告訴你。」

我請內務大臣回奏皇帝，讓他知道，雖然我是個外國人，不便干涉他國的黨派紛爭，但爲了保衛他和他的國家，我願意冒著生命危險抵抗一切入侵者。

第 5 章

　　布列夫斯卡帝國是小人國東北方的一個島國，兩國間只隔著一條八百碼寬的海峽。我沒見過這座島，自從得知他們企圖侵略的消息之後，我就避免到那一帶沿海地區，以防被敵人的船隻發現。他們尚未得知有關我的消息，因為戰爭期間兩國嚴禁任何往來，違者將處以死刑，而且皇帝又下封港令，任何船隻不得進出港口。我向皇帝提出一個奪取敵人艦隊的計畫，因為根據偵察員的報告，敵人的艦隊正停泊在港灣，一遇順風就起航。我向經驗豐富的海員請教有關海峽深度的問題，因為他們經常進行探測。他們告訴我，海峽中央高水位時有七十「格蘭姆勒夫」深，相當於歐洲的六呎左右，其他地方最深是五十格蘭姆勒夫。我朝東北方正對著布列夫斯卡的海岸走去，然後在一座小山丘背面趴下，取出我的袖珍望遠鏡，看到了停泊在港口的敵艦，有五十艘左右的戰艦和大量的運輸艦。

　　然後我回到住所，因為有授權令，所以我下令準備大量堅固的纜繩和鐵條。纜繩的粗細與包裹繩差不多，鐵條的長

度大小則與縫衣針一樣。我把三根纜繩編成一根使它更結實；同樣地，我也把三根鐵條扭在一起，然後兩端彎成鉤狀，再把五十只鐵鉤固定在五十根纜繩上之後，又來到了東北海岸。我脫下外套、鞋子和襪子，只穿著皮背心走進海裡，這時離漲潮大約還有半個小時，我盡速涉水而過，在海峽中央游了大約三十碼，我的腳就踩到海底了。不到半個小時，我已到達敵艦停泊的地方。敵人看見我時，嚇得紛紛跳下船朝岸邊游去，總數不下三萬人。接著我拿出工具，在每一艘船的船頭套上一個鐵鉤，再把所有纜繩的另一端收攏在一起，這個時候，敵人朝我放了幾千支箭，有許多支射中了手和臉，使我疼痛萬分，也擾亂了工作進行。我最擔心的是眼睛，要不是突然想到了應對措施，恐怕早就失明了。於是我拿出眼鏡戴在鼻子上。有了這項防備，就可以繼續勇敢地工作，儘管好多支箭射中了鏡片，但除了造成一些小麻煩外，並沒有任何不良後果。我把所有鐵鉤都固定好，便拿起繩結，開始用力拉，可是船一動也不動，因為它們全都下了錨，被緊緊地扣住了，看來最艱難的工作還在後頭。因此我先放下繩索，但是必須讓鐵鉤繼續鉤在船上，再用小刀割斷綁住鐵錨的纜索，這時我的臉上和手上又中了兩百多支箭，然後我重拾繫著鐵鉤的繩索，輕輕鬆鬆地把敵人最大的五十艘戰艦拖走。

布列夫斯卡人一點都沒料到我的企圖，起初只是驚慌失

措。當他們看見錨索被割斷時，以為我只是想讓軍艦隨波漂流或是互相撞擊沉沒，但是當他們發現整個艦隊整整齊齊地移動起來，又看見我在前頭拉著時，立刻悲痛絕望地尖叫起來，那種情形實在難以形容。脫離險境之後，我稍微停了一下，拔出射在手上和臉上的箭，並且擦了一些初到小人國時他們給我的那種藥膏。然後摘下眼鏡，等了大約一個小時，直到海潮稍退，我才拖著敵人的艦隊涉水走過海峽，安全返回小人國皇家港口。

皇帝和全朝官員都站在岸邊，等待這次偉大冒險的結果。他們看見敵艦成半月形大規模地往前進，可是卻看不到我，因為海水已經淹到了胸脯，當我走到海峽中央時，他們更加焦急了，因為此時我從脖子以下全都淹沒在海水中。皇帝斷定我已經溺死，而半月形的艦隊不斷朝他們逼進，但是不久之後他就放心了，因為我越往前走，海水越淺，很快地走到可聽見彼此聲音的地方，並且舉起繫著軍艦的纜繩，高聲呼喊：「小人國帝王萬歲！」這位偉大的皇帝迎接我上岸，並且竭力讚揚，當場授予我最高榮譽封號「那達克」。

皇帝希望再找機會把敵人的其他軍艦全都拖回他的港口。他的野心實在深不可測，因為他似乎想把布列夫斯卡整個帝國貶為一個行省，派一位總督前往治理：他想要消滅大端派的流亡者，強迫那個國家的人也都打破雞蛋較小的一端，這樣他就可以成為世界上唯一的君王。但是我從政策和正義方面列舉了許多論點，盡力使他打消這個念頭，坦白地

表示，我永遠不會成爲別人的工具，使得一個自由、勇敢的民族淪爲奴隸。會議 針對這個議題辯論的時候，部分明智的大臣都和我抱持相同的看法。

我這大膽的公開聲明，完全和皇帝的計畫與政策背道而馳，因此他絕不會原諒我。據說，有幾位明智的大臣以沉默的方式表示贊成我的意見，但是其他幾位因爲是我的死敵，就趁機迂迴地說一些中傷我的話。從此，皇帝與其他不懷好意的大臣就策劃一項陰謀，不到兩個月，陰謀暴露，卻差點以我的澈底消失而告終。你一旦拒絕滿足皇帝的野心，那麼就算你曾獲得再大的功勳，也會立刻變得微不足道。

在我立下功勞的三個星期後，布列夫斯卡正式派遣大使謙恭地前來求和。不久後，兩國簽訂了對小人國極爲有利的和約，和約內容我就不再贅述了。布列夫斯卡國派來的大使有六位，隨行人員大約有五百人，場面十分隆重，與該國皇帝的威嚴相符，也表示使命重大。簽約之後，有人私下告訴那幾位大使，說我其實是他們的朋友，因爲我憑藉著自己在宮廷中的聲望，在訂約過程中幫了他們一些忙，因此他們便禮貌性地前來拜訪。先是讚揚我的英勇和寬大，然後以布國皇帝的名義邀請我訪問他們的王國，並且表示很希望我能爲他們表演一番。我欣然答應了這個請求。

我花了些時間款待這幾位大使，他們十分滿意，並對我的一切感到十分驚奇，我則請他們代我向布國皇帝致上最誠

摯的敬意。布王仁德遠播，舉世欽佩，在我返回祖國前一定
會去拜見他。於是，我在下一次謁見小人國皇帝時，請他准
許我前去拜會布列夫斯卡的皇帝。雖然獲得了同意，但是我
看得出來，他的態度十分冷淡。後來有人偷偷告訴我，是弗
林奈普和博格蘭姆把我和布國大使往來的情形呈報給皇帝，
說那是我背叛的表現。不過這件事情我自認問心無愧，這是
我第一次對宮廷和大臣們產生不好的觀感。

值得一提的是，這些大使是透過翻譯員和我交談的。兩個
帝國的語言和歐洲任何兩國之間的語言一樣，有很大的差異，
而且每一國都以自己的語言歷史最悠久、最優美、最有活力而
自豪，甚至公然蔑視鄰國的語言。不過小人國皇帝仗著奪取布
國艦隊的優勢，迫使他們在遞交國書或發言時都必須使用小人
國的語言。除此之外，由於兩國間的商貿往來頻繁，而且彼此
都接納對方的流亡者，又因為兩國都會互派貴族子弟及富紳到
對方國家留學，以增廣見聞、了解異國風土民情，所以名門望
族和住在沿海地區的商人、海員幾乎都會說兩國語言，這個情
形是我在幾個星期後去拜見布列夫斯卡皇帝時發現的。

某天深夜，我被門外數百人的叫喊聲驚醒，有些膽戰。
我聽見人們不斷喊著「勃格蘭姆」，好幾位官員從人群中走
來，懇求我立即趕到皇宮，原來女僕在讀羅曼史時一不注意
睡著了，導致皇后的寢宮著火。我即刻動身，並要求所有人
讓道，那晚明月皎皎，我火速趕往皇宮，途中並未踏傷任何

人。我見他們已在皇宮的圍牆外架起梯子，水桶已準備好，只不過離水源有一段距離。那些水桶只有頂針的大小，可憐的人們疲於奔命只為了盡快供應水源，但火勢相當凶猛，無異於杯水車薪。我本可以用大衣撲滅火勢，不巧我因為來的匆忙而沒有穿上，身上只有一件皮革背心。眼見情勢不妙，這座雄偉的皇宮定會被燃燒殆盡、夷為平地，我卻意外地處變不驚，腦海中閃過一個權宜之計。

前一天晚上，我喝了很多一種名叫「格麗姆格瑞姆」的美酒（布列夫斯卡人稱它叫「福祿奈克」，但我們的名稱比較受到推崇），這種酒相當利尿。更巧的是在那之前我還沒有排泄過。於是我馬上靠近火焰，待了一會兒，我全身被烤得暖烘烘的，一肚子的酒馬上化作尿意。我對準皇宮小便，不到三分鐘火就全熄了，這座宏偉的宮殿才倖免於難。

此時天已經亮了，我不待向皇帝道賀便回了住處，因為儘管我立了大功，但我無法確定皇帝對我的處理方式是否有微詞，畢竟小人國的法律規定，任何人無論地位高低，只要在皇宮區域內小便，一律以死論處。但皇帝通知我，說他將會命令審判庭赦免我，這讓我稍微放寬了心，然而我卻一直沒收到赦免令。而我私下得知，皇后對我的行為深惡痛絕，已搬離皇宮，表示絕對不會修復燒毀的宮殿收為己用，並在心腹面前立誓要向我報仇。

第 6 章

　　小人國當地人的身高不超過六吋，因此動物和植物都有與之相稱的嚴格比例。例如，最高大的馬和牛約四到五吋，綿羊大約一吋半，鵝只有麻雀那麼大，依次往下推，一直到最小的種類，我就幾乎看不見了。不過，大自然使這個族類的眼睛能適應所看到的一切，他們可以看得非常清楚，只是看不太遠。有一次，我看到一位廚師在拔雲雀的羽毛，而那隻還不及普通蒼蠅那般大；又有一次，我看到一個女孩拿著一條細到看不見的絲線，在穿一根小得看不見的針，這些都說明了他們對近處物體的視力十分敏銳。這裡最高的樹木約有七呎，我指的是御花園裡的那幾棵，我舉起手臂時剛好碰得到樹頂，其他植物也依此比例生長。

　　他們的學術經歷許多年代的發展，已經相當發達。不過他們書寫的方法非常特別，既不像歐洲人從左寫到右，也不像阿拉伯人從右寫到左，或像中國人從上往下寫，更不像卡斯凱吉人從下往上寫，而是像英國婦女一般 從紙的一角斜著寫到另一角。

　　他們埋葬死人時是將死人的頭垂直朝下，因為他們認為，一萬一千個月之後死人會復活，屆時地球（他們認為是扁平的）會上下翻轉過來，所以使用這種埋葬法，死人復活的時候就會直接站在地上。當然，一些學識淵博的人也承認這種說法很荒誕，但是這個習俗還是一直延續下去。

　　他們把欺詐看得比偷竊更為嚴重，因此犯下欺詐罪的人幾乎都會被處死。他們認為，一個人只要小心謹慎，提高警惕，再加上一些普通常識，就能保護自己的東西不被偷；但是誠實卻無法對抗狡猾的騙術。既然生活中必然會有買賣和借貸的行為，因此，如果我們縱容欺詐而沒有法律加以制裁，那麼誠實的商人永遠吃虧，狡猾的騙子反倒占了便宜。記得有一次，我在皇帝面前替一個拐騙主人一大筆錢的罪犯說情，那個人奉主人之命出外收款，結果最後竟然捲款潛逃。我對皇帝說，那只是一種背信的行為，希望能減輕對他的刑責。皇帝覺得我太過荒謬，竟然把最能加重此人罪行的理由提出來替他辯護，當時我真的無言以對，只能回答說，不同的國家有不同的風俗吧。我承認，當時確實感到非常羞愧。

　　我們通常都認為賞與罰是政府運作的兩大關鍵，但是除了小人國，我還沒有看過哪個國家確實將這一準則付諸實行。在這裡，任何人只要能提出充分證據，證明自己在七十三個月內一直嚴守國家法律，就可以要求某種特權，根

據他的身分地位和生活狀況，從專用的基金中領取相稱的金額，並且可以冠上「守法者」的稱號，不過這個稱號不能傳給後代。我告訴他們，我們的法律只有刑罰沒有獎賞，他們認爲這是我們政策上的一大缺點。因爲這個緣故，他們法院裡的正義女神雕像有六隻眼睛，兩隻在前，兩隻在後，左右還各有一隻，這代表正義女神是謹愼小心的。女神右手拿一袋金子，袋口開著；左手持一柄寶劍，劍插在鞘內，這表示她喜歡獎賞而不是懲罰。

在人事任用方面，他們注重良好品德更甚於優異才能。因爲他們認爲，人類既然需要政府，那麼只要具有一般才能的人就可以勝任各種公職；而且，上帝也無意把管理公衆之事弄成一門複雜難懂，只有少數傑出天才才能理解的高深學問。他們認爲每個人都有誠實、正義和節制等美德，只要實踐這些美德，加上經驗和善心，任何人都能爲國服務，只不過需要一些訓練罷了。他們還認爲，一個人如果缺乏德行，那麼就算他有再好的資質也沒有用，任何職務都不能交到那些危險分子手中。相反的，一個正直良善的人如果由於無知而犯了錯，也不會像那些道德淪喪，還企圖掩飾自己腐敗行徑的人那樣，給大衆福祉造成無可挽回的後果。

不相信天命的人也不能擔任公職，因爲這裡的人認爲，既然皇帝宣稱自己是上帝的代表，若是他任用的人不承認他所憑藉的權威，那就太荒謬了。

　　說到上述和以下的這些法律時，指的是他們原先的制度，並非指之後人性墮落而終歸淪為惡名昭彰的政治腐敗。那些憑借在繩子上跳舞謀取官職、在御杖上下跳躍爬行而獲得皇家勳章的卑劣行為，是由當今皇帝的祖父開啟先例，而隨著黨派之爭越演越烈，才走向如今逢迎諂媚的極端。

　　忘恩負義是會被判死罪的，他們的理由是：對於自己的恩人以怨報德，絕對是人類的公敵，他們不懂得感激別人施予的恩德，根本不配活在這個世界上。

　　他們對於親子關係互相應負的責任觀念也與我們天差地別。小人國人民認為，雄性與雌性結合是自然法則，是為了繁衍後代；與動物相同，男人與女人的結合都是出於慾望，而照料年幼的後代也是大自然的定律。但孩子不必因為父母生養他們而盡什麼義務，人生已經充滿苦難，生兒育女本身並無益處、也不在一心談情說愛的父母的計畫之內。出於這些理由，他們認為子女的教育絕不可以交給他們的親生父母。因此，每個市鎮上都有公立托兒所，除了農民和勞工，所有父母都必須把年滿二十個月的兒女送到學校裡去受教育，因為個年齡的兒童基本上能聽從教導。這些學校又分成好幾種，以適應不同的階級和性別，學校裡有經驗豐富的教師，他們訓練孩子們各自的生活方式，既能與其父母地位相符合，又能符合他們自身能力和愛好。

　　我在小人國住了九個月又十三天，因為生活上的需要，我用皇家公園裡最大的樹木為自己做了一套便利的桌椅。他們雇了兩百個女裁縫為我製作襯衫、床單和桌巾，他們用的是最粗且最硬的布料，但還是得把好幾層疊在一起縫製，因為他們最厚的布都比我們最細的棉布還要薄。他們的亞麻布一捲通常是三吋寬三呎長，我躺在地上讓女裁縫們量尺寸，其中一個站在脖子上，一個站在腿中央，兩人各拉著一根粗線的一端，再由第三個拿一把一吋長的尺來量這根粗線的長度。接著，她們又量我右手的大拇指，之後就不需再量了，因為根據數學原理來計算，大拇指周長的兩倍等於手腕的周長，以次類推，她們又算出了脖子和腰圍的大小。再加上我把一件舊襯衫攤在地上讓她們做樣本，所以她們做好的襯衫非常合身。他們又雇了三百個男裁縫以同樣的方式幫我做外套，不過他們用另一種方法為我丈量。我跪在地上，他們豎起一把梯子靠在脖子上，然後一個人爬上梯子，從我的領口垂下一根錘線直到地上，這就是我的外套長度，不過腰身和臂長我得自己量。這些衣服全都是在我的住所縫製的，做好的衣服看起來很像英國婦人們做的補綴衣。

　　我有三百名廚師替我料理飲食，他們和家人一起住在我房子附近的簡便小屋裡。每位廚師為我煮兩盤菜。我把二十個男侍者舉起來放到桌上，另外還有一百多名在地面上侍候著，有的端著一盤盤的肉，有的扛著一桶桶的酒。我要吃什

麼，桌上的侍者就用繩索巧妙地把食物吊到桌上，就像我們
歐洲人從井裡拉起吊桶一樣。他們的一盤肉只夠我吃一大
口，一桶酒也只夠我喝一口。他們的羊肉沒有我們的好吃，
不過牛肉倒是美味極了。我曾經吃到一塊很大的牛腰肉，要
咬三口才吃得完，不過這種機會很少。像在祖國吃雲雀的腿
肉一樣，連肉帶骨一起吞下肚，他們看了都非常驚訝。他們
的鵝和火雞我通常都一口一隻，而且我必須承認，那味道比
我們的好太多了，至於其他較小的禽肉，我用刀尖一次可以
叉起二、三十隻。

　　皇帝聽說了我的生活情形後，有一天，他突然想帶皇后
和年輕的王子、公主們來和我一起用餐。他們駕臨之後，我
把他們放置到桌面的椅子上和我面對面坐著，四周有侍衛保
護。財政大臣弗林奈普手裡拿著他那根白手杖也隨侍在側，
我發覺他不時以敵對的目光瞪著我，我並不理會，反而吃得
比平常還要多，一方面是為了光耀我親愛的祖國，另一方面
是想讓小人國的廷臣們欽佩。我相信皇帝這次的駕臨又給了
弗林奈普一個算計我的好機會，這位大臣一向暗地裡與我為
敵，但是表面上卻對我相當客氣，與他陰暗乖僻的本性有很
大的出入。他對皇帝說，目前的財政狀況非常窘迫，撥付款
項都得大打折扣，貨幣實際價值也比票面價值低百分之九才
能流通，短時間內我已經耗掉皇帝一百五十多萬「斯普魯
格」（這是他們最大的金幣，大約是一個亮片的大小。），

總之，皇帝應該盡快找機會把我打發走。

　　在此我必須證明一位貴夫人的清譽，她因為我人蒙受了不白之冤。財政大臣總愛猜忌自己的妻子，受到一些奸詐小人的挑撥離間，他聽聞自己的妻子熱烈地愛上我，謠傳她曾祕密地前往我的住所，這樁宮廷醜聞傳了好一陣子，我鄭重澄清這都是造謠，這位夫人與我之間只有一段真摯的友誼。我承認她常到我的住處來，但一直都是光明正大地來往，馬車裡總有三四個人同往，通常包括她的妹妹、小女兒，或者一些閨密。這對宮廷裡的貴婦人而言再正常不過，我還可以讓我身邊的僕人作證，他們什麼時候看見我門口停著馬車卻不知是哪位貴客。 每當有人來訪，僕人便會先行通報，我就立刻到門口迎接。行禮問安之後，我便非常小心地用雙手拿起馬車和兩匹馬，放到桌子上。為了防止意外發生，我在桌面周圍釘了一道五吋高的活動桌邊。我的桌上經常同時有四輛馬車，裡面全坐滿了客人，這時我得坐到椅子上，然後把臉靠近他們，我和第一輛馬車中的客人交談時，馬車夫就駕著其他的車子，在桌子上慢慢地兜圈子。我就在這樣的交談中度過了許多愉快的下午。

第 7 章

在我說明自己離開這個王國的情況之前，請容我先將一樁兩個月來針對我的陰謀詭計娓娓道來。

我對於宮廷裡的事情一直都很陌生，而且礙於身分其實也沒有資格了解。不過，有關皇帝和大臣們性情與脾氣的故事，我倒是聽過也讀過不少，但實在沒想到，對如此偏遠的一個國家，竟然也會有這麼可怕的影響。我本來還以爲這個國家的統治原則與歐洲國家完全不一樣呢。

就在我準備謁見布列夫斯卡皇帝的時候，宮廷裡的一位重要人士夜裡坐著轎子十分隱秘地來到我家。他並沒有通報姓名，便直接要求會面。打發走轎夫之後，我把他連同乘坐的轎子一起放進上衣的口袋裡，然後吩咐一個可靠的僕人，要他說我身體不太舒服已經入睡了，之後我關緊大門，依照平常的習慣，把轎子放到桌上，然後在桌子旁邊坐下來。彼此寒暄過後，我發現這位大人滿臉憂慮，就問他發生了什麼事。他要我耐心地聽他講，因爲這件事攸關我的榮譽和生命。

「要知道，爲了你的事，國務會議的幾個委員最近召集了一次極爲秘密的會議，皇帝兩天前已經作出了決定。

「相信你也很清楚，從一開始海軍上將斯開瑞奇‧博格蘭姆就成了你的死對頭。起因是什麼我並不知道，不過自從你大敗了布列夫斯卡，使得這個海軍上將的顏面盡失，他對你的仇恨也就更深了。這位大將和財政大臣弗林奈普、將軍林托克、內侍大臣拉爾康以及大法官巴爾穆夫向皇帝提了一份彈劾書，指控你犯有叛國罪和其他重大罪行。」

這一段開場白讓我無法接受，因爲我覺得自己只有功沒有罪，於是急著想辯駁，但是他請我不要講話。

「爲了報答你的恩情，我冒著生命危險打聽到全部的消息，還拿到了一份彈劾書的副本。」

巨人彈劾書

第一條：

陛下卡琳‧德法‧布魯恩在位時曾制定法令：凡在皇宮範圍內小便者，一律處以嚴重叛國罪。巨人藉撲滅皇后殿下寢宮火災之名，公然違反該法令，竟以尿滅火，實屬居心不良、罪大惡極。當事人不僅違

犯該項法令，並有擅專越權之舉動等等。

第二條：

巨人曾擄獲布列夫斯卡皇家艦隊，並帶回皇家港口，之後皇帝陛下命令他將殘餘的船隻也奪取過來，將布列夫斯卡貶為我國的一個行省，從此由總督管轄，並且將大端派亡命之徒及該國不願立即放棄大端主義的異端，全部消滅處死，然而巨人就像個狡詐的叛徒，以不願違背良心摧毀一個無辜民族的自由與生命為託辭，違抗了尊貴的皇帝陛下。

第三條：

布列夫斯卡派遣使臣前來我國求和時，巨人就像個狡詐忤逆之徒，明知道這些人是最近與皇帝陛下公開宣戰的敵國子民，竟然還幫助他們、慰勉他們，甚至款待他們。

第四條：

巨人違反了忠臣的本分，僅是取得皇帝陛下的口諭，就準備前往布列夫斯卡帝國。他以取得此允諾為藉口，其實存心不良，真正目的是為了前去援助、安慰、教唆布列夫斯卡皇帝。然而，如同前面所說的，該國近日與我國為敵，甚至公然向陛下宣戰。

「另外還有其他條文，不過這幾條是最重要的，我已經把重點都唸給你聽了。

「在這宗彈劾案的幾次辯論中，不可否認的，皇帝多次表現出寬大慈悲的態度，不止一次強調你爲他立下的功績，企圖減輕你的罪行。但是財政大臣和海軍上將卻堅持用最痛苦的方式、最不名譽的罪行將你處死，他們要在夜裡放火燒你的房子，並由林托克將軍率兩萬名士兵用毒箭射你的臉和手。他們還私下命令你的幾個僕人將毒汁灑在你的襯衫上，很快地你就會把自己的皮肉扯爛，極端痛苦地死去。將軍也贊成這些意見，所以有很長一段時間，大多數人都是與你對立的。不過皇帝決定盡可能地保全你的性命，最後取得了內侍大臣的支持。

「關於這件事，皇帝還徵詢了內務大臣瑞爾德索的意見，大家都公認他是你的忠實朋友。而從他說的那番話看來，你對他印象不錯也是有道理的。他承認你罪行重大，但是尚有可以寬恕之處，而寬恕是一個皇帝最值得稱頌的美德，吾王陛下也正以此美名而馳名天下。他說，大家都知道你和他是朋友，或許大部分的閣員會認爲他偏袒你，不過爲了遵從皇帝的命令，他也願意把自己的看法坦白地說出來。他謙恭地建議皇帝是否能體念你所立下的功績，寬宏大量地饒你一命，僅要求你挖出雙眼作爲懲處。這個權宜之計不僅讓正義得以伸張，天下百姓還會歌頌陛下的仁慈，甚至有幸

參與這場會議的閣員們也備感光榮。而你雖然失去了雙眼，但這不妨礙你的體能，以後仍然可以為皇帝效勞，失明使你看不見危險，反倒可以增加你的勇氣，當初你奪取敵國戰艦時最大的困難不就是害怕眼睛被射瞎嗎？以後你依靠大臣們的眼睛就足夠了，就連偉大的君王也不過如此。

「這個建議遭到全體閣員強烈反對，海軍上將博格蘭姆甚至控制不住情緒，怒沖沖地站起來說，他不明白內務大臣怎麼膽敢主張要保全一個叛徒的性命。他認為，從國家的立場來考量，你所立下的那些功勞其實也等於加重了你的罪行，既然你能把敵艦拖來，同樣的，一旦你不高興，也可以把敵艦再送回去。

「財政大臣也抱持相同的看法。他指出，為了負擔你的生活，皇帝的稅收已經大大縮減，很快就沒有辦法再供養你了。他們秉著良知確信你有罪，那麼這就足以判你死刑，並不需要嚴守法律提出正式證據。

「但是皇帝陛下堅決反對死刑，他仁慈地說。這時你的朋友內務大臣謙遜地要求再次發言，他說，既然財政大臣能全權處理國家的稅收，應該也可以漸漸減少你的飲食，一旦你沒有足夠的食物，就會變得虛弱或昏厥過去，也會變得沒有食慾，結果不出幾個月就會被餓死。屆時，你的體重只剩下一半，屍體發出的惡臭也不會造成太大的危害。你一死，

五六千個百姓兩三天內就可以把你的肉從骨頭上割下來，用貨車運到遠處埋掉，以防傳染病發生，只留下你的骸骨當做紀念，供後代子孫瞻仰。

「因此，由於內務大臣與你的深厚友誼，整個事件才得以有折衷的解決方法。除了海軍上將博格蘭姆之外，所有閣員一致同意這個方法。皇帝嚴令，逐步將你餓死的計畫必須祕密進行，不過刺瞎你雙眼的判決卻寫在彈劾書中。

「三天後，你的朋友內務大臣就會奉命前來，當面宣讀彈劾書，同時表明皇帝以及閣員們有多麼的寬大與仁慈，因此你才會只被判處弄瞎眼睛。皇帝相信你會心存感激地接受這個判決，到時候，二十名御用外科醫生將會前來監督，確保手術順利進行。他們會讓你躺在地上，然後用十分銳利的箭射入你的眼球。

「要採取什麼應對方法，你自己審慎考慮吧。為了不引起懷疑，我得立刻像剛才來的時候那樣祕密地回去。」

這位大人走了，只留下我一個人，心中充滿了困惑。

坦白說，由於我的出身和所受的教育，我從來都沒有想過要當官。雖然我不擅於判斷事理，但我實在看不出來這個判決有任何寬大和恩典可言。有些時候，我無法否認彈劾書上的那幾條指控，但還是希望他們能減輕我的刑罰，我也曾

經閱讀過許多由國家提出起訴的審判案件，發覺最後都是法官自以爲是的結案。在這關鍵時刻，面對如此有權勢的敵人，我恐怕不能相信這麼一個危險的決定。我一度想極力反抗，由於我現在還是自由的，因此就算用上整個帝國的力量也很難將我制服，我只要用一些石頭就可以輕易地把首府砸毀。但是一想到我曾經對皇帝宣誓，想起他賜予我的恩典以及「那達克」的封號，就又立刻打消這個念頭。但我也沒有這麼快就學會朝臣們那種報恩的辦法，於是安慰自己說，既然現在皇帝對我如此殘酷，一切應盡的義務也就免除了。

　　爲了保全雙眼和自由，我也顧不得那麼多了。因爲皇帝曾經准許我前去拜謁布列夫斯卡皇帝，我就利用這個機會，趁三天期限還沒到來之前，寫了一封信給我的朋友內務大臣，告訴他我決定次日早晨就動身前往布列夫斯卡。還沒等他回覆，我就來到了艦隊停泊的海邊，我抓起一艘大戰艦，在船首綁了一根纜繩，拔起船錨，脫掉衣服，把衣服連同夾在腋下的被子一起放入船裡，然後拉著船，半涉水半游泳地來到了布列夫斯卡的皇家港口。當地的人民早已期待我的到來，他們派了兩名嚮導帶我前往京城，該國京城也叫布列夫斯卡。我把這兩人拿在手裡，一直走到離城門不及兩百碼的地方，我請他們去通報一位大臣說我到了，讓他知道我在這裡等候皇帝的命令。

　　大約過了一個小時，我得到的回應是，皇帝已經帶著皇

室和大臣們出來迎接了，於是我又往前走了一百碼，皇帝和隨扈們從馬上下來，皇后和貴婦們也都下了車，我看不出他們有任何害怕或不安的樣子。我臥在地上親吻皇帝和皇后的手，告訴皇帝我得到了小人國皇帝的許可，因此如約前來拜見他這位偉大的君主，我心中感到萬分榮幸，並且表明願意竭力為他效勞。但是，關於我在小人國受辱的事則隻字未提，因為我到那時為止仍未接到正式通知，所以可以裝作完全不知道這件事。我現在不在他的勢力範圍內，所以我想小人國的皇帝也不可能公開那件密謀，然而不久之後我就發現我錯了。

第 8 章

　　到達後三天，由於好奇心的驅使，我來到了這座島的東北海岸。在離海岸大約半里格的海面上，我發現了一樣東西，看起來像是一艘翻覆的船隻。我脫下鞋子和襪子，涉水走了兩、三百碼，只見那東西被潮水沖得更近，已經可以清楚地看見確實是一艘小船，我想大概是被暴風雨從大船上吹落下來的。於是我立刻回到城裡，請求皇帝把上次艦隊損傷後剩下的二十艘最大的軍艦借給我，並請海軍中將率領三千名水兵前來協助。艦隊繞道而行，我則抄近路回到原先發現小船的海邊，此時潮水把小船推得離岸邊更近了。水兵們都攜帶著我事先搓綁緊實的繩索，軍艦抵達的時候，我脫掉衣服，涉水走到離小船不到一百碼的地方，然後游到小船邊。水兵們將繩索的一端丟給我，我將繩索繫在小船前面的洞孔裡，再把另一端綁在一艘軍艦上，可是我發現這麼做沒什麼用，因為我的腳踩不到水底，沒辦法工作。我只好游到小船後面，用一隻手盡可能地把小船往前推，順著潮水的力量，我一直往前進，直到雙腳可以探著水底，下巴也剛好可以露

出水面。休息兩、三分鐘後，我又推行了一陣子，一直把船推到海深只及腋下的地方，最吃力的工作已經完成，我又拿出放在一艘軍艦上的另外一些繩索，將一端繫著小船，另一端繫在伴隨我的九艘軍艦上。這時正值順風，水兵們在前面拉，我在後面推，一直前進到離岸不到四十碼的地方。等潮水退後，我把小船拉出水中，在兩千名水兵的繩索和機器協助下，我將它底朝天地翻了過來，這時發現小船只有輕微損傷。

我花了十天功夫做了幾把槳，才把小船划進了布列夫斯卡皇家港口。入港的時候，只見人山人海，群眾看見這麼龐大的一艘船全都驚嘆不已。我對皇帝說，上天賜給我這艘船真是太幸運了，它可以載我到其他地方，也許可以從那裡返回祖國。因此我請求皇帝提供修船的材料，並且准許我離境。他好心地勸說了一番，後來仍答應了我的請求。

這段期間我一直覺得很納悶，為什麼沒聽說小人國皇帝告知布列夫斯卡宮廷關於我的事。後來有人私下告訴我，原來小人國皇帝根本沒想到計畫已經曝光，還以為我只是履約前來布列夫斯卡，等朝見儀式結束，過幾天我就會回去。然而過了這麼久我都沒回去，他終於開始苦惱起來，和財政大臣以及那幫密謀者商量之後，派遣了一名特使帶著那份彈劾書前來，向布列夫斯卡皇帝傳達他只判了我「刺瞎雙眼」一罪的寬大與仁慈，而我卻逃脫正義的制裁，若兩小時內我仍

不返回，就要取消我「那達克」的封號，並宣布我為叛國犯。那位特使還說，為了維持兩帝國間的和平友好，他的君王希望布列夫斯卡皇兄下令將我的手腳綁　送回小人國，以叛國罪懲治。

布列夫斯卡皇帝和大臣們商議了三天後，回以一封充滿禮儀和託辭的信函。他說，小人國皇帝應該知道，要把我捆綁起來送回去是不可能的，雖然我曾經奪走布列夫斯卡的艦隊，但議和時我也幫了不少忙，他對我是非常感激的。然而兩國君王很快就可以寬心了，因為我在海邊發現了一艘巨船，已經準備出航，而且他已下令在我的指導和幫助下修復這艘船，希望再過幾個星期，兩國就可以擺脫這個無法經受的累贅。

特使帶著答覆返回小人國。布列夫斯卡皇帝把事情的經過全都告訴我，同時表示，如果我願意繼續為他效勞，他會盡力保護我。雖然相信他的真誠，但是我已下定決心，盡可能避免和帝王或大臣推心置腹，因此我對他的好意表示感謝，同時謙卑地請求原諒。我說，既然命運賜給我一艘船，不論是吉是凶，我都決心冒險出航，不願兩位偉大的君主因我而爭鬥。我覺得皇帝並沒有因為這番話而生氣，後來我還意外發現，他和多數大臣們都很高興這樣的決定。

大約一個月後，一切都準備好了，我便派人向皇帝請示

告別。皇帝帶著皇室成員出了宮，我趴在地上，皇帝親切地
伸出手讓我親吻，皇后和王子也讓我行了吻手禮。皇帝賜我
五十隻各裝有兩百個「斯普魯格」的錢袋，還送了一幅他的
全身畫像，我立即把畫像放進一隻手套裡以免損毀。

　　我在船上放了宰好的一百頭牛和三百隻羊，相當數量的
麵包和飲料以及四百名廚師盡可能烹調好的熟肉。我又帶了
六頭活母牛和兩頭活公牛以及同樣數量的活母羊和活公羊，
打算回祖國繁殖，再加上一大捆乾草和一袋玉米，以便在船
上餵牠們。雖然我很想帶走十幾個當地人，可是皇帝堅決反
對；他除了仔細搜查每個口袋之外，還要我以名譽保證，即
使他的臣民願意，也不能帶走任何一個人。

　　我盡可能地把一切都準備好，清晨六點，船起航了。我
向北行駛了約十二英里遠，那時正刮著東南風，西北方約
一‧五英里遠的地方有一座小島，我往前駛去，在小島的背
風面下錨，看來似乎是座無人島。我吃了些東西後便陷入沉
睡，這一覺睡得相當好，醒來後不到兩小時天就亮了，所以
我推估自己睡了六個小時。夜晚天空一片晴朗，我在太陽升
起前吃過早餐，然後就起錨了。風向很順，我照著袖珍羅盤
按前一天的路線行駛，當時我的計劃是，順利的話能抵達位
於凡迪門蘭東北面的一個小島。

　　一整天我一無所獲，不過第二天下午三點鐘左右，據我

推算離開佈雷夫斯克已經有七十二英里遠。我朝著正東方行駛，這時忽然發現一艘帆船正朝東南方開去，我大聲呼叫，但是沒有人回應，不過由於風勢轉弱，我才能漸漸靠近那艘船。我開始全速前進，半個小時過後，那艘船上的人才終於發現我，於是掛起了一面旗幟並且鳴放了一槍。萬萬沒想到我還有機會再次見到親愛的祖國和留在那裡的親人，我內心的喜悅實在難以形容！

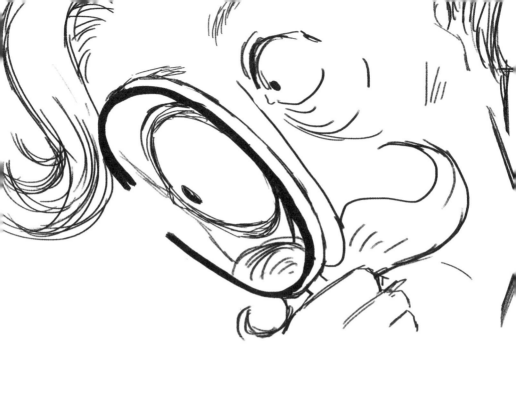

巨人國遊記

第 9 章

　　返家才兩個月我又再次啓程離開。卻因爲遇上了許多問題，而在海上迷失了方向，連船上最有經驗的水手也無法判斷我們的位置。

　　一名男孩在船桅上發現了一座島，接著我們清楚地看到一座大島，陸地南岸有個小半島延伸進入海中，還有一個深度不夠上百噸船停泊的小港灣。我們在離港灣不到幾英里的地方下錨，船長派出十幾名裝備齊全的水手，帶著各種容器坐上長舢板去找水，我與他們同行。

　　上岸之後，並沒發現任何河流或泉水，也沒有人類居住的跡象，水手們沿著岸邊來回尋找飲水，我則獨自走往另一邊，放眼所見盡是岩石，是個不毛之地。我開始覺得無趣，便慢慢返回港灣，大海上一覽無遺，我看見同伴們已經搭上了舢板，拚命朝大船划去，我想要呼喊他們，但是一點用處也沒有，此時卻看到一個巨人飛快地走進海裡跟在他們後面。他邁著大步，水深還不及他的膝蓋，但是水手們比他領

先了幾哩遠，海水裡又滿是鋒利的岩石，所以那怪物沒有追上小船。我趕緊轉身沿著原路狂奔，爬上一座陡峭的小山，發現四周都是耕地，令人驚訝的是，一片似乎保留作為乾草的田地裡，草的高度竟然超過二十呎。

　　我走上了一條大路，以為是一條大路，但那其實只是當地人穿越大麥田的小徑。我在路上走了一段時間，兩邊什麼也看不到，因為收割時節快到了，麥子至少有四十呎高。我走了大約一個小時才到麥田的盡頭，田的四周有一道至少一百二十呎高的籬笆圍著；樹木就更高聳了，無法估算它們的高度。這塊田與另一塊田間有一個階梯相通，階梯共有四級，每一級都有六呎高，爬到最高一級還得跨過一塊二十呎高的石頭，所以根本無法爬上去。我竭力在籬笆間尋找縫隙，因為我看見一個當地人從隔壁的田裡朝台階走過來，這個人和剛才在海邊追趕小船的那個巨人一樣高大，有一般教堂尖塔那麼高，估計他跨一步約有十碼長。我驚恐萬分，連忙跑到麥田中間躲起來，我看到他站在台階頂端回頭望著右邊那塊田，又聽到他發出比擴音器還要響好幾倍的叫喊聲，起初我還以為是在打雷。他這一喊，就有七個和他一樣的怪物走過來，他們手裡拿著鐮刀，是我們長柄鐮刀的六倍大。裝束沒有第一個人的好，看起來像是傭人或雇工，因為他只說了幾句話，他們就來到我藏身的這塊麥田裡收割了。我盡可能地遠離他們，但是麥稈與麥稈之間有時相隔不到一呎，

我很難擠過身子。不過，我還是盡力往前移動到一片被風雨吹倒的麥子裡，可是這裡的麥稈交纏在一起，我根本無法往前進，落在地上的麥芒又硬又尖，刺穿了我的衣服並且扎進肉裡。此時，我聽出割麥子的人已經在我身後不到一百碼的地方。

我精疲力竭，絕望透頂，於是躺在兩道田壟中間，心想自己就要命喪於此，留下孤苦無依的妻子和沒有父親的孩子，我懊悔自己的愚蠢、任性，不聽親友勸阻而執意二度出航。內心極度混亂不安，不由得想起了小人國，那裡的居民視我為奇蹟；在那裡，我可以單手拖動一支皇家艦隊，其他功績也將永遠在那個帝國流傳，也許後人會覺得難以置信，但有數百萬人可以作證。然而，現在的我顯得渺小無助，就像一個小人國的人處在我們當中一樣無足輕重，要是被其中一個巨人抓到，除了成為他口中的一小塊美食，我還能期望什麼？

我既害怕又困惑，無法克制腦海裡的這些念頭。這時，一個割麥人已經走到我躲藏的田壟的附近，他只要再往前一步，我就會被踩死，或者被鐮刀砍成兩段。因此當他移動時，我嚇得尖聲驚叫，巨人忽然停住腳步，朝下方搜索了好一會兒，終於看到躺在地上的我。他遲疑了一下，就像捉住一隻危險小動物卻又怕被牠抓咬一樣小心翼翼。最後，他大膽地用拇指和食指捏住我的腰，將我拿到他眼前三碼處看個

清楚，我盡量保持冷靜，雖然他把我舉到離地六十呎的高空，並且緊捏著我的腰部，深怕我從他的指間滑落，但我決心不掙扎。唯一能做的就是抬眼望著太陽，雙手合攏擺出祈求的姿態，以卑微的語調說了幾句話，雖然還是擔心他會隨時把我摔到地上，就像我們平常把討厭的小動物弄死一樣。幸好，他似乎覺得我的聲音和動作很有趣，把我當成珍奇之物，雖然完全聽不懂我的話，但是感到相當驚訝。此時他撩起上衣的下擺，把我輕輕地放在上面，然後立即帶著我跑向他的主人。他的主人是個富裕的農夫，也就是我在麥田裡最先看到的那個巨人。

　　農夫聽完僕人說的話後，拿起一根約有拐杖那麼粗的麥稈，挑起我上衣的下擺，把我的頭髮吹開，以便看清楚我的臉。他召喚所有雇工，問他們是否曾在田裡看過像我這樣的小動物。接著，他把我輕輕地放在地上趴伏。但我立刻又站起來了，緩慢地踱步，讓這些人明白我沒有逃跑的意圖。他們坐了下來，全都圍著我，以便更清楚地看到我的舉動。我脫下帽子，向那農夫深深地鞠了個躬。我又雙膝跪地，舉起雙手，抬起雙眼，以我最大的音量說了幾句話。我從口袋裡掏出一袋金幣，十分謙恭地呈給他。他用手掌接過去，拿到眼前看看到底是什麼，後來又用一枚取自他的衣袖上的別針撥弄了好幾次，還是沒弄明白那究竟是什麼東西。於是我示意他把手放在地上，我再拿過錢袋，打開來，將金幣盡數倒

入他的手掌。除了二三十枚小金幣以外，還有六枚西班牙大金幣，每枚值四個比斯脫。我看見他用舌頭舔了一下小指尖，拈起一枚最大的金幣，隨後又拈起另一枚；可他似乎全然不懂這是些什麼東西。他做手勢讓我將它們放回錢袋，又叫我把錢袋放回衣袋。我好幾次遞過去，請他收下，可他堅決不肯，我沒辦法只好收起來。

農夫這時才相信我是有理智的生物，時而和我說話，聲音如雷貫耳，不過倒很清晰。我用幾種不同語言儘量大聲地回答，他也把耳朵湊到離我不及兩碼的地方，但是都白費力氣，因為我們完全聽不懂對方的話。之後，他差遣僕人們回去工作，自己則從口袋裡掏出一條手帕，摺起來鋪在左手心，再將手心朝上平放在地上，示意我走上去。他的手掌不到一吋厚，我很輕易地跨了上去，但是怕跌落下來，於是挺直身子躺在手帕上。為了確保安全，他用手帕四周多出來的部分裹住我的身體，只露出頭部，然後把我帶回家。他一到家就叫喚妻子前來，把我拿給她看，她嚇得放聲尖叫，轉頭跑開，跟英國婦女看到蟾蜍或蜘蛛的反應一樣。然而，當她觀察我一會兒，見我很聽從她丈夫的指示，就放下心來，態度也漸漸變得很親切。

中午十二點左右，僕人將午餐送了上來。一個直徑約二十四吋的盤子裡裝滿了肉，這是全部的菜餚，與農家簡樸的生活相稱。一起用餐的包括農夫和他的妻子、三個孩子以

及一位老奶奶。他們就坐之後，農夫把我放在離他不遠的桌面上，桌子離地約有三十呎高，我盡量遠離桌子邊緣以免跌落。

農夫的妻子切下一小塊肉，又弄碎一點麵包，然後擺放在我面前。我對她深深一鞠躬，接著拿出自己的刀叉吃了起來，他們看了十分開心。女主人吩咐女僕拿來一只容量約三加侖的小酒杯，為我斟滿了酒；我十分吃力地用雙手捧起酒杯，極為恭敬地以英文高聲祝福女主人身體健康，所有人開懷大笑，我的耳朵幾乎要被震聾了。那酒嘗起來像蘋果酒，並不難喝，接著主人示意我走到他的餐盤旁。我因為飽受驚嚇而不小心絆到一塊麵包屑，所以直挺挺地撲倒在桌上，幸好沒有受傷。我立刻站了起來，發覺大家都一臉擔心，於是拿起帽子在頭頂上揮了揮，歡呼三聲，表示沒有跌傷。但是就在我走向主人的時候，坐在他旁邊的小兒子，一個十歲大的頑皮男孩，突然一把抓住我的雙腿，高高地舉到半空中，嚇得我全身顫抖。他的父親連忙從他手中把我搶回來，同時狠狠地賞了他左臉頰一記耳光，然後叫人把他帶離餐桌。我擔心這男孩會記仇，又想到孩子生性本來就愛捉弄麻雀、兔子、小貓和小狗等動物，於是我跪了下來，手指著男孩，盡可能地讓主人明白我希望他原諒他的兒子。主人答應了，小男孩才又回到座位上，我隨即走過去親吻他的手，我的主人也拉過男孩的手，讓他輕輕撫摸我。

　　用餐時，我聽到身後一陣吵雜聲，像是十幾架織襪機轉動的聲音，轉頭一看，發現原來是一隻比母牛還大上三倍的貓，因為女主人的餵食和撫摸而發出呼嚕聲。我遠遠地站在桌子的另一邊，與貓相距五十多呎，女主人也緊緊地抱住牠，以防牠跳過來用爪子傷害我，但那動物兇猛的容貌仍使我感到不安。根據我的經驗以及人家常告戒的，當著猛獸面前逃跑或顯露恐懼，必定會招來追逐或攻擊。因此，在這危險關頭，我要裝得若無其事，放大膽子在那隻貓面前晃了五、六回，甚至走到離牠不到半碼遠的地方，但是牠好像更怕我似的，把身子縮了回去。這時，三、四隻狗進了屋子，這在農家是常見的事，其中一隻是獒犬，身體有四頭大象那麼大，還有一隻是獵犬，比獒犬更高一些，但是沒牠那麼龐大。

　　午餐快吃完的時候，保姆抱著一個一歲大的嬰兒走了進來。嬰兒一看到我就想拿來當玩具，於是大聲啼哭起來。女主人寵愛孩子，就把我拿到小孩面前，他立刻將我攔腰抓住，想把我的頭往嘴裡塞，我大吼一聲，嚇得那小鬼鬆手扔了我。要不是他母親張開圍裙接住我，一定早就跌死了。保姆為了哄孩子，趕緊耍起撥浪鼓，那是繫在嬰兒腰間一個裝滿石頭的容器，但是一點作用也沒有，她只好使出最後一招——讓孩子吃奶。

　　午餐後，主人前往麥田監督雇工之前，我從他的聲音和

手勢可以看出，他一再囑咐妻子要好好照顧我。女主人看出我很累、想睡覺了，就把我放到了她自己的床上，用一條乾淨的白色手帕蓋住我，但那手帕比戰艦上的主帆還要大而且粗糙。

我睡醒之後，發現自己孤零零地置身在一個約莫兩三百呎寬、兩百多呎高的巨大房間裡，躺在一張二十碼寬的床上。女主人忙於家務，所以把我一個人鎖在房裡，因為生理上的需要，我不得不下床，但是這張床離地面有八碼高。我不敢擅自叫嚷，即便我喊了，以這房間到這家人所在的廚房這麼遙遠的距離，憑我的聲音，也只會是徒勞無功。 這時，兩隻老鼠沿著帷幔爬了上來，在床上東聞西嗅，其中一隻差點跑到我臉上，嚇得我趕緊跳起來，立刻拔出短劍自衛。這兩隻可怕的生物竟膽敢從我的兩側夾擊， 其中一隻的前爪抓住了我的衣領，幸好在牠傷害我之前，我就劃破牠的肚皮；另一隻見狀後立刻拔腿就跑，但是我在牠的背上留下一道大傷口，鮮血直流。凱旋歸來後，我輕輕地在床上踱步，以平復呼吸以及受驚的情緒。這些生物體形堪比大型獒犬，卻比獒犬敏捷凶狠多了，要不是我睡前沒有脫下腰帶，現在早就被撕成碎片吞下肚了。我測量了一下死老鼠的尾巴，發現只差一英吋便有兩碼長。老鼠還橫屍在床上，不停流血，雖然感到惡心，但我卻無法把它拖下床去。後來我見它還沒死透，就舉刀朝牠的脖子用力一砍，它這才澈底一命嗚呼了。

　　不久之後，女主人來到了房間，看見我渾身是血，趕緊跑過來把我拿到手中。我指著老鼠的屍體露出笑容，並且作手勢讓她知道我沒有受傷。她喊來女僕用鉗子夾起老鼠屍體扔到窗外，然後把我放到桌子上，我舉起沾滿血跡的短劍給她看，又用上衣的下襬把劍擦乾淨再放回劍鞘。經過這場打鬥，我的內急尚未解決，因此請她把我放到地上。站到地上之後，我害羞地指指門，並向她連連鞠躬。這個好心的女人終於明白我的意思了，於是用手拿起我走進花園，把我放到地上，我急忙躲在兩片樹葉之間解決了生理需求。

第 10 章

　　女主人有個九歲的女兒，是個聰明的小孩，擅於做針線活，也很會打扮她的洋娃娃。她和她母親設法把洋娃娃的搖籃整理一下，好讓我晚上有地方睡覺。搖籃放在櫃子的一個小抽屜裡，因為擔心老鼠侵擾，她們又把抽屜放在一個懸吊的架子上。與這家人住在一起的日子裡，這搖籃一直是我的床鋪；後來我開始學習他們的語言，讓他們明白我的需要，那張床也就漸漸變得更加舒適了。小女孩的手十分靈巧，她幫我做了七件襯衫和一些內衣，用的都是最精細的布料，不過仍然比我們的麻袋布還要粗；她還親手幫我洗這些衣物，同時也是我的語言老師，我每指向一樣東西，她就用當地語言告訴我那東西的名稱。多虧了她，短短幾天內我便能夠說出我需要的物品的名稱。她性格溫厚，身量不超過四英尺，以她的年紀而言算是十分嬌小。　她幫我取名叫「格里瑞格」，全家人也都這麼稱呼我。這個名字的涵義就是「矮子」的意思，我能在那個國家活下來得歸功於她。那段時間裡，我們幾乎形影不離，我稱她為我的「格蘭達莉琦」，也就是小保姆的意思。

　　附近的居民知道了我的消息，紛紛討論我的主人在田裡發現了一隻奇怪的動物，大小有如「斯普拉克那克」，模樣卻像極了人類，還能模仿人類的動作；牠用兩條腿直立行走，性情溫順，叫牠來就來，叫牠做什麼就做什麼，四肢纖細，膚色比貴族的三歲女孩還要白皙。住在附近的另一個農夫，他是主人的一位好朋友，特地前來探究事情的真相。主人立即把我放到桌上，我依照他的命令在桌上走動，抽出短劍再放回劍鞘，並且向主人的賓客鞠躬致敬，用小保姆教我的當地語言問候他，歡迎他的到來。這個人人老眼花，想把我看個究竟便戴上眼鏡；我忍不住大笑了起來，因為他的眼睛就像兩輪滿月，正從窗戶照進房間來。當這家人弄清楚緣由，也和我一同大笑起來，這個呆頭呆腦的老頭子竟勃然大怒，變了臉色。這個人是個守財奴，他建議主人把我帶到離家約二十二哩、騎馬半個鐘頭才會到的市集去展示。我看見他和主人竊竊私語了老半天，有時還指指點點。我心中的恐懼大到彷彿我已經聽見他們的談話並理解其意了。

　　第二天早晨，我的小保姆格蘭達莉琦就把整件事情告訴了我。可憐的小女孩把我抱在懷裡，羞愧難過地哭了起來，她擔心我被那些粗鄙的人拿在手裡時，會被捏死或者弄斷手腳，或是受到其他傷害。她認為我謙遜善良，現在為了錢把我展示給那些卑鄙的人賞玩，這是多麼羞恥啊。她說，爸爸媽媽已經答應把「格里瑞格」給她，但是現在他們又像去年

那樣欺騙了她，那時他們假裝給她一隻小羊，但是一等到羊長得肥壯，他們就把牠賣給了肉販。不過老實說，我並沒有像我的小保姆那樣擔心，我一直抱持著強烈的希望，認為總有一天會重獲自由。

我的主人聽從了他朋友的建議，在下一個趕集的日子，把我裝進一個盒子裡，帶著他的女兒，也就是我的小保姆，一起前往鄰近的市鎮。盒子各面都封起來，只留一扇供我進出的小門，還有幾個讓空氣流通的洞孔。小女孩很細心，她把洋娃娃床上的被褥放進盒子，讓我可以躺臥，雖然只有半小時路程，我卻被晃盪得非常不舒服，因為那匹馬跨出一步就有四十呎，而且起伏很大，有如船隻置身暴風雨中，只不過顛簸得更為頻繁。我們的旅程比從倫敦到聖奧爾本斯還要遠些。主人在一家他常光顧的客棧前下馬，跟客棧主人商量片刻，又做了些必要的準備，接著雇用了一名宣傳員通知全鎮民眾，「綠鷹客棧」將要展示一頭怪物，身長不及六呎，人類的模樣，會說幾句話，能耍上百種有趣的把戲。

我被放到客棧裡最大房間的一張桌子上，桌面約三百平方呎。我的小保姆站在桌子旁的一張矮凳上照顧我。主人每次只讓三十個人進來觀賞以免太過擁擠。我依照小保姆的指令在桌子上走動，問問題時，她還特地配合我的語言程度，因此我也盡量大聲回答。我多次轉身向觀眾敬禮、致謝歡迎，還說了些其他的話。格蘭達莉琦給我一個頂針大小的容

器當作酒杯，讓我舉杯祝賀觀眾身體健康；我拔出短劍，以英國劍術家的姿態舞弄了一番；小保姆又給我一段麥稈，我把它當作長槍耍了一陣，好在這項技藝我年輕時曾經學過。

那天一共表演了十二場，被迫重複那些把戲，使得我又疲累又苦惱。看過表演的人都嘖嘖稱奇，所以外頭的人都想衝進門來觀賞，主人為了自身的利益，規定除了小保姆外不准任何人碰我，並使觀眾的長凳與桌子四周保持一段距離，以防我被觀眾碰到而發生意外。然而，還是有一個頑皮的男學生用一個榛果對準我的頭扔了過來，害我差點被擊中。那榛果像一顆小南瓜那麼大，而且來勢兇猛，要是被擊中一定當場腦漿迸裂。因此我很高興看到那小流氓被痛打一頓並被趕出門去。

我的主人當眾宣布，下個市集的日子會再帶我來表演；同時，他也為我準備了一輛較為舒適的車子。然而，即使在家中也無法休息，因為方圓百里內的居民聽聞消息後，都紛紛攜家帶眷前來主人家看我。在這裡，一個家庭的總人口數不會少於三十人，每次主人讓我表演時，即使是給一家人看，也要求按照滿屋子的人數收費。所以，即使沒被帶到鎮上演出，一星期除了星期三的安息日之外，每天都不得休息。

主人發現我能為他賺進大把鈔票，就決定帶我到全國各大城市演出。他準備好長途旅行所必需的東西，並且打點好

家中事務後，向妻子告別，我們動身前往離家約三千哩的首
都。主人讓女兒坐在他身後的馬背上，她把裝著我的盒子綁
在腰間放在大腿上，並在盒子四周襯上最柔軟的布料，於底
部鋪上被褥，並把洋娃娃的床放在裡面，又為我準備了些內
衣和其他必需品，盡可能讓我覺得舒適。除了我們三人，還
有一個男僕同行，他騎馬跟在後面看顧行李。

　　我的主人計畫在沿途的各個城市展示我，只要有生意還
要到離大路五十或者一百英里的村莊裡，或者大戶人家去
演。 我們一路輕鬆前進，一天的路程不超過一百六十英
里，因為格蘭達莉琦疼惜我，故意抱怨說馬快步疾走會使她
很疲憊。她時常順從我的要求，把我從箱子裡拿出來呼吸新
鮮空氣，欣賞鄉村風光。我們渡過了五、六條河，每條都比
尼羅河或恆河更寬更深。我們走了十個星期，在許多村莊和
私宅，還有十八個大城市表演過。

　　後來我們抵達首都「羅布魯格魯德」，意思是「宇宙的
驕傲」。主人在離皇宮不遠的城內大街上找了住處，一如往
常發出傳單，上面詳細地描述了我的外貌和才能。他租了一
間三、四百呎寬的大房間，裡面擺了一張直徑六十呎的桌子
作為我的表演舞台，並在離桌緣三呎的地方圍了一圈三呎高
的護欄以防止我跌下去。我一天演出十場，所有觀眾都驚歎
不已，我已經可以把當地語言說得不錯，也能完全理解他們
的問話。此外，我還學會了他們的字母，偶爾還能解釋幾個

句子。因為,不論在家裡或旅途中空閒的時候,格蘭達莉琦
都是我的老師,她在口袋裡放了一本小書,不比尼古拉斯·桑
鬆的地圖冊大多少,那是供年輕女孩們看的一本簡要敘述他
們宗教的普通讀物,她就用這本書 教我字母、講解詞義。

第 11 章

　　由於每天頻繁地演出，幾個星期下來我的健康起了很大的變化。主人賺的錢越多，就越貪得無厭。我沒有胃口吃東西，幾乎瘦得只剩下一把骨頭了。主人發現這個情形，想盡快從我身上多撈一筆。這時宮廷派了一位傳令官前來，命令他立刻帶我進宮，為皇后和貴婦們表演取樂。有幾位貴婦已經把我的容貌、舉止和智慧等奇妙的事情報告給皇后。皇后和隨侍一旁的人對我的行為舉止非常欣喜，我跪下請求皇后恩准我親吻她的腳，但是被放到一張桌上後，仁慈的皇后卻把她的小指伸到我的面前，我雙臂環抱住，畢恭畢敬地在她的指尖上親吻了一下。

　　皇后問了幾個問題，我盡量清楚簡要地回答。她還問我是否願意住進宮中，我深深鞠躬至桌面，謙遜地回答說，若能自己做主，我願意終身為皇后效勞並引以為榮。她隨即問我的主人願不願意將我高價出售，主人認定我活不過一個月，早就想脫手了，於是他開價一千個金幣，當場成交。每枚金幣大約有八百個摩伊多 那麼大。但是，如果按照這個

國家和歐洲的所有東西的比例，再按照金子在他們那兒的高價來計算一下，這一千塊金幣的數目還不抵英國的一千個幾尼 。隨後我對皇后說，既然現在是皇后陛下最卑微的奴僕了，希望陛下開恩，讓一直細心照料我的格蘭達莉琦也留下來為陛下效勞，同時讓她繼續做我的保姆和老師。

皇后答應了我的請求，並且輕易地取得農夫的同意。對於女兒能留在宮中，他當然很高興，女孩也難掩喜悅之情。我昔日的主人一邊向我告別，一邊說是他替我找了這麼好的一個地方，然後退了出去。對此我不置一詞，只是朝他冷冷地鞠了個躬。

皇后把我拿在手中，帶我到皇帝那兒。皇帝神情莊重嚴肅，他一開始沒看清楚我的樣子，只是冷淡地問皇后什麼時候喜歡上「斯普拉克那克」了，機智幽默的皇后把我輕輕放在桌上，令我向皇帝自我介紹。我簡要地說明了幾句；一刻也離不開我的格蘭達莉琦正站在門口，這時她也被叫了進來，證實我到她父親家之後的全部經歷。

皇帝博學多聞，研究過哲學，對於數學尤其感興趣；儘管如此，在我尚未開口說話之前，他看到我的樣子，又見我站直身子走路，以為我大概是哪位天才工匠設計的發條機械，在這個國家，這類機械製造技術已發完善。不過當他聽到我說話，並且說得有條有理時，不禁大感驚訝。我向他陳

述自己來到這個王國的經過，但是他不相信，認為這是格蘭達莉琦和她父親串通編造的故事，他們教我這套說詞，以便把我賣個好價錢。又問了我其他幾個問題，可是我說話除了帶有外國口音，還夾雜著一些與宮廷文雅風格不相稱的鄉下土話，並沒有什麼破綻。

皇帝召來了三位當週值班的大學者，這幾位先生仔細地看過我的模樣之後，各有不同的見解，但是他們一致認為，我不可能是自然法則下誕生的產物，因為我沒有自衛的能力：不僅行動不敏捷、不會爬樹，也不會挖地洞。他們對我的牙齒進行精密的檢視之後，認為我是肉食性動物，但是和大多數四足動物相比，我根本敵不過牠們，即使是田鼠也比我來得靈敏，他們無法想像我該如何維生，除非餵我吃蝸牛或其他昆蟲；不過他們又提出了許多論據，證明我不可能吃那些東西。其中一位學者認為我可能是個胚胎或早產兒，不過這個看法立即遭到另外兩位學者的反駁，因為他們看到我的四肢發育健全，並且透過放大鏡清楚看見我的鬍子，表示我已經有些年歲。他們也不認為我是侏儒，因為我實在小得無人可比，即使是皇后寵愛的一名侏儒，他是全國最矮小的人，也都還有三十呎高。經過一番激辯，他們最後做出一致的結論，認為我只是「瑞爾普倫·斯開爾卡斯」，字面意思就是「造物者的玩笑」。

皇帝要皇后下令特別照顧我，並表示格蘭達莉琦應留下

來，因爲他看出我們倆的感情非常好。皇后爲她準備了一間
舒適的房間，有一名女教師負責她的教育，一名宮女爲她更
衣梳妝，還有兩名僕人幫她做些粗活，但是照顧我的事則全
部由她負責。

　　皇后命令她的細木工依照我和格蘭達莉琦喜歡的樣式，
設計一個箱子作爲我的臥房。那名巧匠是個能手，經由我的
指示，他在三個星期內就做了一間十六呎平方、十二呎高的
木造房間，有幾扇窗戶，一扇門，還有兩個櫥櫃，就像一般
倫敦的臥室。天花板上有兩個鉸鏈，所以可以上下開合，皇
后的裝潢師爲我設計的床就是從上面放進去的。格蘭達莉琦

每天親手把床拿出來透氣，晚上再放回去，並為我把屋頂鎖
上。一位以製造袖珍物品出名的工匠用類似象牙的材料，幫
我做了兩張有靠背和扶手的椅子、兩張桌子和一個可以放東
西的櫃子。房間的四壁、地板和天花板都鋪上了襯墊，以防
搬運我的人不小心而發生事故，而且在我乘馬車時也可減緩
顛簸。我要求他們在門上加一道鎖，以防老鼠跑進來，為此
鐵匠試了好多次，才打造出一把他們從未見過的小鎖。我設
法把鑰匙留在自己口袋裡，因為我擔心格蘭達莉琦會把它弄
丟。皇后又下令拿最細的絲綢為我縫製衣服，雖然那絲綢沒
比英國的毛毯厚多少，卻十分笨重，我穿了好一陣子才習
慣。那些衣服是照該國樣式做的，有點像波斯服，也有點像
中國服，顯得相當體面大方。

　　皇后很喜歡我陪伴她，少了我就無法用餐。她在餐桌上
靠近左手肘的地方，特地為我擺了一張桌子和椅子，格蘭達
莉琦便站在一張凳子上，緊挨著我的桌子協助照料。我有一
整套銀製餐具，和皇后的比較起來，就好像我在倫敦玩具店
內看到的洋娃娃房裡擺設的餐具一樣。我的小保姆把這套餐
具放在她口袋裡的一個銀盒裡，要用餐時才拿出來，而且總
是親手清洗乾淨。和皇后一起用餐的只有兩位公主，大公主
十六歲，小公主十三歲零一個月。皇后習慣把一小塊肉放到
我的盤子裡，讓我自己切著吃，把看我小口小口地吃東西的
模樣當成一種娛樂，因為皇后一口吃下的東西，是十二個英

國農夫一餐的分量,有一段時間我看了都覺得噁心。她可以把一隻雲雀的翅膀連骨帶肉一口咬得粉碎,而那翅膀有九隻火雞那麼大;她往嘴裡送進一小片麵包,但那也有兩條價格十二便士的麵包那麼大;她用金杯飲酒,一口可以喝掉一大桶量那麼多;她的餐刀有兩把長柄鐮刀那麼長,湯匙、叉子和其他餐具也是同樣比例的大小。記得有一次,我因為好奇而讓格蘭達莉琦帶我去宮裡看其他人用餐的情形,十幾把像這樣巨大的刀叉同時舉起,心想那是我從未見過的恐怖景象。

　　每逢星期三安息日,皇帝、皇后依照慣例和王子、公主要在陛下的內宮裡一起用餐。如今我已是皇帝寵愛的人物了,每到這時候,我的小桌椅就會被擺放到他左手邊的一瓶鹽罐前面。這位君王很喜歡和我交談,詢問我一些關於歐洲的風俗習慣、宗教、法律、政府和學術之事,我也盡我所能地答覆。他的理解力敏銳,判斷精確,對我所說的話總有睿智的反應與意見。不過我得承認,每當我談起摯愛的祖國,說起貿易、戰爭、宗教和政黨,我便開始滔滔不絕。因為所受教育而懷有成見的皇帝,忍不住用右手把我舉起來,並用另一手輕輕撫摸我,一陣大笑。並問我是輝格黨還是托利黨。然後,他轉頭對隨侍在後的首相,接著回過頭對站在身後的首相說,人類的尊嚴竟如此微不足道,像我這麼小的昆蟲都能模仿。「不過,」他又說,「我敢說這些小傢伙們也

有爵位和官銜；他們造了一些蜂窩蟻穴，稱之為樓宇城市；他們也裝模作樣的打扮一番；他們也談戀愛、打仗、辯論、欺詐甚至背叛！」他口若懸河，氣得我臉色一陣青一陣白。我們那宏偉的祖國，文明和武力的主宰者，是法蘭西的剋星，歐洲的仲裁者，是道德、信仰、榮譽和真理的中心，是世界的驕傲和榮耀，難以置信他竟然如此地藐視。

然而，我當時的處境不允許我對這種侮辱表示出任何憤慨，仔細考慮過後，我甚至開始懷疑我是不是真的受到了傷害。 幾個月下來，我已經看慣了他們的外表，聽慣了他們的談話，每一件事物看起來都等比例的碩大，當初因他們的身軀和面孔所感到的恐懼已逐漸消失。如果我那時看見一群英國貴族男女穿著華服，在那裡裝模作樣，趾高氣揚，空談閒聊，老實說，我也很可能像這位皇帝和他的大臣一樣，大聲嘲笑他們。事實上，皇后經常把我拿在手裡站在鏡子前，這時候我也忍不住要笑自己，因為再沒有比這幅對照畫面更滑稽的了，因此我不禁開始幻想自己的身材比原來縮小了好幾倍。

最令我感到氣憤和屈辱的，莫過於皇后寵愛的侏儒了。他是該國有史以來身高最矮的人，可是自從看見我比他矮了許多，開始變得傲慢無禮。每當我站在皇后前廳的桌子上和宮裡的爵爺貴婦們談話時，他總喜歡擺出高傲的姿態故意從旁邊走過，假裝自己很高大，並且說幾句譏諷我矮小的話。

這時候我只能叫他一聲兄弟,向他挑戰摔角,或說些挑釁的話作為報復,這在宮廷男侍之間很常見。一天晚餐的時候,這個惡毒的小子被我說的話給惹火了,竟然站到皇后座椅的扶手上,一把將我攔腰抓起,扔進一個裝有奶油的大銀碗裡,然後拔腿就跑。我整個人掉進碗裡,幸好我是個游泳健將,否則不知要吃多少苦頭。格蘭達莉琦那時正好在房間另一頭,皇后則嚇得不知如何救我。最後還是我的小保姆飛奔過來把我救起,但是我已經吃下超過一夸脫的奶油,我被送到了床上,除了損壞一套衣服,倒沒有受傷。侏儒被痛打了一頓,並且被罰吃下那一大碗奶油;不久之後就把他送給一名貴婦。我很高興再也不會見到他。

在這之前,他也曾以下流的伎倆對付過我,雖然引得皇后哈哈大笑,但也令她非常生氣,要不是我寬宏大量替他求情,他早就被趕出宮了。那次是皇后拿起盤子裡的一根髓骨,挖出骨髓後,又把骨頭立在盤子裡;此時格蘭達莉琦正好走到餐具櫃邊,侏儒見機不可失,便悄悄登上她專門照顧我所站的腳凳,雙手將我捧起,併攏我的兩腿,隨即猛地往骨頭裡塞,一直塞到我的腰際。我困在裡面好一陣子,樣子十分滑稽好笑。因為我覺得大呼小叫有失身分,所以大約一分鐘之後才有人發現我出了事。幸好御 少有熱的肉食,我的腿並沒有因此燙傷,只是襪子和褲子被弄得一團糟。侏儒因為有我替他求情,只有被痛打了一頓。

扶手上，一把將我攔腰抓起，扔進一個裝有奶油的大銀碗裡，然後拔腿就跑。我整個人掉進碗裡，幸好我是個游泳健將，否則不知要吃多少苦頭。格蘭達莉琦那時正好在房間另一頭，皇后則嚇得不知如何救我。最後還是我的小保姆飛奔過來把我救起，但是我已經吃下超過一夸脫的奶油，我被送到了床上，除了損壞一套衣服，倒沒有受傷。侏儒被痛打了一頓，並且被罰吃下那一大碗奶油；不久之後就把他送給一名貴婦。我很高興再也不會見到他。

在這之前，他也曾以下流的伎倆對付過我，雖然引得皇后哈哈大笑，但也令她非常生氣，要不是我寬宏大量替他求情，他早就被趕出宮了。那次是皇后拿起盤子裡的一根髓骨，挖出骨髓後，又把骨頭立在盤子裡；此時格蘭達莉琦正好走到餐具櫃邊，侏儒見機不可失，便悄悄登上她專門照顧我所站的腳凳，雙手將我捧起，併攏我的兩腿，隨即猛地往骨頭裡塞，一直塞到我的腰際。我困在裡面好一陣子，樣子十分滑稽好笑。因為我覺得大呼小叫有失身分，所以大約一分鐘之後才有人發現我出了事。幸好御　少有熱的肉食，我的腿並沒有因此燙傷，只是襪子和褲子被弄得一團糟。侏儒因為有我替他求情，只有被痛打了一頓。

第 12 章

　　這個王國是個半島，東北邊境是三十哩高的山脈，山頂有火山，因此完全無法通行，即使最博學的人也不知道山的另一頭住著什麼人，或者究竟有沒有人住。王國的另外三面環海，但卻一個海港也沒有，因為河川出海的沿岸布滿尖銳的岩石，而且海上波濤洶湧，根本沒有人敢冒險駕船出海，所以這裡的人沒有跟任何國家有商業往來。不過大河裡到處是船隻，這裡盛產鮮美的魚，因此幾乎不用到海裡捕魚，因為海魚的大小和歐洲的一樣，並不值得捕捉。由此可見，這塊大陸得天獨厚，自然界的動植物長得如此碩大。他們偶爾會抓到撞上岩石的鯨魚，並且大快朵頤一番，百姓便可以打撈上來，吃上一頓。當然了，這些鯨魚的身體是很大的，雖然當地人力大無比，但背起一條鯨魚來也頗為吃力。鯨魚在當地是稀有產品，有的人打撈上鯨魚後，用有蓋子的大籃子裝著送到羅布魯格魯德去。我曾在國王餐桌上的一隻盤子裡見過一條，那真可謂是一味珍品，不過我注意到他並不愛吃。我想一定是這東西大得叫他討厭，儘管我在格陵蘭還見過一條更大一點的。

　　皇宮是佔地約有七哩方圓的建築群；主要宮殿一般約兩百四十呎高，長和寬也都與之相稱。皇帝賜給格蘭達莉琦和我一輛馬車，她的女教師經常帶她和待在箱子裡的我到城裡逛逛或到商店購物，不過，格蘭達莉琦經常順應我的要求，把我從箱子裡拿出來放在手上，讓我更方便觀看沿途的房屋和路人。我估計這輛馬車有英國國會大廳那麼大，不過沒那麼高。雖然我無法說得更精確。

　　除了平常裝載我的那只大箱子外，皇后又下令同一位工匠為我做一個較小的箱子，方便旅行時使用，因為大箱子放在格蘭達莉琦的腿上稍大了些，放在馬車裡也嫌累贅。這個旅行用的小盒是正方形，三面的中央都各開有一扇窗戶，外邊再釘上鐵絲框，避免長途旅行時發生意外。第四面沒有窗戶，不過裝上了兩個堅固的鉤環；如果我想到馬背上，攜帶我的人可以用一條皮帶穿過鉤環把箱子扣在腰間。不論是陪同皇帝皇后出巡、遊賞花園，還是拜訪宮中達官貴婦，如果遇上格蘭達莉琦身體不適，就會把照料我的事交付給一些穩健可靠的僕人。旅途中，當我坐厭了馬車，騎馬的僕人就會把小箱子扣在腰間，放到他前面的墊子上，這樣我就可以從三面窗戶飽覽沿途的景色。我的小房間裡有一張床、一個吊床、兩把椅子和一張桌子，桌椅都用螺絲釘固定在地板上，以免被車馬的震動搖得東倒西歪。

　　每當我想到市區逛逛，也總是坐在這個旅行用的小箱子

裡，由格蘭達莉琦抱著放在大腿上，乘坐一種由四人抬行的
敞篷轎子，另有皇后的兩名侍從隨行。民眾時常聽聞我的
事，總是好奇地湧到轎子四周，格蘭達莉琦則會客氣地請轎
夫停下來，把我拿在手裡好讓大家更方便觀看。

　　我一直嚮往這個國家一座很重要的廟宇，尤其是它那據
說舉國最高的鐘樓。這樣，一天我的小保姆就帶我去了，不
過老實說，我回來以後感到大失所望。因為從地面到最高的
塔頂還不到三千英尺，從本國人和歐洲人的高矮差別看來，
這並不值得驚奇，若按比例加以比較，它根本沒法與索利茲
波立教堂 1 的尖閣相提並論（倘若我沒有記錯的話）。但是
對於這個國家我終身都將感激不盡，所以我不能貶損它的名
譽，應當承認，無論這座名塔在高度上有什麼欠缺，其美觀
與堅固都足以補償它的不足。廟宇的牆壁將近有一百英尺
厚，都是用每塊約四十英尺見方的石頭砌成，四周的壁龕裡
放著用大理石刻成的比真人還要高大的神像和帝王之像。有
一尊雕塑的小拇指脫落下來，掉在一堆垃圾裡無人注意，我
量了一下，足有四英尺一英吋長。格蘭達莉琦用她的手帕把
小拇指包了起來，放在口袋裡帶了回來，和其他一些小玩意
兒放在一起。像她這個年齡的孩子，對這些小玩意兒通常都
是非常感興趣的。

　　御膳廚房是一座宏偉的建築，屋頂呈拱形，約有六百呎
高，裡面的大烤爐比聖保羅教堂的圓頂約窄十步，這是我返

回英國後特地去量的。不過，如果我把廚房裡的大爐、大鍋大壺、鐵叉上的大塊烤肉以及其他許多細節都寫出來，恐怕沒有人會相信，旅人經常都會被懷疑誇大不實。　而為了避免諸如此類的責難，恐怕有時我又會走向另一極端。如果這本書有機會譯成布羅布丁奈格語（布羅布丁奈格是王國的一般名稱）流傳到那裡，國王和他的臣民們都會埋怨我侮辱他們，把他們描寫得太渺小、太失實了。

　　皇帝馬廄裡飼養的馬，一般不會超過六百匹，每匹馬的高度大多在五十四呎到六十呎之間。皇帝逢重大節慶出巡時，為了顯示其皇威，總會出動五百名騎兵部隊護衛，在還沒看到皇帝的軍隊操演之前，真的以為那是我生平所見最壯觀的場面了。

第 13 章

　　在該國，我本來可以過得相當如意，但由於身材矮小，弄出了幾件滑稽可笑的麻煩事。恕我冒昧，現在就來說一說其中的幾件。格蘭達莉琦經常把我放在小箱子裡帶到御花園，有時會把我拿出來放在手上，或是到地上走一走。我記得，在那個侏儒被皇后趕走以前，有一天他也跟著我們來到花園裡。我的保姆放下我來，和他緊挨在一起走到幾棵矮蘋果樹旁邊。我故意賣弄聰明，跟他開起了玩笑，我暗示他和這蘋果樹有某相似之處，碰巧這說法在他們的語言中也同樣適用。一聽這話，這壞傢伙就瞄準我正從一棵樹下走過的當兒，在我頭頂上搖起樹來，這一搖，十二顆蘋果，每隻差不多都有布里斯托爾大酒桶那麼大，就劈頭蓋臉地砸了下來。我一彎腰，一隻蘋果砸到我背上，於是我面朝地摔了一跤，不過倒沒受到別的傷害。由於這事由我挑起，所以在我的懇求下，侏儒得到了寬恕。

　　有一天，她把我放在一塊平整的草地上自己玩耍，忽然下起一陣猛烈的冰雹，我立刻被砸倒在地，冰雹殘酷地襲擊

我的全身，就好像網球打在身上一樣，我設法爬到百里香花壇的背風面，臉朝下趴著躲在那裡，不過仍然渾身是傷，整整十天不能出門。這也沒什麼好驚訝的，因為這個國家的大自然事物都是等比例地巨大，一顆冰雹差不多是歐洲冰雹的一千八百倍大。

同樣在這座花園裡，我遇上了一件更危險的意外。有一次，小保姆把大箱子留在家裡，把我放到了一個她認為安全的地方之後，就和她的女教師以及幾個女性友人到花園的另一處去了，我經常要求她這麼做，好讓我獨自沉思。當她離開時，園丁總管養的一條白色小獵犬突然闖進花園，來到我躺著的地方，那隻狗循著氣味直奔而來，隨即將我叼在嘴裡，搖著尾巴跑回主人跟前，輕輕地把我放到地上。幸好牠受過良好的訓練，雖然把我銜在齒間，卻絲毫沒有傷到我，連衣服也沒有扯破，但是那可憐的園丁嚇壞了，他原本就認識我，而且對我很不錯，他用雙手將我輕輕地捧起，問我怎麼樣了；我則是驚魂未定，氣都喘不過來，一個字也說不出。幾分鐘後等我回過神，他才把我安全地送回小保姆身邊，這時，小保姆已經回到原先放置我的地方，正心急如焚，她把園丁狠狠地訓斥了一頓。

這件意外發生之後，格蘭達莉琦決心再也不讓我離開她的視線，我早就擔心她會這麼做，所以隱瞞了之前遇到的幾件小意外。有一次，一隻在花園上空盤旋的鳶鳥突然俯身朝

我衝來，要不是我果斷地拔出短劍，並且跑到花棚下尋求掩護，牠一定會伸出爪子把我攫走。又有一次，我爬上一座新築起的鼴鼠丘頂，一不小心掉進了鼠洞裡，把衣服全弄髒了，我只好撒謊為自己找了個藉口；還有一次，我獨自走在路上，正想著可憐的英國，結果被一個蝸牛殼絆倒，把右脛骨給摔斷了。

也不知道該高興或是尷尬，當我獨自行走的時候，那些較小的鳥一點都不怕我，牠們會跳到離我不到一碼的範圍內尋找蟲子和其他食物，非常安閒自在，似乎無視於我的存在，真不知道應該覺得高興還是屈辱。記得有一回，一隻畫眉鳥竟然從我手中啄走格蘭達莉琦給我當早餐的一塊餅乾，當我想抓這些鳥時，牠們大膽地反抗，企圖啄我的手指，使我不敢靠近，然後又毫不在乎地跳回去繼續覓食。不過，有一天我拿了一根粗棍子，全力一揮正巧擊中一隻紅雀；我雙手抓緊牠的脖子，得意洋洋地提著牠跑向我的保姆。然而，那隻鳥一甦醒過來，就用翅膀不停地拍打我的頭和身子，儘管伸直了手臂使鳥爪搆不到我，但是鬆手放掉牠的念頭出現了二十次。幸好一個僕人即時趕來搭救，把紅雀的脖子給扭斷；皇后下令以那隻鳥做為我次日的晚餐，就我記憶所及，那隻紅雀似乎比英國的天鵝還要大。

皇后時常聽我談及航海的經歷，所以每當我心情鬱悶的時候，她總會想辦法為我解悶，問我能否操作船帆或船槳，

划船運動是否有益我的健康。我回答說，這兩樣我都很擅長，雖然真正的職業是隨船醫生，但是如果遇到緊急狀況，我也得像普通水手一樣工作。皇后說，如果我能設計一艘船，她的木工就能製造出來，而且她會提供划船的場所。那名木工聰明靈巧，在我的指導下，十天內就造好了一艘足以乘載八個歐洲人的遊艇，而且船具齊備。船造好之後，皇后興高采烈地抱著它去見皇帝，皇帝下令把船放入一個蓄滿水的池子，讓我到船上試驗一下，但是池子太小了，我根本無法操作那兩把船槳。不過皇后早已備好另一個方案，她吩咐木工做了一個三百呎長、五十呎寬、八呎深的木質水槽，塗上瀝青以防漏水，放在皇宮外殿牆邊的地板上。靠近槽底處有一個活栓，可以讓久放汙濁的水排掉；兩個僕人不到半個小時就能將水槽灌滿水，我時常在這裡划船消遣，皇后和貴婦們也很欣賞我的划船技術和敏捷身手，並以此為樂。有時候我會揚起船帆，貴婦們會用扇子為我搧起陣陣強風，此時我只要專心掌舵就可以了，貴婦們如果累了，就由幾名男侍用嘴吹氣推帆前進，我則隨心所欲向左向右，展現駕船本領。每次划完船，格蘭達莉琦都會把船拿進她的房間，並且掛在釘子上晾乾。

有一次，由於負責每隔三天為水槽換水的一名僕人太過粗心，沒有發現水桶裡有一隻大青蛙，竟然將牠倒進了水槽裡。我坐船下水之後，一直躲藏著的青蛙看見有個地方可以休息，便想爬上船來，使得船身嚴重傾斜，我不得不站到船

的另一邊，用身體的重量保持平衡，以免船隻翻覆。青蛙上船之後，一跳就是半條船的距離，在我的頭頂上來回跳躍，噁心的黏液塗得我一身都是。牠那肥大的身軀，看起來真是所有動物中最畸形醜陋的，我要求格蘭達莉琦讓我單獨對付牠，於是用船槳狠狠地打了牠一頓，終於逼得牠跳出船外。

然而，我在這個王國所遭遇到最危險的事件，是由御膳廚房裡一名人員飼養的猴子所引起的。格蘭達莉琦外出辦事或探訪某人時，會把我鎖在她的房間裡，當天天氣很暖和，房間的窗戶都敞開著，我住的那個大箱子的門窗也都敞開著。我靜靜地坐在桌前沉思，突然聽到有東西從房間的窗戶跳了進來，然後就在房裡跳來跳去。我十分驚慌害怕，沒有離開座椅，但還是壯著膽子向外看了一眼，接著，我看到了那隻淘氣的動物在那裡跳上跳下，最後來到了箱子前。牠似乎對這個箱子很好奇，從門口和每扇窗戶往裡頭張望，我退縮到箱子的角落，然而當那猴子從四面往裡頭瞧，驚慌失措的我竟忘了躲到床底下，這對我來說是很容易的事。那猴子又是張望，又是齜牙咧嘴，還發出吱吱的叫聲，一段時間後終於發現了我，牠從門口伸進一隻爪子，就像貓逗老鼠一樣捉弄我；儘管我一直閃躲，牠最後還是抓住了我的外套下襬，把我給拖了出去。牠用右前爪將我抓起，像保姆餵孩子吸奶般地抱著我，也和我在歐洲看到大猴抱小猴的情形一樣，只要一掙扎，牠就把我抱得更緊。我想牠把我當成是小

猴子了，因為牠不時用另一隻爪子輕撫我的臉頰，這時候，房門突然傳來一陣聲響，好像是有人開門，牠立刻跳上原先進來的那扇窗戶，然後再跳上屋簷的滴水溝，用三隻腳走路，第四隻腳抱著我，一直爬到隔壁的屋頂上。

猴子抱著我往外逃的那一刻，我聽到格蘭達莉琦尖叫了一聲，那可憐的女孩幾乎要發狂了，而皇宮也陷入一片騷亂，僕人們連忙跑去找梯子。宮裡有數百人看著猴子坐在屋脊上，一隻前爪像抱嬰孩般地緊抱著我，另一隻前爪餵我吃東西，把一側頰囊中擠出的食物往我嘴裡塞，我不肯吃，牠還輕輕地拍打我，使得下面圍觀的人都忍不住哈哈大笑。我想這也不能怪他們，因為當時的情景，除了我以外，任誰看了都會覺得很可笑。有幾個人往上面丟石頭，希望把猴子趕下來，但是立刻就被制止，否則我可能已被砸得頭破血流。

梯子架妥之後，幾個人爬了上來；猴子見狀，發現自己幾乎被包圍，於是把我丟在屋脊的瓦片上，自己逃命去了。我在離地面三百碼的瓦片上坐了一陣子，隨時可能被風吹落，或者因為自己頭昏目眩而摔倒，從屋脊一直翻滾到屋簷。幸好，一個誠實的小夥子爬了上來，他是小保姆的男僕，他把我放進他的褲袋裡，安全地帶了下來。

猴子硬把髒東西塞到我嘴裡，差點把我噎死，幸好小保姆趕緊用一根細針把它們挑出來，我吐了一陣之後才覺得舒

服許多，不過還是很虛弱，身體兩側也被那可惡的畜牲搯傷，被迫臥床休息了兩個星期。在我生病期間，皇帝、皇后以及宮廷每天都派人前來慰問我的健康，皇后還親自駕臨好幾次。那隻猴子最後被處死了，而且皇宮裡再也不准飼養這種動物。

我每天都為宮裡提供荒謬可笑的故事。格蘭達莉琦雖然對我十分愛護，但是每當我做了什麼蠢事，她就會淘氣地向皇后報告，以便討皇后開心。有一次小女孩身體不適，女教師帶她出城到三十哩外、約一小時車程的地方透透氣，她們在一條田野小徑附近下了車，格蘭達莉琦放下我的旅行箱子，讓我到外面走動。小徑上有一堆牛糞，我試圖跳過去一展身手；我向前跑去，可惜跳得不夠遠，結果正好落在牛糞中央，深及膝蓋，我費力地從牛糞堆裡走出來，雖然一個男僕用手帕盡量替我擦拭乾淨，我仍然滿身污穢，所以小保姆把我關在箱子裡，直到我們返回宮裡。皇后很快就知道了事情的經過，那幾個男僕更將此事傳遍宮廷，所以我的糗事一連好幾天又成為大家的笑柄。

第 14 章

　　我每星期晉見皇帝一次或兩次，經常看到理髮師幫他刮鬍子，初次看到那情形著實令我嚇了一跳，因為那把剃刀約有兩把普通鐮刀那麼長，根據這個國家的習俗，皇帝一星期只刮兩次鬍子。有一次，我說服理髮師給我一些刮下來的肥皂沫，從裡面挑選了四、五十根最粗硬的鬍渣，然後找來一塊好木頭，把它削成梳背的形狀，又向格蘭達莉琦要了一根最小的針，在梳背上鑽了幾個等距離的孔，再把鬍渣固定在小孔裡，最後用小刀把鬍渣末端削尖，如此就做成了一把很不錯的梳子。我原本那把梳子的梳齒已經嚴重毀損，幾乎不能使用，這把新梳子正好能派上用場，我不認為這個國家有哪位工匠的精巧技藝，能幫我另製一把好用的梳子。

　　這使我想到了一個有趣的點子，我花了許多閒暇時間在上面，我請皇后的女僕替我把皇后梳頭時掉落的頭髮保留起來，沒多久便收集了很多。我和奉命來幫我做點零碎工作的木匠朋友商量了一下，指導他做出兩張和我箱子裡那幾把椅子差不多大小的椅架，並在設計作為椅背和椅座的地方，用

細鑽子鑽一些小孔，接著，我挑選出最堅韌的幾根頭髮，將它們穿過這些小孔，就像英國人製做籐椅那樣。椅子完成之後，我把它們當成禮物送給了皇后，她把椅子擺在櫥櫃裡當成奇珍異物來展示，而事實上，看過的人無不嘖嘖稱奇。皇后要我坐上其中一把椅子，但我堅定地拒絕，表示寧死也不願把身體不潔的部位放到那些寶貴的頭髮上，那可是曾經為皇后的頭部增輝的東西啊！此外，我又利用那些頭髮做了一個約五呎長的小錢包，並用金線織上皇后的名字，徵得皇后同意之後，我把錢包送給了格蘭達莉琦，不過說實話，這個錢包中看不中用，因為它承受不了大錢幣的重量，所以格蘭達莉琦只放了一些女孩們喜歡的小玩物在裡面。

皇帝喜好音樂，經常在宮裡舉行音樂會，有時他們也讓我出席，把箱子放在桌子上好讓我聆聽演奏。不過音樂聲太大了，我幾乎分辨不出是什麼曲調。我相信，即使皇家軍隊所有鼓號在耳邊齊奏，也沒有這麼大聲。因此，我請他們讓箱子盡量遠離演奏者，然後關上門窗，放下窗簾，這才覺得他們的音樂並不難聽。

我年輕時曾學過一點古鍵琴，格蘭達莉琦的房裡就有一架，一名教師每星期來教她兩次，我把那架琴也叫做古鍵琴，是因為它們的外型相似，彈奏的方法也一樣。我突然有個想法，可以用這台樂器彈奏一首英國曲子取悅皇帝和皇后，不過這件事相當困難，因為那架古鍵琴有六十呎長，每

第 14 章

個琴鍵幾近一呎寬，就算我兩臂伸直，最多也只能觸及五個琴鍵，而且非得用拳頭猛擊才能按下琴鍵，這樣實在太費力了，也不會有什麼效果。後來我想出一個辦法，準備了兩根和普通棍棒差不多大小的圓棍，一頭比較粗一頭比較細，較粗的一頭用老鼠皮包起來，這樣敲打時才不會傷到琴鍵，也不會干擾音樂，琴鍵前擺了一張比鍵盤約低四呎的長凳，然後我就在上面左右盡量快跑，並用那兩根圓棍敲擊正確的琴鍵，設法演奏了一首快步舞曲。皇帝和皇后非常開心，不過對我來說，這可是我做過最劇烈的運動，即使如此，我仍然無法敲擊超過十六個琴鍵，所以無法像其他音樂家那樣同時彈奏出低音和高音，這使得我的演出大為失色。

皇帝的領悟力很強，時常叫人把我連人帶盒擺到房間的桌上，再命令我從箱子裡搬出一張椅子坐在盒頂，這樣我和他的臉就差不多在相同高度。我們以這種方式交談了幾次，有一天，我直率地對皇帝說，他對歐洲及世界其他各地所顯露的鄙視態度，似乎與他卓越的心靈不相符，一個人的心智才能並不隨著他的身材成長，相反地，在我們國家，我們發現最高大的人往往最缺乏才智；在動物界，蜜蜂和螞蟻比起許多較大的動物更具有勤勉、靈巧和聰慧的好名聲。因此，雖然我在他眼中微不足道，我還是願意竭盡心力為他效勞，皇帝專心地聽我說完，對我的評價比以往更高了，他希望我把英國政府的情況盡量仔細地告訴他，雖然君王們都喜歡自

己的風俗制度，但是如果有值得效法之處，他也樂意聽取。

　　我首先啓稟陛下，我國領土包括兩大海島，三大王國統歸一位君王治理，除此之外，我們在美洲還有殖民地。我們的土地肥沃，氣候溫和，就此我又嘮叨了半天。接下來，我又談到英國議會。議會的一部分由貴族組成，稱爲上議院。上議員都有貴族血統，他們世襲最古老而富足的祖傳產業。我還告訴他，這些人文武雙全，因爲在他們一直接受針對這兩方面的特殊教育，這樣，他們生來就具有做國王及王國的參議的資格，因而他們能幫助國家立法，能成爲完滿處理一切上訴的最高法庭的法官，能具有勇敢、正直、忠誠的品格，隨時準備成爲捍衛他們的君王和國家的戰士。他們是整個王國的驕傲和棟樑，是他們偉大祖輩的優秀繼承者。他們的祖輩因爲種種美德而享譽盛名，故而子孫後代也一直興盛不衰。除此之外，上議院中還有一些人是享有主教頭銜的神職人員，負責管理宗教事務，率領教士們向人民布傳教義。君王和最英明的參議員們從全國生活最聖潔、學識最淵博的教士中選拔出這些人，他們確實是教士和人民的精神領袖。

　　議會的另一部分由一個集會組成，稱爲下議院。下議員都是些德高望重的紳士，是人民自己自由選舉出來的。這些人才能非凡、熱愛祖國，能夠代表全國人民的智慧。這兩院人士組成了歐洲最嚴正的議會，而這一立法機關則由議員們和君王一起掌管。

我又談到法庭。法官們都賢明而精通法律，是極為可敬的人士，他們主持審判，對人們的權利及財產糾紛作出判決，以此懲罰罪惡，庇護無辜。我提到了我國節儉的財政管理制度，也提到了我國海陸軍隊的勇武與功績。我先估算出我們每個教派或政黨大約擁有幾百萬人，然後再統算出我國的總人口。我甚至沒有忘記提到我們的體育和娛樂，以及其他一些我認為能為本國爭光的小事例。最後，我對英國過去一百年來的主要事件做了一番簡要的歷史評述。

為了講述這些，我一共被召見了五次，每次都持續好幾個小時。國王對我講述的一切都很感興趣，聽得津津有味，有時還作一些筆記，把他不懂的問題寫成備忘錄，以便與我進一步探討。

他想知道，我說的那些下議員是如何選舉產生的？假如一個外地人，只要他有錢，是否就可以使得普通的選民選他為代表，而不選他們自己的地主或鄰近最值得考慮的紳士？既然我承認這事既麻煩又很費錢，沒有薪金或年俸的人往往弄得傾家蕩產，可是，人們為什麼還是那麼強烈渴望往這個議會裡擠呢？這看起來像是大家品德極高，都有為公眾服務的精神，但陛下卻懷疑那可不可能總是出於忠誠？同時他也想知道，這些熱心的紳士們會不會犧牲公利，來迎合一位軟弱、邪惡的君王和腐敗的內閣的意志，使他們付出的金錢和精力得到補償？他又問了諸多問題，就這一題目，他從各個

方面細細地考問我，提出了無數的疑問和異議，不過我想在此複述他的話會有失謹慎也不大方便。

有關我說到的我國法庭的情況，陛下也頗有幾個問題想要瞭解。在這方面我比較在行，我從前曾在大法官法庭打過一場歷時很久的官司，砸了不少錢才得到判決，差點傾家蕩產。他問我裁定一樁案子一般歷時多久，耗資多少？倘若判決明顯不公，故意刁難欺壓人，辯護律師或原告是否有申辯的自由？有沒有發生過教派或政黨影響執法公正的事？那些替人辯護的律師是否接受過公平法律的常識性教育？還是只略通一些省、國家或其他地方性的知識？既然律師和法官認為自己有隨意解釋、任意理解法律的自由，那麼他們是否參與法律的制定呢？他們是否會對相同的案件，有時辯護，有時反駁，援引先例來證明相反的觀點？他們是有錢人還是窮人？他們為人辯護，或者發表意見，是否會得到金錢報酬？尤其是，他們能否被選為下議院成員？

接下來，他又攻擊了我國的財政管理。他說，他以為我的記性欠佳，我算出我們的稅收每年大概是五六百萬，可是後來當我談到各項支出，他發現，有時會超支一倍還多。關於這一點他的筆記記得非常詳細，他告訴我，他本來希望知道我們採取了什麼措施，因為這對他或許有些借鑒之用，這樣他在籌劃時就不會被人欺蒙。但是，如果我對他說的是實情，他還是弄不明白，一個王國怎麼也會像私人那樣超支

呢？他追問誰是我們的債權人？我們又如何弄來還債之錢？聽我談及那些耗資巨大的大規模戰爭時，他驚愕非常，斷定我們一定是一個好鬥的民族，否則就是住在我們四周的都是壞人，最後我們的將軍一定比國王還富有。他問，除了進行貿易、簽訂條約和用軍艦保衛海岸線外，我們在自己的島國以外還幹什麼？最令他感到大惑不解的是，我談到在和平時期自由民族中間還需要有一支僱傭的常備軍隊。他說，既然我們的統治者是按照我們自己的意願選舉產生的，那麼他不能想像，在這樣的君王統治下，我們還怕誰，又要和誰去作戰？他想聽聽我對下面這個問題的看法：一個家庭，它的安全靠全家人來保護，難道不比花錢胡請幾個街上的小流氓來保護強？倘使這些流氓把全家人都殺了，他們不就可以多賺一百倍的錢嗎？

為推算我國的人口總數，我先計算了幾個教派和政黨的人數，他嘲笑這種計算方法，說這方法著實奇怪。他說，他不明白為什麼一定要強迫那些對公眾懷有惡意的人改變他們的主張，而不是強迫他們把自己的主張隱瞞下來。一個政府要做第一點那是專制，但它做不到第二點卻是軟弱：因為，可以允許一個人在家裡私藏毒藥，卻不能讓他拿毒藥當興奮劑去四處兜售。

他又談到，提及我們貴族紳士的各種娛樂中我曾說到賭博，他想知道，他們大概多大歲數開始玩這遊戲？玩到什麼

時候方肯罷休？要玩掉他們的多少時光？會不會賭得傾家蕩產？那些卑鄙邪惡的小人會不會因為賭技高超而成為巨富，使我們的貴族老爺們有時也要對他們另眼相看，甚至習慣與這幫下流人為伍？這會不會使貴族老爺們完全喪失進取心，輸了之後不得不去學那些卑劣伎倆，再用於對付其他人？

我講述了我國過去一百年來發生的歷史，令他震驚非常。他斷言，那只不過是一堆詭計、叛變、謀害、屠殺、造反和流放，都是貪婪、黨爭、虛偽、背叛、凶殘、憤怒、瘋狂、仇怨、妒忌、淫慾、陰險和野心所能產生的最壞後果。

當陛下另一次召見我，他又不厭其煩地將我所說的一切簡明扼要地總結了一下，對比了一番他所提的問題和我的作答。然後，他把我捧在手中，輕輕地撫摸著我，說了幾句話，這番話和他說這番話時的神情我將永遠難以忘懷：「我的朋友格立錐格，你為你的國家譜寫了一篇極其華麗的頌詞。你清楚地證明：無知、懶惰和腐化有時也許正是做一個立法者所必備的條件；那些有興趣並有能力曲解、顛倒和逃避法律的人，才能最好地解釋、說明和應用法律。我認為，你們原先有幾條規章制度還說得過去，可它們一半已被廢除，一半被腐敗所玷污。照你所說，在你們國家，似乎獲取任何職務都無需一絲一毫的道德。人們不是因為品德優秀而得到爵位，教士不是因為虔誠或博學而陞遷，士兵不是因指揮得力和勇猛善戰而晉級，法官不是因為廉潔奉公而高昇，

上議員不是因爲熱愛國家而當選，參議員也不是因爲英明領導而受獎。至於你自己嘛，」國王接著說，「大半生的時間都耗費在了航海旅行中，我多麼希望你能在你們國家的諸多污穢中出污泥而不染。從你自己的言談舉止，以及我費了很大的勁才從你口中得到的回答來看，我只能如此定論：你的大部分同胞們，是大自然古往今來容忍其於地面爬行的小害蟲中，最最惡毒的那一種。」

第 15 章

　　為了證實我目前所說的話，同時進一步證明狹隘的教育會產生怎樣悲慘的結果，我將在此添加一段敘述，雖然它幾乎令人難以相信。為了討好皇帝以獲得更多寵幸，我告訴他：三、四百年前有人發明了一種粉末，即使只有一點火花，也會立刻被點燃，把山那麼大的物體炸得飛到半空中，聲響和震動比打雷還厲害。按照管子的大小，把適當份量的粉末裝進中空的銅管或鐵管，就可以將鐵彈或鉛彈推射出去，力道之強與速度之快，沒有任何東西可以抵擋，以這種方法發射最大砲彈，不僅可以摧毀一整支軍隊，還能把堅固的城牆夷為平地，把可乘載一千名士兵的大船隻擊沉海底，如果用鏈條把所有船隻串在一起，子彈擊出能打斷桅杆和索具，攔腰截斷數百人的身軀，將一切都摧毀。我們經常把這種粉末裝入中空的大鐵球中，用機器發射到我們正在圍攻的城市，就可以將道路、房舍炸毀，碎片紛飛，鄰近的人都會被炸得腦漿迸裂。我說可以指導皇帝的工人製造出比例相稱的砲管，最長不會超過一百呎，備有二、三十支這種砲管，填裝一定數量的粉末和砲彈，就可以在數小時內摧毀王國裡

第 15 章

最堅固的城牆，如果城裡的人膽敢抗拒陛下的命令，甚至可以把整個城鎮炸毀。我謙卑地獻出此策略，以回報陛下對我的恩寵和庇護。

皇帝對於我描述的那些可怕武器和提議大為震驚。他很驚訝我這個卑微無能的小蟲竟有如此殘酷的想法，而且在描繪那些毀滅性武器所造成的殺戮和破壞時，似乎顯得無動於衷。他說發明這種機器的人，一定是邪惡的天才、人類的公敵。他堅決表示寧可失去半個王國，也不願知道這種武器的秘密，於是他命令我，如果珍惜自己的性命，以後就不要再提這件事。

想狹隘和目光短淺竟會導致如此怪事！一位具有令人崇敬愛戴的所有品質的君王，他有卓越的才能，至上的智慧，淵博的知識，統治國家的雄才大略，他的臣民幾乎都崇拜他。但他出於一種完全子虛烏有的顧慮，竟將到手的機會輕易放過了。這真是我們歐洲人絕對意想不到，那機會會使他成為他的子民的生命、自由和財產的絕對主宰！我這樣說絲毫不想貶低這位卓越的國王的若干美德，我很清楚，只因為這一點，一位英國讀者免不了會小看這位國王的品德。不過，我認為他們有這種缺陷是由於無知，他們至今還沒能像歐洲一些比較精明的才子那樣把政治變成一門科學。

有一天我和皇帝談話時，提到英國有幾千本論述政治的

119

書籍，沒想到竟使他鄙視我們的智慧。他痛恨且鄙視君王或大臣的一切秘密和陰謀，他們既沒有敵人也沒有敵國，所以不明白我所謂的國家機密是什麼意思。他把治理國家的知識局限在很小的範圍裡，認為那只不過是常識和道理，公正和仁慈，盡快裁決民事糾紛和刑事案件，以及其他一些無關緊要的簡單事務罷了。他還提出了這麼一種觀點：誰能讓原來只能長一串谷穗和一片草葉的土地長出兩串谷穗和兩片草葉來，誰就比所有的政客更有功於人類，對國家的貢獻也更大。他還認為，任何能使原來只生產一串稻穗、一片草葉的土地長出兩串稻穗、兩片草葉，那麼他對國家和全人類的貢獻，遠比所有政客加起來還要多。

這個國家和中國一樣，在很久以前就發明了印刷術，可是他們的圖書館並不大，規模最大的皇家圖書館，藏書也不超過一千冊，全都陳列在一個一千二百呎長的長廊裡，我可以在那裡自由借閱圖書。王后的木工在格蘭達莉琦的房間裡設計了一架二十五呎高的木製器具，外型就像一架直立的梯子，每一階梯都有五十呎長，這其實是一架可以搬動的梯子，梯腳離房間牆壁約十呎，我把想看的書斜靠在牆壁上，先爬到梯子最上層，然後面朝書本從頁首開始，根據每行不同的長度，左右來回大約走八到十步，直到文字低於視線，再慢慢一階一階往下降，直到最底層，然後，我重新爬上梯子，用同樣的方法閱讀另一頁。我能輕易地用雙手翻動書

頁，因為書頁像紙板一樣又厚又硬，最大的開本也不過十八到二十呎長。

他們的文風清新、雄健、流暢，但是不怎麼華麗，因為他們最忌諱不必要的詞彙或太多樣化的表達方法。我仔細閱讀過他們的許多書籍，尤其是歷史和道德方面的，至於其他方面的書，我最喜歡的是一直擺在格蘭達莉琦臥室裡那本女教師的小舊書，這位莊重年長的女士喜歡閱讀道德和信仰方面的書籍，這本書主要探討人性的弱點，不過除了婦女和庶民外，並不怎麼受到重視。

然而對於這樣一個題目，該國的一個作家能談出些什麼，我倒很是好奇。這位作者論述了歐洲道德學家經常談論的所有主題，指出人本質上是一個十分渺小、卑鄙而無能的動物。他們既無法抗禦惡劣的天氣，也不能抵擋兇猛的野獸。而其他動物，論力量，論速度，論視力，論勤勞，各有優勢，都遠勝人類。

他又說，近代以來，世界一切都在走下坡路，大自然也退化了，較之古時候的人類，現在大自然只能降生矮小的、不足月的產兒。他寫到，有充足之證，不僅原始人種的體格比現代人種大得多，從前也確實存在過巨人，不但歷史和傳說裡記載過此點，王國各處偶然挖出的巨大骨胳和骷髏也足以證明原始人種遠遠大於當今縮小了的人種。他認定，毫無疑問，當初

的自然法則要求我們長得更高更壯，而不是像現在這樣，連屋頂上掉下的一片瓦，小孩子手裡扔過來的一塊石子，或者失足掉進一條小溪這樣小小的意外都能使我們喪命。根據這種推論，作者提出了幾條對人生處世有益的道德法則，不過在此就不加贅述了。至於我自己，心裡卻不由自主地想，這裡爲何處處充斥這種講道德的才能，實際上與其說這是善於談論道德，倒不如說這只不過是我們在和自然發生口角，發發牢騷，吐吐苦水罷了。經過嚴密的調查研究，我相信他們跟自然之間的爭吵，也和我們的一樣，毫無根據。

至於軍事，他們則誇耀說，皇帝的大軍包括十七萬六千名步兵和三萬兩千名騎兵。事實上，這支軍隊是由幾個城市的技工和鄉下的農夫所組成，指揮官則是當地的貴族和鄉紳，他們沒有薪俸或賞賜，所以不知道能不能稱做軍隊。不過他們確實操練精實、紀律嚴明，但我看不出有什麼其他特別的優點，因爲每一個農民都由他們的地主指揮，每一個市民都由所在城市的首長統率。

我常常看到羅布魯格魯城的民兵部隊在郊外一塊二十平方哩的大原野上操練，總共不超過兩萬五千名步兵和六千名騎兵，不過他們占的範圍太廣，我無法計算出確切的數目。騎在大戰馬上的騎兵約有一百呎高；我曾見過全部騎兵在一聲令下後，同時拔出劍在空中揮舞的景象，沒有人能想像如此壯觀驚人的場面，彷彿是萬道閃電同時在天空中奔馳。

　　我感到納悶的是，既然這個國家與世隔絕，沒有路可以通往這裡，爲什麼這位君王想要擁有軍隊，還讓百姓接受軍事訓練。但是藉由與人交談和閱讀他們的歷史，我很快就知道了其中的道理，因爲許多世代以來，他們也犯了全人類的通病，也就是：貴族爭權、人民爭自由、君王爭絕對專制。儘管這三方面都受到王國的法律規範，但有時總有一方會違反法律，造成不止一次的內戰發生。最後一次內戰幸而被現任皇帝的祖父平定了，於是三方面一致同意設立民兵部隊，從此嚴格執行各自的職責。

第 16 章

　　我一直懷有一個強烈的衝動，希望自己有朝一日能恢復自由，雖然我毫無辦法，也設計不出任何有一點點成功希望的計劃來。據說，我原先乘坐的那艘船是第一艘被刮到這一帶海岸附近的船，國王嚴令，無論何時倘若再有這樣的一艘船出現，一定要把它俘虜到岸上，把水手和旅客全都裝進囚車押到羅布魯格魯德。他一心一意要找一個跟我一樣大小的女人，來為我傳宗接代，但是我卻想，我寧死也不願遭受這樣的恥辱，留下一些後代，像馴順的金絲雀一樣讓人養在籠子裡，也許到時還得當稀罕玩物在顯貴人物間轉手交易。確實，我很受優侍：我是一位偉大的國王和皇后的寶貝，整個宮裡的人也都很喜歡我，然而我所處的地位卻有辱整個人類的尊嚴。我永遠也忘不了我曾經給家人立下的那些誓言。我希望跟能與我平等交談的人們在一起，我渴望走在在街上或田間時不用懼怕自己會像青蛙或小狗一樣被人踩死。然而我根本沒想到我這麼快就會獲救，獲救的方法也是那麼地不同尋常。下面我就來如實地敘述事情的全部經過。

　　我在這個國家已經待了兩年；邁入第三年的時候，格蘭達莉琦和我陪同皇帝皇后到王國的南方海岸巡視。他們一如往常把我放在旅行箱子裡帶著。我吩咐他們替我準備一張吊床，用絲繩固定在盒子的四個角落，外出時我會要求騎馬的僕人把我擺在他的前面，藉以減輕顛簸，途中我也經常睡在吊床裡。在屋頂上方，並非吊床正上方，我要求細木工開了一個一呎平方的洞，這樣可以讓我在天熱睡覺時透透氣。洞上有一塊木板，可以順著溝槽前後推移，方便隨時把它關上。

　　行程將盡之際，皇帝認為應該到弗蘭夫拉斯尼克，一座離海邊不到十八哩的城市。格蘭達莉琦和我都已疲憊不堪，我有點感冒，可憐的格蘭達莉琦則病得出不了門，我渴望看到大海，如果有機會，那也是我唯一可以逃走的地方。我假裝病得很嚴重，希望由一位我很喜歡的男僕帶我到海邊呼吸新鮮空氣，我永遠忘不了格蘭達莉琦是多麼不情願地答應，也忘不了她是如何嚴令僕人小心照顧我：她當時淚如雨下，好像預感即將發生的事。

　　男僕提著我的旅行箱子走出行宮，大約半個小時後便來到海邊的岩石上，我吩咐他把箱子放下，然後打開一扇窗子，滿懷憂愁地望著大海。我覺得很不舒服，便對僕人說想在吊床上睡一會兒，希望會好一點。爬上吊床後，男僕為我關上窗子以防著涼，我很快的睡著了，可以猜想的是在我睡著的時候，僕人認為不會有什麼危險發生，就跑到岩石堆裡

尋找鳥蛋，因為我剛才從窗口看到他在那裡四處尋找，並且在岩縫間揀到了一、兩顆。

過了一會兒我突然驚醒，因為旅行箱頂上便於攜帶的鐵環被猛烈地扯了一下，我感覺箱子被高舉到空中，然後飛快地往前移動。先前那一下震動差點使我從吊床上跌下來，不過隨後倒很平穩，我用盡力氣大喊了幾聲，然而卻一點用也沒有。我朝窗外望去，除了天空和雲朵，什麼也看不見，我聽到頭頂上彷彿有翅膀拍動的聲音，這才意識到自己置身在多麼悲慘的處境，原來是一隻老鷹用嘴銜住了旅行箱上的鐵環。這種鳥很聰明，嗅覺也十分敏銳，從很遠的地方就能發現獵物，即使獵物藏身在比我這兩吋厚的木板更安全的地方也難逃一劫。

不久之後，我覺得翅膀拍撲的聲音變得更快，旅行箱子就像狂風中的路標一樣上下晃盪，接著聽到了幾聲撞擊的聲音，我想是老鷹遭到了攻擊，隨後猛然感覺到自己垂直往下墜超過一分鐘，那速度快得令人難以置信，我差點喘不過氣。突然啪的一聲巨響，擋住了我的墜落，那聲音聽起來比尼亞加拉瀑布還要響，隨後又是一分鐘漆黑的情況，接著箱子高高升起，光線從最上面的窗子透射進來，這時我才發現自己掉進了海裡。那只箱子由於我的體重和裡面的東西，以及釘在頂部與底部四角的寬鐵板，大約有五呎浸泡在水裡。我當時猜想，那隻抓走我箱子的老鷹被另外兩、三隻同類追

趕，牠們也想分一杯羹，那隻老鷹為了保衛自己，不得不扔下我和牠們搏鬥。箱子底部的鐵板很堅實，所以下墜時得以保持平衡，落到海面時也沒有被砸得粉碎，箱子的接縫處都很嚴密，門也不是靠鉸鏈開關的，而是像窗戶那樣上下拉動，所以我這間小屋緊密得幾乎沒有水滲進來。我費力的爬出吊床，冒險拉開屋頂上那塊活動木板讓空氣透進來，否則感覺就要被悶死了。

那時我多麼希望能和親愛的格蘭達莉琦在一起啊！才一個小時我們就分隔如此遙遠。老實說，雖然自己正遭遇不幸，但還是忍不住要為我那可憐的保姆感到哀傷，失去了我她會多麼痛苦啊！而皇后說不定也會遷怒於她，她的未來也將因此受到摧毀。我每分每秒都擔心箱子會被撞得粉碎，一陣狂風或一個巨浪都會將它掀翻；只要窗戶上出現一道裂痕，我就會立刻送命，幸虧當初為防止旅行時出意外而在窗戶外加裝了堅固的鐵絲網，否則窗戶早就保不住了。此時，

我看到幾處縫隙已經開始滲水，雖然不嚴重，我還是盡全力將它堵住，我無法推開屋頂，否則絕對會立刻坐到箱子頂上，這樣至少可以多活幾個小時，總比在這裡「關禁閉」來得好。可是，就算我度過了這些危險而多活一、兩天，最後仍會饑寒交迫悲慘地死去外，還能有什麼希望呢？過了四個小時，時時刻刻都在等待末日來臨。

我正發著愁，忽然聽到，至少我以為自己聽到了，箱子安著鉤環的那一面在嘎嘎作響。我馬上意識到是什麼東西在海水中拖拉箱子，而且我時不時地還能感受到那種拖拽的力量，窗外激起的浪濤幾乎湧到窗頂，箱子裡幾乎一片黑暗。這給了我一絲獲救的希望，雖然我推斷不出究竟是怎麼回事。我大費周章，把固定在箱底的椅子上的螺絲擰開，又耗費氣力把它搬到正對著我剛才打開的活動木板的下面，重新用螺絲固定在地上。我爬上椅子，將嘴盡盡量湊近那個孔，用我所掌握的各種語言大聲呼救。接著我又將手帕系到我平時一直隨身攜帶著的一根手杖上，伸出孔去，在空中晃了好幾下，要是附近有什麼大小船隻，水手們見了就會猜到這箱子裡可能關著一個倒霉的人。

我發現我能做的都沒什麼作用，但我明顯感覺到我的小房間在往前移動。過了一個小時，也許還要久一點，箱子裝有鉤環的那面撞上了什麼堅硬的東西，我擔心那是塊礁石，因為這時我感覺搖晃得更厲害了，且清楚地聽到箱子頂上發

出聲響，像是纜繩穿過那鉤環發出的摩擦聲。接著，我覺得
自己慢慢地往上升，至少比原來高了三呎，於是我再次把手
杖伸出去，大聲呼救，直到嗓子都快喊啞了。這次呼救有了
回應，我聽到頭頂上有腳步聲，有人從洞口用英語大喊：
「下面如果有人，請快說話！」我回答說我是英國人，哀求
他們把我從這暗牢中救出去。那聲音回答說我已經安全了，
箱子已經繫到他們的船上，木匠馬上就過來，會在箱子頂上
鋸一個大洞，然後把我拉出去。我回答說，用不著那麼麻
煩，只要請一名水手用手指鉤住鉤環，把箱子提出海面放到
船上，再提到船長室就行了。他們聽到我這般胡言亂語，以
為我瘋了，有些人則哈哈大笑，因為我確實完全沒有想到，
那時已經遇上了與我身材和力氣相當的人。木匠抵達之後，
沒幾分鐘就鋸開了一個四呎平方的通口，並且放下一個小梯
子，身體虛弱的我爬了上去，就這樣被帶到船上。

　　水手們都非常驚奇，問了一大堆問題，我卻感到困惑，
因為長久以來我已看慣了那些龐然大物。船長見我快要暈倒
了，就把我帶到他的艙室，給我喝了一杯甘露酒以便覺得舒
適些，並且讓我躺到他的床鋪上休息。入睡之前告訴他，那
箱子裡有幾件珍貴的家具，丟了未免可惜，包括一張吊床、
一張行軍床、兩把椅子、一張桌子，還有一個櫥櫃，而且箱
子四處都鋪著絲綢和棉花；如果他請一名水手去把那箱子拿
到艙室，我會當面打開，把那些東西展示給他看。他走到甲

板上，派幾個人下去箱子把所有東西都搬了出來，牆壁上的襯墊也都扯了下來；不過椅子、櫥櫃還有床架都是用螺絲釘在地板上的，無知的水手們卻硬生生地將它們拆下來，結果損毀得非常嚴重。他們還拆下幾塊木板帶回船上使用，把想要的東西都拿走，然後再把空箱子扔進了海裡，因為箱底和四壁有不少裂縫，所以箱子立刻就沉入海裡。

　　我睡了幾個小時，不斷被惡夢所擾；夢見經歷的種種危險。一覺醒來，我感覺自己好多了。當時正好晚上八點，船長想起我已經很長一段時間沒有進食，立即吩咐準備晚飯。他相當好心地招待我，見我看起來並沒有失控，說話也不至於顛三倒四，便我倆獨處時，詢問我述說旅行的經過，以及為何會被困在那只大木箱中漂流海上，他說，大概中午十二點時，他正用望遠鏡對著海面瞭望，發現遠處海面漂浮著一樣東西，起先他以為是帆船呢，便盤算自己船上的餅乾快吃完了，這船離他們的航線不遠，不如追上去購些回來。誰料到近前一看，卻發現完全不是那麼回事兒。於是他派了幾名水手坐長舢板去看看那究竟是什麼東西，水手們回來後都驚恐不已，詛咒發誓說他們看見了一座漂在水上的房子。他笑他們滿嘴傻話，便親自乘小船去看，還吩咐水手們隨身帶一根結實的纜繩。那當兒風平浪靜，他環繞我劃了幾圈，發現了我箱子上的窗戶和保護窗戶的鐵線框格，又發現它的一面全是木板，毫無透光之處，卻安著兩個鉤環。於是他吩咐水

手們劃到那一面去，用纜繩拴住一個鉤環，又命令水手把我的櫃子（他們如此稱呼）向大船拖去。拖到船邊以後，他命令再用一根纜繩拴在箱頂的鐵環上，利用滑車把我的箱子托起來，然而全體水手一齊用力仍然抬不起，只略抬高了兩三英尺。他說，當他們見到我從孔裡伸出來的手杖和手帕時，斷定一定有個不幸的傢伙被關在那洞裡了。我問他起初發現我的時候，他和他的部下可曾注意到天上什麼大鳥沒有。他回答說，我睡覺時，他同水手們談過這事，其中一個提及他曾看到有三隻鷹朝北方飛去，可他並沒有說它們比普通的鷹要大，我認為那定是因為它們飛得太高而沒能看得清楚。至於他，則搞不懂我問這個問題幹什麼。

我又問船長，我們離陸地大概有多遠。他說，據他最精確的估算，至少得有一百里格。我斷言，他肯定搞錯了，多估算了近一半路程，因為從我離開那個國家到掉進海裡，最多不超過兩小時。此話一出，他立馬又開始犯嘀咕了，暗示我他認為我的腦子糊塗了，並且建議我再躺下來休息一下，我休息的房間他已安排好了。我讓他放心，他這麼友好地招待我、陪伴我，我早已恢復徹底，神志也跟平時一樣清醒得很。這時他卻嚴肅起來，他坦率地問我是不是犯了什麼大罪，所以被某個君王下令關到箱子裡作為懲罰。船長說，他很遺憾把我這個惡人搭救上船，但他還是會讓我安全上岸不過還是相當守信，保證等到了第一個港口就送我平安上岸。

他又說，我起初對水手們胡說八道，後來又對他講了一些關於小房間或者櫃子的胡話，加上我在吃晚飯時的舉止怪異，他就越發懷疑了。

我懇請船長耐心聽我講個故事，於是把自己最後一次離開英國到他發現我為止的那些經過，詳實地說了一遍。為了進一步證實我所說的一切，我請他派人把我的櫥櫃抬進來，櫥櫃的鑰匙還在我的口袋裡，我當著他的面打開櫥櫃，把我在大人國收集的幾項珍奇玩物拿給他看，裡面有一把用皇帝的鬍渣做成的梳子、幾根一呎到半碼長的縫衣針和別針、四根像細木工用的大頭釘般的黃蜂刺、皇后的幾根頭髮，還有一枚皇后送我的金戒指，皇后從小指上取下來套到我頭上，像個項圈似的。我請船長收下這枚戒指，以回報他殷勤的款待，可是他堅決不收。我又拿出一顆親手從一位宮女腳趾割下來的雞眼給他看，那和英國肯特郡生產的蘋果一樣大，但變得非常堅硬，我回英國後把它挖空做成了一個杯子，並且用白銀鑲嵌起來。最後，我又請他看我在那兒穿的緊身褲，那是用一隻老鼠的皮做成的。

我硬要船長收下一顆僕人的牙齒，因為我見他十分好奇地端詳而且很是喜歡，最後他千恩萬謝地接受了。其實那只是件小東西，他根本不必如此，那牙齒是一位笨拙的醫生從一個牙痛的僕人嘴裡誤拔下來的，它其實是一顆好牙，約有一呎長，直徑四吋，我把它洗淨後擺到櫥櫃裡。

　　船長說希望我回英國後能把這一切寫下來公諸於世。我的回答是：現在的旅行書數量氾濫，但真正有新意的旅行書卻還鮮見。因此我懷疑有些作家寫出的書沒有任何可信度，為了沽名釣譽、或者為了博得無知讀者的歡心而胡編亂造。我的故事呢，只有一些普普通通的事實，別的很少，我不會效仿大多數作家，盡寫些奇怪的草、木、鳥、獸，或者野蠻民族的野蠻風俗、偶像崇拜等等華而不實的東西。儘管如此，我還是很感謝他的好意，並且答應他會考慮這件事。

　　不過有件事他覺得很奇怪，為什麼我說話總是那麼大聲，他問我是不是大人國的皇帝和皇后都有重聽，我跟他說，兩年多來我一直都用這種音量說話，我也覺得很奇怪，他和水手們說話的聲音低得像是耳語，不過我還是可以聽得很清楚。可是在那個國家，我說話就得像站在大街上跟另一個從教堂的塔頂向外探望的人說話一樣，除非他們把我放在桌上，或者托於手中，才不必那麼大聲。我還對他說，我剛上船那會兒水手們把我圍在身邊時，我還真以為他們是我生平所見到的最不足掛齒的小矮子呢。確實，我在那個巨人國裡已看慣了龐然大物，從來不敢照鏡子，因為相比之下實在自慚形穢。船長說，剛才吃晚飯時，他就觀察到我行為怪異，看什麼東西都好像很驚奇似的，並且似乎有種忍不住要譏笑的意思，當時他不明就理，還當我確實神經不正常呢。

　　我對他的這種說法點頭稱是，你瞧那些飯菜和器具，盤

子還沒有三個銀幣大，一條豬腿幾乎不夠一口吃的，酒杯還沒有胡桃殼大，你倒說說我如何才能忍住不笑。我接著又以同樣的方式把他們的其餘家用器皿和食物形容了一番。在我為皇后效命時，雖然她吩咐人給我預備了一整套小型日用必需品，我卻一心只關注周圍那些大東西，這就像人們對待自己的錯誤一樣，對於自己的渺小視而不見。船長很能領會我這些挖苦話，就引用了一句古老的英國諺語來挖苦我，說他懷疑我的眼睛比我的肚子還大，因為我雖然餓了一天，我的胃口看起來卻並不大好。他還繼續開玩笑，堅決的表示他很樂意出一百英鎊看看鷹如何叼著我那小房間，又如何從高空中把它丟進海裡。他說，那情景勢必驚心動魄，值得一寫以流傳後世，簡直可以和法厄松的故事相提並論，但我倒並不欣賞他這種牽強附會的說法。

船長是從東京灣一帶返回英國的途中，我提出留下我的東西，作為乘船費，但是船長堅決分文不取。我們親切話別，並邀約他日後造訪我在瑞德里夫的家，還向他借了五先令雇用一匹馬和一位嚮導回家。

一路上，我覺得房屋、樹木、牲口和人都很渺小，有置身小人國的感覺。我深怕踩到路上行人，所以常常大聲叫喊要他們讓路。有一、兩次，我差點因為這種無禮的舉動被打得頭破血流。

　　到家後，一名僕人開了門，我像鵝穿越籬笆門一樣彎著腰走進去，唯恐撞到了頭。妻子跑出來擁抱我，我彎腰低到她的膝蓋，以免她摟不到我的嘴唇。女兒跪下來向我請安，我長久以來已習慣於仰看六十呎以上的高處，所以等到她站起來之後我才看見她，才走上前一手將她攔腰抱起。我俯視僕人和家裡來的一、兩個朋友，好像他們都是矮子，我是巨人。我告訴我妻子，她節儉過了頭，因為我發現她把她自己和女兒都餓得快找不著了。總之，我的舉動非常不可思議，大家都和船長初次見到我一樣，斷定我精神失常。我之所以提起這一點，是為了舉例說明習慣和偏見的力量是很大的。

Gulliver's Travels

A VOYAGE TO LILLIPUT

CHAPTER 1

My name is Gulliver. I was surgeon successively in two ships and made several voyages to the East and West Indies, by which I got some addition to my fortune. My hours of leisure I spent in reading the best authors, ancient and modern, being always provided with a good number of books; and when I was ashore, in observing the manners and dispositions of the people, as well as learning their language; wherein I had a great facility, by the strength of my memory.

Once, I accepted an advantageous offer from Captain William Prichard, master of the Antelope. Our voyage was at first very prosperous.

The weather was very hazy, and the wind was so strong, that we were driven directly upon it, and immediately split. Six of the crew, of whom I was one, having let down the boat into the sea, made a shift to get clear of the ship and the rock. We rowed, by my computation, about three leagues, till we were able to work no longer, being already spent with labour while we were in the ship. We therefore trusted ourselves to the mercy of the waves, but the boat was overset by a sudden flurry.

What became of my companions in the boat, I cannot

tell. For my own part, I swam as fortune directed me, and was pushed forward by wind and tide. I often let my legs drop and could feel no bottom; but when I was almost gone, and able to struggle no longer, I found myself within my depth; and by this time the storm was much abated.

The declivity was so small, that I walked near a mile before I got to the shore, which I conjectured was about eight o'clock in the evening. I then advanced forward near half a mile, but could not discover any sign of houses or inhabitants. I was extremely tired, and I found myself much inclined to sleep. I lay down on the grass, which was very short and soft, where I slept sounder than ever I remembered to have done in my life.

When I awaked, it was just day-light. I attempted to rise, but was not able to stir: for, as I happened to lie on my back, I found my arms and legs were strongly fastened on each side to the ground; and my hair, which was long and thick, tied down in the same manner. I likewise felt several slender ligatures across my body, from my arm-pits to my thighs. I could only look upwards; the sun began to grow hot, and the light offended my eyes.

I heard a confused noise about me; but in the posture I lay, could see nothing except the sky. In a little time I felt something alive moving on my left leg, which advancing gently forward over my breast, came almost up to my chin; when, bending my eyes downwards as much as I could, I perceived it to be a human creature not six inches high, with a bow and arrow in his hands, and a quiver at his back. In the

mean time, I felt at least forty more of the same kind (as I conjectured) following the first.

I was in the utmost astonishment, and roared so loud, that they all ran back in a fright; and some of them were hurt with the falls they got by leaping from my sides upon the ground.

However, they soon returned, and one of them, who ventured so far as to get a full sight of my face, lifting up his hands and eyes by way of admiration, cried out in a shrill but distinct voice, the others repeated several times, but then I knew not what they meant.

At length, struggling to get loose, I had the fortune to break the strings, and wrench out the pegs that fastened my left arm to the ground; for, by lifting it up to my face, I discovered the methods they had taken to bind me, and at the same time with a violent pull, which gave me excessive pain, I a little loosened the strings that tied down my hair on the left side, so that I was just able to turn my head about two inches.

But the creatures ran off a second time, before I could seize them; whereupon there was a great shout in a very shrill accent, like an order; when in an instant I felt above a hundred arrows discharged on my left hand, which, pricked me like so many needles; and besides, they shot another flight into the air, as we do bombs in Europe, whereof many, I suppose, fell on my body, (though I felt them not), and some on my face, which I immediately covered with my left hand.

When this shower of arrows was over, I fell a groaning with grief and pain; and then striving again to get loose, they

discharged another volley larger than the first, and some of them attempted with spears to stick me in the sides; but by good luck I had on a buff jerkin, which they could not pierce. I thought it the most prudent method to lie still, and my design was to continue so till night, when, my left hand being already loose, I could easily free myself: and as for the inhabitants, I had reason to believe I might be a match for the greatest army they could bring against me, if they were all of the same size with him that I saw.

But fortune disposed otherwise of me.

When the people observed I was quiet, they discharged no more arrows; but, by the noise I heard, I knew their numbers increased; and about four yards from me, over against my right ear, I heard a knocking for above an hour, like that of people at work; when turning my head that way, as well as the pegs and strings would permit me, I saw a stage erected about a foot and a half from the ground, capable of holding four of the inhabitants, with two or three ladders to mount it: from whence one of them, who seemed to be a person of quality, made me a long speech, whereof I understood not one syllable.

He appeared to be of a middle age, and taller than any of the other three who attended him, whereof one was a page that held up his train, and seemed to be somewhat longer than my middle finger; the other two stood one on each side to support him. He acted every part of an orator, and I could observe many periods of threatenings, and others of promises, pity, and kindness.

I answered in a few words, but in the most submissive manner, lifting up my left hand, and both my eyes to the sun, as calling him for a witness; and being almost famished with hunger, having not eaten a morsel for some hours before I left the ship, I found the demands of nature so strong upon me, that I could not forbear showing my impatience (perhaps against the strict rules of decency) by putting my finger frequently to my mouth, to signify that I wanted food.

He understood me very well. He descended from the stage, and commanded that several ladders should be applied to my sides, on which above a hundred of the inhabitants mounted and walked towards my mouth, laden with baskets full of meat, which had been provided and sent thither by the king's orders, upon the first intelligence he received of me. I observed there was the flesh of several animals, but could not distinguish them by the taste. There were shoulders, legs, and loins, shaped like those of mutton, and very well dressed, but smaller than the wings of a lark. I ate them by two or three at a mouthful, and took three loaves at a time, about the bigness of musket bullets. They supplied me as fast as they could, showing a thousand marks of wonder and astonishment at my bulk and appetite. I then made another sign, that I wanted drink. They found by my eating that a small quantity would not suffice me; and being a most ingenious people, they slung up, with great dexterity, one of their largest hogsheads, then rolled it towards my hand, and beat out the top; I drank it off at a draught, which I might well do, for it did not hold half a pint, and tasted like a small wine of Burgundy, but much more

delicious. They brought me a second hogshead, which I drank in the same manner, and made signs for more; but they had none to give me.

When I had performed these wonders, they shouted for joy, and danced upon my breast.

I confess I was often tempted, while they were passing backwards and forwards on my body, to seize forty or fifty of the first that came in my reach, and dash them against the ground. But the remembrance of what I had felt, which probably might not be the worst they could do, and the promise of honour I made them - for so I interpreted my submissive behaviour - soon drove out these imaginations. Besides, I now considered myself as bound by the laws of hospitality, to a people who had treated me with so much expense and magnificence. However, in my thoughts I could not sufficiently wonder at the intrepidity of these diminutive mortals, who durst venture to mount and walk upon my body, while one of my hands was at liberty, without trembling at the very sight of so prodigious a creature as I must appear to them.

After some time, his excellency, having mounted on the small of my right leg, advanced forwards up to my face, with about a dozen of his retinue; and producing his credentials under the signet royal, which he applied close to my eyes, spoke about ten minutes without any signs of anger, but with a kind of determinate resolution, often pointing forwards, which, as I afterwards found, was towards the capital city, about half a mile distant; whither it was agreed by his majesty in council that I must be conveyed. I answered in few words,

but to no purpose, and made a sign with my hand that was loose, putting it to the other (but over his excellency's head for fear of hurting him or his train) and then to my own head and body, to signify that I desired my liberty.

It appeared that he understood me well enough, for he shook his head by way of disapprobation, and held his hand in a posture to show that I must be carried as a prisoner. However, he made other signs to let me understand that I should have meat and drink enough, and very good treatment.

Whereupon I once more thought of attempting to break my bonds; but again, when I felt the smart of their arrows upon my face and hands, which were all in blisters, and many of the darts still sticking in them, and observing likewise that the number of my enemies increased, I gave tokens to let them know that they might do with me what they pleased. Upon this, he and his train withdrew, with much civility and cheerful countenances.

Soon after I heard a general shout, with frequent repetitions of the words Peplom selan; and I felt great numbers of people on my left side relaxing the cords to such a degree, that I was able to turn upon my right, and to ease myself with making water; which I very plentifully did, to the great astonishment of the people; who, conjecturing by my motion what I was going to do, immediately opened to the right and left on that side, to avoid the torrent, which fell with such noise and violence from me. But before this, they had daubed my face and both my hands with a sort of ointment, very pleasant to the smell, which, in a few minutes, removed

all the smart of their arrows. These circumstances, added to the refreshment I had received by their victuals and drink, which were very nourishing, disposed me to sleep. I slept about eight hours, as I was afterwards assured; and it was no wonder, for the physicians, by the emperor's order, had mingled a sleepy potion in the hogsheads of wine.

It seems, that upon the first moment I was discovered sleeping on the ground, after my landing, the emperor had early notice of it by an express; and determined in council, that I should be tied in the manner I have related, (which was done in the night while I slept;) that plenty of meat and drink should be sent to me, and a machine prepared to carry me to the capital city.

These people are most excellent mathematicians, and arrived to a great perfection in mechanics, by the countenance and encouragement of the emperor, who is a renowned patron of learning. This prince has several machines fixed on wheels, for the carriage of trees and other great weights. He often builds his largest men of war, whereof some are nine feet long, in the woods where the timber grows, and has them carried on these engines three or four hundred yards to the sea. Five hundred carpenters and engineers were immediately set at work to prepare the greatest engine they had. It was a frame of wood raised three inches from the ground, about seven feet long, and four wide, moving upon twenty-two wheels. The shout I heard was upon the arrival of this engine, which, it seems, set out in four hours after my landing. It was brought parallel to me, as I lay. But the principal difficulty was

to raise and place me in this vehicle. Eighty poles, each of one foot high, were erected for this purpose, and very strong cords, of the bigness of packthread, were fastened by hooks to many bandages, which the workmen had girt round my neck, my hands, my body, and my legs. Nine hundred of the strongest men were employed to draw up these cords, by many pulleys fastened on the poles; and thus, in less than three hours, I was raised and slung into the engine, and there tied fast. All this I was told; for, while the operation was performing, I lay in a profound sleep, by the force of that soporiferous medicine infused into my liquor. Fifteen hundred of the emperor's largest horses, each about four inches and a half high, were employed to draw me towards the metropolis, which, as I said, was half a mile distant.

We made a long march the remaining part of the day, and, rested at night with five hundred guards on each side of me, half with torches, and half with bows and arrows, ready to shoot me if I should offer to stir. The next morning at sunrise we continued our march, and arrived within two hundred yards of the city gates about noon. The emperor, and all his court, came out to meet us; but his great officers would by no means suffer his majesty to endanger his person by mounting on my body.

At the place where the carriage stopped there stood an ancient temple, esteemed to be the largest in the whole kingdom; which, having been polluted some years before by an unnatural murder, was, according to the zeal of those people, looked upon as profane, and therefore had been

applied to common use, and all the ornaments and furniture carried away. In this edifice it was determined I should lodge. The great gate fronting to the north was about four feet high, and almost two feet wide, through which I could easily creep. On each side of the gate was a small window, not above six inches from the ground: into that on the left side, the king's smith conveyed fourscore and eleven chains, like those that hang to a lady's watch in Europe, and almost as large, which were locked to my left leg with six-and-thirty padlocks. Over against this temple, on the other side of the great highway, at twenty feet distance, there was a turret at least five feet high. Here the emperor ascended, with many principal lords of his court, to have an opportunity of viewing me, as I was told, for I could not see them. It was reckoned that above a hundred thousand inhabitants came out of the town upon the same errand; and, in spite of my guards, I believe there could not be fewer than ten thousand at several times, who mounted my body by the help of ladders. But a proclamation was soon issued, to forbid it upon pain of death.

When the workmen found it was impossible for me to break loose, they cut all the strings that bound me; whereupon I rose up, with as melancholy a disposition as ever I had in my life. But the noise and astonishment of the people, at seeing me rise and walk, are not to be expressed. The chains that held my left leg were about two yards long, and gave me not only the liberty of walking backwards and forwards in a semicircle, but, being fixed within four inches of the gate, allowed me to creep in, and lie at my full length in the temple.

.

CHAPTER 2

When I found myself on my feet, I looked about me, and must confess I never beheld a more entertaining prospect. The country around appeared like a continued garden, and the enclosed fields, which were generally forty feet square, resembled so many beds of flowers. These fields were intermingled with woods of half a stang, and the tallest trees, as I could judge, appeared to be seven feet high. I viewed the town on my left hand, which looked like the painted scene of a city in a theatre.

The emperor was already descended from the tower, and advancing on horseback towards me, which had like to have cost him dear; for the beast, though very well trained, yet wholly unused to such a sight, which appeared as if a mountain moved before him, reared up on its hinder feet: but that prince, who is an excellent horseman, kept his seat, till his attendants ran in, and held the bridle, while his majesty had time to dismount.

When he alighted, he surveyed me round with great admiration; but kept beyond the length of my chain. He ordered his cooks and butlers, who were already prepared, to give me victuals and drink, which they pushed forward in a

sort of vehicles upon wheels, till I could reach them. I took these vehicles and soon emptied them all; twenty of them were filled with meat, and ten with liquor; each of the former afforded me two or three good mouthfuls; and I emptied the liquor of ten vessels, which was contained in earthen vials, into one vehicle, drinking it off at a draught.

The emperor is taller by almost the breadth of my nail, than any of his court; which alone is enough to strike an awe into the beholders. His features are strong and masculine, with an Austrian lip and arched nose, his complexion olive, his countenance erect, his body and limbs well proportioned, all his motions graceful, and his deportment majestic. He was then past his prime, being twenty-eight years and three quarters old, of which he had reigned about seven in great felicity, and generally victorious.

He stood but three yards off. His dress was very plain and simple, and the fashion of it between the Asiatic and the European; but he had on his head a light helmet of gold, adorned with jewels, and a plume on the crest. He held his sword drawn in his hand to defend himself, if I should happen to break loose; it was almost three inches long; the hilt and scabbard were gold enriched with diamonds. His voice was shrill, but very clear and articulate; and I could distinctly hear it when I stood up.

The ladies and courtiers were all most magnificently clad; so that the spot they stood upon seemed to resemble a petticoat spread upon the ground, embroidered with figures

of gold and silver.

His imperial majesty spoke often to me, and I returned answers: but neither of us could understand a syllable. There were several of his priests and lawyers present (as I conjectured by their habits), who were commanded to address themselves to me; and I spoke to them in as many languages as I had the least smattering of, which were High and Low Dutch, Latin, French, Spanish, Italian, and Lingua Franca, but all to no purpose.

After about two hours the court retired, and I was left with a strong guard, to prevent the impertinence, and probably the malice of the rabble, who were very impatient to crowd about me as near as they durst; and some of them had the impudence to shoot their arrows at me, as I sat on the ground by the door of my house, whereof one very narrowly missed my left eye. But the colonel ordered six of the ringleaders to be seized, and thought no punishment so proper as to deliver them bound into my hands; which some of his soldiers accordingly did, pushing them forward with the butt-ends of their pikes into my reach. I took them all in my right hand, put five of them into my coat-pocket; and as to the sixth, I made a countenance as if I would eat him alive. The poor man squalled terribly, and the colonel and his officers were in much pain, especially when they saw me take out my penknife: but I soon put them out of fear; for, looking mildly, and immediately cutting the strings he was bound with, I set him gently on the ground, and away he ran. I treated the rest in the same manner, taking them one by one out of my

pocket; and I observed both the soldiers and people were highly delighted at this mark of my clemency, which was represented very much to my advantage at court.

Towards night I got with some difficulty into my house, where I lay on the ground, and continued to do so about a fortnight; during which time, the emperor gave orders to have a bed prepared for me. Six hundred beds of the common measure were brought in carriages, and worked up in my house; a hundred and fifty of their beds, sewn together, made up the breadth and length; and these were four double: which, however, kept me but very indifferently from the hardness of the floor, that was of smooth stone. By the same computation, they provided me with sheets, blankets, and coverlets, tolerable enough for one who had been so long inured to hardships.

As the news of my arrival spread through the kingdom, it brought prodigious numbers of rich, idle, and curious people to see me; so that the villages were almost emptied; and great neglect of tillage and household affairs must have ensued, if his imperial majesty had not provided, by several proclamations and orders of state, against this inconveniency. He directed that those who had already beheld me should return home, and not presume to come within fifty yards of my house, without license from the court; whereby the secretaries of state got considerable fees.

In the mean time the emperor held frequent councils, to debate what course should be taken with me; and I was afterwards assured by a particular friend, a person of great

quality, who was as much in the secret as any, that the court was under many difficulties concerning me. They apprehended my breaking loose; that my diet would be very expensive, and might cause a famine. Sometimes they determined to starve me; or at least to shoot me in the face and hands with poisoned arrows, which would soon despatch me; but again they considered, that the stench of so large a carcass might produce a plague in the metropolis, and probably spread through the whole kingdom.

In the midst of these consultations, several officers of the army went to the door of the great council-chamber, and two of them being admitted, gave an account of my behaviour to the six criminals above-mentioned; which made so favourable an impression in the breast of his majesty and the whole board, in my behalf, that an imperial commission was issued out, obliging all the villages, nine hundred yards round the city, to deliver in every morning six beeves, forty sheep, and other victuals for my sustenance; together with a proportionable quantity of bread, and wine, and other liquors; for the due payment of which, his majesty gave assignments upon his treasury: for this prince lives chiefly upon his own demesnes; seldom, except upon great occasions, raising any subsidies upon his subjects, who are bound to attend him in his wars at their own expense.

An establishment was also made of six hundred persons to be my domestics, who had board-wages allowed for their maintenance, and tents built for them very conveniently on each side of my door.

It was likewise ordered, that three hundred tailors should make me a suit of clothes, after the fashion of the country; that six of his majesty's greatest scholars should be employed to instruct me in their language; and lastly, that the emperor's horses, and those of the nobility and troops of guards, should be frequently exercised in my sight, to accustom themselves to me.

All these orders were duly put in execution; and in about three weeks I made a great progress in learning their language; during which time the emperor frequently honoured me with his visits, and was pleased to assist my masters in teaching me. We began already to converse together in some sort; and the first words I learnt, were to express my desire "that he would please give me my liberty;" which I every day repeated on my knees. His answer, as I could comprehend it, was, "that this must be a work of time, not to be thought on without the advice of his council, and that first I must swear a peace with him and his kingdom." However, that I should be used with all kindness. And he advised me to "acquire, by my patience and discreet behaviour, the good opinion of himself and his subjects."

He desired "I would not take it ill, if he gave orders to certain proper officers to search me; for probably I might carry about me several weapons, which must needs be dangerous things, if they answered the bulk of so prodigious a person."

I said, "His majesty should be satisfied; for I was ready to strip myself, and turn up my pockets before him." This I

delivered part in words, and part in signs.

He replied, "that, by the laws of the kingdom, I must be searched by two of his officers; that he knew this could not be done without my consent and assistance; and he had so good an opinion of my generosity and justice, as to trust their persons in my hands; that whatever they took from me, should be returned when I left the country, or paid for at the rate which I would set upon them."

I took up the two officers in my hands, put them first into my coat-pockets, and then into every other pocket about me, except my two fobs, and another secret pocket, which I had no mind should be searched, wherein I had some little necessaries that were of no consequence to any but myself. In one of my fobs there was a silver watch, and in the other a small quantity of gold in a purse.

These gentlemen, having pen, ink, and paper, about them, made an exact inventory of every thing they saw; and when they had done, desired I would set them down, that they might deliver it to the emperor. This inventory I afterwards translated into English, and is, word for word, as follows:

In the right coat-pocket of the great man-mountain, after the strictest search, we found only one great piece of coarse-cloth, large enough to be a foot-cloth for your majesty's chief room of state. In the left pocket we saw a huge silver chest, with a cover of the same metal, which we, the searchers, were not able to lift. We

desired it should be opened, and one of us stepping into it, found himself up to the mid leg in a sort of dust, some part whereof flying up to our faces set us both a sneezing for several times together.

In his right waistcoat-pocket we found a prodigious bundle of white thin substances, folded one over another, about the bigness of three men, tied with a strong cable, and marked with black figures; which we humbly conceive to be writings, every letter almost half as large as the palm of our hands. In the left there was a sort of engine, from the back of which were extended twenty long poles, resembling the pallisados before your majesty's court: wherewith we conjecture the man-mountain combs his head; for we did not always trouble him with questions, because we found it a great difficulty to make him understand us.

In the large pocket, on the right side of his middle cover, we saw a hollow pillar of iron, about the length of a man, fastened to a strong piece of timber larger than the pillar; and upon one side of the pillar, were huge pieces of iron sticking out, cut into strange figures, which we know not what to make of. In the left pocket, another engine of the same kind. In the smaller pocket on the right side, were several round flat

pieces of white and red metal, of different bulk; some of the white, which seemed to be silver, were so large and heavy, that my comrade and I could hardly lift them. In the left pocket were two black pillars irregularly shaped: we could not, without difficulty, reach the top of them, as we stood at the bottom of his pocket. One of them was covered, and seemed all of a piece: but at the upper end of the other there appeared a white round substance, about twice the bigness of our heads. Within each of these was enclosed a prodigious plate of steel; which, by our orders, we obliged him to show us, because we apprehended they might be dangerous engines. He took them out of their cases, and told us, that in his own country his practice was to shave his beard with one of these, and cut his meat with the other.

There were two pockets which we could not enter: these he called his fobs; they were two large slits cut into the top of his middle cover, but squeezed close by the pressure of his belly.

Out of the right fob hung a great silver chain, with a wonderful kind of engine at the bottom. We directed him to draw out whatever was at the end of that chain; which appeared to be a globe, half silver, and half of some transparent metal; for, on the transparent side, we saw certain strange figures circularly drawn,

and thought we could touch them, till we found our fingers stopped by the lucid substance. He put this engine into our ears, which made an incessant noise, like that of a water-mill; and we conjecture it is either some unknown animal, or the god that he worships; but we are more inclined to the latter opinion, because he assured us, (if we understood him right, for he expressed himself very imperfectly) that he seldom did any thing without consulting it. He called it his oracle, and said, it pointed out the time for every action of his life.

From the left fob he took out a net almost large enough for a fisherman, but contrived to open and shut like a purse, and served him for the same use: we found therein several massy pieces of yellow metal, which, if they be real gold, must be of immense value.

Having thus, in obedience to your majesty's commands, diligently searched all his pockets, we observed a girdle about his waist made of the hide of some prodigious animal, from which, on the left side, hung a sword of the length of five men; and on the right, a bag or pouch divided into two cells, each cell capable of holding three of your majesty's subjects. In one of these cells were several globes, or balls, of a most ponderous metal, about the bigness of our heads, and

requiring a strong hand to lift them; the other
cell contained a heap of certain black grains, but
of no great bulk or weight, for we could hold
above fifty of them in the palms of our hands.

This is an exact inventory of what we found
about the body of the man-mountain, who used
us with great civility, and due respect to your
majesty's commission.

Signed and sealed on the fourth day of the eighty-
ninth moon of your majesty's auspicious reign.

CLEFRIN FRELOCK, MARSI FRELOCK.

When this inventory was read over to the emperor, he
directed me, although in very gentle terms, to deliver up the
several particulars.

He first called for my scimitar, which I took out,
scabbard and all. In the mean time he ordered three thousand
of his choicest troops (who then attended him) to surround
me at a distance, with their bows and arrows just ready to
discharge; but I did not observe it, for mine eyes were wholly
fixed upon his majesty. He then desired me to draw my
scimitar, which, although it had got some rust by the sea
water, was, in most parts, exceeding bright. I did so, and
immediately all the troops gave a shout between terror and
surprise; for the sun shone clear, and the reflection dazzled
their eyes, as I waved the scimitar to and fro in my hand. His

majesty, who is a most magnanimous prince, was less daunted than I could expect: he ordered me to return it into the scabbard, and cast it on the ground as gently as I could, about six feet from the end of my chain.

The next thing he demanded was one of the hollow iron pillars; by which he meant my pocket pistols. I drew it out, and at his desire, as well as I could, expressed to him the use of it; and charging it only with powder, which, by the closeness of my pouch, happened to escape wetting in the sea (an inconvenience against which all prudent mariners take special care to provide,) I first cautioned the emperor not to be afraid, and then I let it off in the air.

The astonishment here was much greater than at the sight of my scimitar. Hundreds fell down as if they had been struck dead; and even the emperor, although he stood his ground, could not recover himself for some time. I delivered up both my pistols in the same manner as I had done my scimitar, and then my pouch of powder and bullets; begging him that the former might be kept from fire, for it would kindle with the smallest spark, and blow up his imperial palace into the air.

I likewise delivered up my watch, which the emperor was very curious to see, and commanded two of his tallest yeomen of the guards to bear it on a pole upon their shoulders, as draymen in England do a barrel of ale. He was amazed at the continual noise it made, and the motion of the minute-hand, which he could easily discern; for their sight is much more acute than ours: he asked the opinions of his

learned men about it, which were various and remote, as the reader may well imagine without my repeating; although indeed I could not very perfectly understand them.

I then gave up my silver and copper money, my purse, with nine large pieces of gold, and some smaller ones; my knife and razor, my comb and silver snuff-box, my handkerchief and journal-book. My scimitar, pistols, and pouch, were conveyed in carriages to his majesty's stores; but the rest of my goods were returned me.

I had as I before observed, one private pocket, which escaped their search, wherein there was a pair of spectacles (which I sometimes use for the weakness of mine eyes,) a pocket perspective, and some other little conveniences; which, being of no consequence to the emperor, I did not think myself bound in honour to discover, and I apprehended they might be lost or spoiled if I ventured them out of my possession.

CHAPTER 3

My gentleness and good behaviour had gained so far on the emperor and his court, and indeed upon the army and people in general, that I began to conceive hopes of getting my liberty in a short time. I took all possible methods to cultivate this favourable disposition. The natives came, by degrees, to be less apprehensive of any danger from me. I would sometimes lie down, and let five or six of them dance on my hand; and at last the boys and girls would venture to come and play at hide-and-seek in my hair. I had now made a good progress in understanding and speaking the language. The emperor had a mind one day to entertain me with several of the country shows, wherein they exceed all nations I have known, both for dexterity and magnificence. I was diverted with none so much as that of the rope-dancers, performed upon a slender white thread, extended about two feet, and twelve inches from the ground.

This diversion is only practised by those persons who are candidates for great employments, and high favour at court. They are trained in this art from their youth, and are not always of noble birth, or liberal education. When a great office is vacant, either by death or disgrace (which often

happens,) five or six of those candidates petition the emperor to entertain his majesty and the court with a dance on the rope; and whoever jumps the highest, without falling, succeeds in the office. Very often the chief ministers themselves are commanded to show their skill, and to convince the emperor that they have not lost their faculty. Flimnap, the treasurer, is allowed to cut a caper on the straight rope, at least an inch higher than any other lord in the whole empire. I have seen him do the summerset several times together, upon a trencher fixed on a rope which is no thicker than a common packthread in England. My friend Reldresal, principal secretary for private affairs, is, in my opinion, if I am not partial, the second after the treasurer; the rest of the great officers are much upon a par.

These diversions are often attended with fatal accidents, whereof great numbers are on record. I myself have seen two or three candidates break a limb. But the danger is much greater, when the ministers themselves are commanded to show their dexterity; for, by contending to excel themselves and their fellows, they strain so far that there is hardly one of them who has not received a fall, and some of them two or three. I was assured that, a year or two before my arrival, Flimnap would infallibly have broke his neck, if one of the king's cushions, that accidentally lay on the ground, had not weakened the force of his fall.

There is likewise another diversion, which is only shown before the emperor and empress, and first minister, upon particular occasions. The emperor lays on the table three fine

silken threads of six inches long; one is blue, the other red, and the third green. These threads are proposed as prizes for those persons whom the emperor has a mind to distinguish by a peculiar mark of his favour. The ceremony is performed in his majesty's great chamber of state, where the candidates are to undergo a trial of dexterity very different from the former. The emperor holds a stick in his hands, both ends parallel to the horizon, while the candidates advancing, one by one, sometimes leap over the stick, sometimes creep under it, backward and forward, several times, according as the stick is advanced or depressed. Sometimes the emperor holds one end of the stick, and his first minister the other; sometimes the minister has it entirely to himself. Whoever performs his part with most agility, and holds out the longest in leaping and creeping, is rewarded with the blue-coloured silk; the red is given to the next, and the green to the third, which they all wear girt twice round about the middle.

The horses of the army, and those of the royal stables, having been daily led before me, were no longer shy, but would come up to my very feet without starting. The riders would leap them over my hand, as I held it on the ground; and one of the emperor's huntsmen, upon a large courser, took my foot, shoe and all; which was indeed a prodigious leap.

I had the good fortune to divert the emperor one day after a very extraordinary manner. I desired he would order several sticks of two feet high, and the thickness of an ordinary cane, to be brought me; whereupon his majesty

commanded the master of his woods to give directions
accordingly; and the next morning six woodmen arrived with
as many carriages, drawn by eight horses to each. I took nine
of these sticks, and fixing them firmly in the ground in a
quadrangular figure, two feet and a half square, I took four
other sticks, and tied them parallel at each corner, about two
feet from the ground; then I fastened my handkerchief to the
nine sticks that stood erect; and extended it on all sides, till it
was tight as the top of a drum; and the four parallel sticks,
rising about five inches higher than the handkerchief, served
as ledges on each side. When I had finished my work, I
desired the emperor to let a troop of his best horses twenty-
four in number, come and exercise upon this plain. His
majesty approved of the proposal, and I took them up, one by
one, in my hands, ready mounted and armed, with the proper
officers to exercise them. As soon as they got into order they
divided into two parties, performed mock skirmishes,
discharged blunt arrows, drew their swords, fled and pursued,
attacked and retired, and in short discovered the best military
discipline I ever beheld. The parallel sticks secured them and
their horses from falling over the stage; and the emperor was
so much delighted, that he ordered this entertainment to be
repeated several days, and once was pleased to be lifted up
and give the word of command; and with great difficulty
persuaded even the empress herself to let me hold her in her
close chair within two yards of the stage, when she was able
to take a full view of the whole performance.

It was my good fortune, that no ill accident happened in

these entertainments; only once a fiery horse, that belonged to one of the captains, pawing with his hoof, struck a hole in my handkerchief, and his foot slipping, he overthrew his rider and himself; but I immediately relieved them both, and covering the hole with one hand, I set down the troop with the other, in the same manner as I took them up. The horse that fell was strained in the left shoulder, but the rider got no hurt; and I repaired my handkerchief as well as I could: however, I would not trust to the strength of it any more, in such dangerous enterprises.

I had sent so many memorials and petitions for my liberty, that his majesty at length mentioned the matter, first in the cabinet, and then in a full council; where it was opposed by none, except Skyresh Bolgolam, who was pleased, without any provocation, to be my mortal enemy. But it was carried against him by the whole board, and confirmed by the emperor. That minister was galbet, or admiral of the realm, very much in his master's confidence, and a person well versed in affairs, but of a morose and sour complexion. However, he was at length persuaded to comply; but prevailed that the articles and conditions upon which I should be set free, and to which I must swear, should be drawn up by himself. These articles were brought to me by Skyresh Bolgolam in person attended by two under-secretaries, and several persons of distinction. After they were read, I was demanded to swear to the performance of them; first in the manner of my own country, and afterwards in the method prescribed by their laws; which was, to hold my right foot in

my left hand, and to place the middle finger of my right hand on the crown of my head, and my thumb on the tip of my right ear. But because the reader may be curious to have some idea of the style and manner of expression peculiar to that people, as well as to know the article upon which I recovered my liberty, I have made a translation of the whole instrument, word for word, as near as I was able, which I here offer to the public.

1st, The man-mountain shall not depart from our dominions, without our license under our great seal.

2d, He shall not presume to come into our metropolis, without our express order; at which time, the inhabitants shall have two hours warning to keep within doors.

3d, The said man-mountain shall confine his walks to our principal high roads, and not offer to walk, or lie down, in a meadow or field of corn.

4th, As he walks the said roads, he shall take the utmost care not to trample upon the bodies of any of our loving subjects, their horses, or carriages, nor take any of our subjects into his hands without their own consent.

5th, If an express requires extraordinary despatch, the man-mountain shall be obliged to carry, in his pocket, the messenger and horse a six days journey, once in every moon, and return the said messenger back (if so required) safe to our imperial presence.

6th, He shall be our ally against our enemies in the island of Blefuscu, and do his utmost to destroy their fleet, which is now preparing to invade us.

7th, That the said man-mountain shall, at his times of leisure, be aiding and assisting to our workmen, in helping to raise certain great stones, towards covering the wall of the principal park, and other our royal buildings.

8th, That the said man-mountain shall, in two moons' time, deliver in an exact survey of the circumference of our dominions, by a computation of his own paces round the coast.

Lastly, That, upon his solemn oath to observe all the above articles, the said man-mountain shall have a daily allowance of meat and drink sufficient for the support of 1724 of our subjects, with free access to our royal person, and other marks of our favour.

Given at our palace at Belfaborac, the twelfth day of the ninety-first moon of our reign.

I swore and subscribed to these articles with great cheerfulness and content, although some of them were not so honourable as I could have wished; which proceeded wholly from the malice of Skyresh Bolgolam, the high-admiral: whereupon my chains were immediately unlocked, and I was at full liberty. The emperor himself, in person, did me the honour to be by at the whole ceremony. I made my acknowledgements by prostrating myself at his majesty's feet: but he commanded me to rise; and after many gracious expressions, which, to avoid the censure of vanity, I shall not repeat, he added, "that he hoped I should prove a useful servant, and well deserve all the favours he had already conferred upon me, or might do for the future."

CHAPTER 4

The first request I made, after I had obtained my liberty, was, that I might have license to see Mildendo, the metropolis; which the emperor easily granted me, but with a special charge to do no hurt either to the inhabitants or their houses. The people had notice, by proclamation, of my design to visit the town. The wall which encompassed it is two feet and a half high, and at least eleven inches broad, so that a coach and horses may be driven very safely round it; and it is flanked with strong towers at ten feet distance. I stepped over the great western gate, and passed very gently, and sidling, through the two principal streets, only in my short waistcoat, for fear of damaging the roofs and eaves of the houses with the skirts of my coat. I walked with the utmost circumspection, to avoid treading on any stragglers who might remain in the streets, although the orders were very strict, that all people should keep in their houses, at their own peril. The garret windows and tops of houses were so crowded with spectators, that I thought in all my travels I had not seen a more populous place. The city is an exact square, each side of the wall being five hundred feet long. The two great streets, which run across and divide it into four quarters, are five feet

wide. The lanes and alleys, which I could not enter, but only view them as I passed, are from twelve to eighteen inches. The town is capable of holding five hundred thousand souls: the houses are from three to five stories: the shops and markets well provided.

The emperor's palace is in the centre of the city where the two great streets meet. It is enclosed by a wall of two feet high, and twenty feet distance from the buildings. I had his majesty's permission to step over this wall; and, the space being so wide between that and the palace, I could easily view it on every side. The outward court is a square of forty feet, and includes two other courts: in the inmost are the royal apartments, which I was very desirous to see, but found it extremely difficult; for the great gates, from one square into another, were but eighteen inches high, and seven inches wide. Now the buildings of the outer court were at least five feet high, and it was impossible for me to stride over them without infinite damage to the pile, though the walls were strongly built of hewn stone, and four inches thick.

At the same time the emperor had a great desire that I should see the magnificence of his palace; but this I was not able to do till three days after, which I spent in cutting down with my knife some of the largest trees in the royal park, about a hundred yards distant from the city. Of these trees I made two stools, each about three feet high, and strong enough to bear my weight. The people having received notice a second time, I went again through the city to the palace with my two stools in my hands. When I came to the side of the

outer court, I stood upon one stool, and took the other in my hand; this I lifted over the roof, and gently set it down on the space between the first and second court, which was eight feet wide. I then stept over the building very conveniently from one stool to the other, and drew up the first after me with a hooked stick. By this contrivance I got into the inmost court; and, lying down upon my side, I applied my face to the windows of the middle stories, which were left open on purpose, and discovered the most splendid apartments that can be imagined. There I saw the empress and the young princes, in their several lodgings, with their chief attendants about them. Her imperial majesty was pleased to smile very graciously upon me, and gave me out of the window her hand to kiss.

One morning, about a fortnight after I had obtained my liberty, Reldresal, principal secretary (as they style him) for private affairs, came to my house attended only by one servant. He ordered his coach to wait at a distance, and desired I would give him an hours audience; which I readily consented to, on account of his quality and personal merits, as well as of the many good offices he had done me during my solicitations at court. I offered to lie down that he might the more conveniently reach my ear, but he chose rather to let me hold him in my hand during our conversation. He began with compliments on my liberty; said "he might pretend to some merit in it;" but, however, added, "that if it had not been for the present situation of things at court, perhaps I might not have obtained it so soon.

"For," said he, "as flourishing a condition as we may appear to be in to foreigners, we labour under two mighty evils: a violent faction at home, and the danger of an invasion, by a most potent enemy, from abroad. As to the first, you are to understand, that for about seventy moons past there have been two struggling parties in this empire, under the names of Tramecksan and Slamecksan, from the high and low heels of their shoes, by which they distinguish themselves. It is alleged, indeed, that the high heels are most agreeable to our ancient constitution; but, however this be, his majesty has determined to make use only of low heels in the administration of the government, and all offices in the gift of the crown, as you cannot but observe; and particularly that his majesty's imperial heels are lower at least by a drurr than any of his court (drurr is a measure about the fourteenth part of an inch). The animosities between these two parties run so high, that they will neither eat, nor drink, nor talk with each other. We compute the Tramecksan, or high heels, to exceed us in number; but the power is wholly on our side. We apprehend his imperial highness, the heir to the crown, to have some tendency towards the high heels; at least we can plainly discover that one of his heels is higher than the other, which gives him a hobble in his gait.

"Now, in the midst of these intestine disquiets, we are threatened with an invasion from the island of Blefuscu, which is the other great empire of the universe, almost as large and powerful as this of his majesty. For as to what we have heard you affirm, that there are other kingdoms and

states in the world inhabited by human creatures as large as yourself, our philosophers are in much doubt, and would rather conjecture that you dropped from the moon, or one of the stars; because it is certain, that a hundred mortals of your bulk would in a short time destroy all the fruits and cattle of his majesty's dominions: besides, our histories of six thousand moons make no mention of any other regions than the two great empires of Lilliput and Blefuscu. Which two mighty powers have, as I was going to tell you, been engaged in a most obstinate war for six-and-thirty moons past.

"It began upon the following occasion. It is allowed on all hands, that the primitive way of breaking eggs, before we eat them, was upon the larger end; but his present majesty's grandfather, while he was a boy, going to eat an egg, and breaking it according to the ancient practice, happened to cut one of his fingers. Whereupon the emperor his father published an edict, commanding all his subjects, upon great penalties, to break the smaller end of their eggs. The people so highly resented this law, that our histories tell us, there have been six rebellions raised on that account; wherein one emperor lost his life, and another his crown. These civil commotions were constantly fomented by the monarchs of Blefuscu; and when they were quelled, the exiles always fled for refuge to that empire. It is computed that eleven thousand persons have at several times suffered death, rather than submit to break their eggs at the smaller end. Many hundred large volumes have been published upon this controversy: but the books of the Big-endians have been long forbidden, and

the whole party rendered incapable by law of holding employments.

"During the course of these troubles, the emperors of Blefusca did frequently expostulate by their ambassadors, accusing us of making a schism in religion, by offending against a fundamental doctrine of our great prophet Lustrog, in the fifty-fourth chapter of the Blundecral (which is their Alcoran). This, however, is thought to be a mere strain upon the text; for the words are these: 'that all true believers break their eggs at the convenient end.' And which is the convenient end, seems, in my humble opinion to be left to every man's conscience, or at least in the power of the chief magistrate to determine. Now, the Big-endian exiles have found so much credit in the emperor of Blefuscu's court, and so much private assistance and encouragement from their party here at home, that a bloody war has been carried on between the two empires for six-and-thirty moons, with various success; during which time we have lost forty capital ships, and a much a greater number of smaller vessels, together with thirty thousand of our best seamen and soldiers; and the damage received by the enemy is reckoned to be somewhat greater than ours. However, they have now equipped a numerous fleet, and are just preparing to make a descent upon us; and his imperial majesty, placing great confidence in your valour and strength, has commanded me to lay this account of his affairs before you."

I desired the secretary to present my humble duty to the emperor; and to let him know, "that I thought it would not

become me, who was a foreigner, to interfere with parties; but I was ready, with the hazard of my life, to defend his person and state against all invaders."

CHAPTER 5

The empire of Blefuscu is an island situated to the north-east of Lilliput, from which it is parted only by a channel of eight hundred yards wide. I had not yet seen it, and upon this notice of an intended invasion, I avoided appearing on that side of the coast, for fear of being discovered, by some of the enemy's ships, who had received no intelligence of me; all intercourse between the two empires having been strictly forbidden during the war, upon pain of death, and an embargo laid by our emperor upon all vessels whatsoever. I communicated to his majesty a project I had formed of seizing the enemy's whole fleet; which, as our scouts assured us, lay at anchor in the harbour, ready to sail with the first fair wind. I consulted the most experienced seamen upon the depth of the channel, which they had often plumbed; who told me, that in the middle, at high-water, it was seventy glumgluffs deep, which is about six feet of European measure; and the rest of it fifty glumgluffs at most. I walked towards the north-east coast, over against Blefuscu, where, lying down behind a hillock, I took out my small perspective glass, and viewed the enemy's fleet at anchor, consisting of about fifty men of war, and a great number of transports.

I then came back to my house, and gave orders (for which I had a warrant) for a great quantity of the strongest cable and bars of iron. The cable was about as thick as packthread and the bars of the length and size of a knitting-needle. I trebled the cable to make it stronger, and for the same reason I twisted three of the iron bars together, bending the extremities into a hook. Having thus fixed fifty hooks to as many cables, I went back to the north-east coast, and putting off my coat, shoes, and stockings, walked into the sea, in my leathern jerkin, about half an hour before high water. I waded with what haste I could, and swam in the middle about thirty yards, till I felt ground. I arrived at the fleet in less than half an hour. The enemy was so frightened when they saw me, that they leaped out of their ships, and swam to shore, where there could not be fewer than thirty thousand souls. I then took my tackling, and, fastening a hook to the hole at the prow of each, I tied all the cords together at the end. While I was thus employed, the enemy discharged several thousand arrows, many of which stuck in my hands and face, and, beside the excessive smart, gave me much disturbance in my work. My greatest apprehension was for mine eyes, which I should have infallibly lost, if I had not suddenly thought of an expedient. I kept, among other little necessaries, a pair of spectacles in a private pocket, which, as I observed before, had escaped the emperor's searchers. These I took out and fastened as strongly as I could upon my nose, and thus armed, went on boldly with my work, in spite of the enemy's arrows, many of which struck against the glasses of my spectacles,

but without any other effect, further than a little to discompose them. I had now fastened all the hooks, and, taking the knot in my hand, began to pull; but not a ship would stir, for they were all too fast held by their anchors, so that the boldest part of my enterprise remained. I therefore let go the cord, and leaving the looks fixed to the ships, I resolutely cut with my knife the cables that fastened the anchors, receiving about two hundred shots in my face and hands; then I took up the knotted end of the cables, to which my hooks were tied, and with great ease drew fifty of the enemy's largest men of war after me.

The Blefuscudians, who had not the least imagination of what I intended, were at first confounded with astonishment: They had seen me cut the cables, and thought my design was only to let the ships run adrift or fall foul on each other: but when they perceived the whole fleet moving in order, and saw me pulling at the end, they set up such a scream of grief and despair as it is almost impossible to describe or conceive. When I had got out of danger, I stopped awhile to pick out the arrows that stuck in my hands and face; and rubbed on some of the same ointment that was given me at my first arrival, as I have formerly mentioned. I then took off my spectacles, and waiting about an hour, till the tide was a little fallen, I waded through the middle with my cargo, and arrived safe at the royal port of Lilliput.

The emperor and his whole court stood on the shore, expecting the issue of this great adventure. They saw the ships move forward in a large half-moon, but could not

discern me, who was up to my breast in water. When I advanced to the middle of the channel, they were yet more in pain, because I was under water to my neck. The emperor concluded me to be drowned, and that the enemy's fleet was approaching in a hostile manner: but he was soon eased of his fears; for the channel growing shallower every step I made, I came in a short time within hearing, and holding up the end of the cable, by which the fleet was fastened, I cried in a loud voice, "Long live the most puissant king of Lilliput!" This great prince received me at my landing with all possible encomiums, and created me a nardac upon the spot, which is the highest title of honour among them.

His majesty desired I would take some other opportunity of bringing all the rest of his enemy's ships into his ports. And so unmeasureable is the ambition of princes, that he seemed to think of nothing less than reducing the whole empire of Blefuscu into a province, and governing it, by a viceroy; of destroying the Big-endian exiles, and compelling that people to break the smaller end of their eggs, by which he would remain the sole monarch of the whole world. But I endeavoured to divert him from this design, by many arguments drawn from the topics of policy as well as justice; and I plainly protested, "that I would never be an instrument of bringing a free and brave people into slavery." And, when the matter was debated in council, the wisest part of the ministry were of my opinion.

This open bold declaration of mine was so opposite to the schemes and politics of his imperial majesty, that he could

never forgive me. He mentioned it in a very artful manner at council, where I was told that some of the wisest appeared, at least by their silence, to be of my opinion; but others, who were my secret enemies, could not forbear some expressions which, by a side-wind, reflected on me. And from this time began an intrigue between his majesty and a junto of ministers, maliciously bent against me, which broke out in less than two months, and had like to have ended in my utter destruction. Of so little weight are the greatest services to princes, when put into the balance with a refusal to gratify their passions.

About three weeks after this exploit, there arrived a solemn embassy from Blefuscu, with humble offers of a peace, which was soon concluded, upon conditions very advantageous to our emperor, wherewith I shall not trouble the reader. There were six ambassadors, with a train of about five hundred persons, and their entry was very magnificent, suitable to the grandeur of their master, and the importance of their business. When their treaty was finished, wherein I did them several good offices by the credit I now had, or at least appeared to have, at court, their excellencies, who were privately told how much I had been their friend, made me a visit in form. They began with many compliments upon my valour and generosity, invited me to that kingdom in the emperor their master's name, and desired me to show them some proofs of my prodigious strength, of which they had heard so many wonders; wherein I readily obliged them.

When I had for some time entertained their excellencies,

to their infinite satisfaction and surprise, I desired they would do me the honour to present my most humble respects to the emperor their master, the renown of whose virtues had so justly filled the whole world with admiration, and whose royal person I resolved to attend, before I returned to my own country. Accordingly, the next time I had the honour to see our emperor, I desired his general license to wait on the Blefuscudian monarch, which he was pleased to grant me, as I could perceive, in a very cold manner; but could not guess the reason, till I had a whisper from a certain person, "that Flimnap and Bolgolam had represented my intercourse with those ambassadors as a mark of disaffection;" from which I am sure my heart was wholly free. And this was the first time I began to conceive some imperfect idea of courts and ministers.

It is to be observed, that these ambassadors spoke to me, by an interpreter, the languages of both empires differing as much from each other as any two in Europe, and each nation priding itself upon the antiquity, beauty, and energy of their own tongue, with an avowed contempt for that of their neighbour; yet our emperor, standing upon the advantage he had got by the seizure of their fleet, obliged them to deliver their credentials, and make their speech, in the Lilliputian tongue. And it must be confessed, that from the great intercourse of trade and commerce between both realms, from the continual reception of exiles which is mutual among them, and from the custom, in each empire, to send their young nobility and richer gentry to the other, in order to

polish themselves by seeing the world, and understanding men and manners; there are few persons of distinction, or merchants, or seamen, who dwell in the maritime parts, but what can hold conversation in both tongues; as I found some weeks after, when I went to pay my respects to the emperor of Blefuscu.

At one night, I was alarmed at midnight with the cries of many hundred people at my door; by which, being suddenly awaked, I was in some kind of terror. I heard the word Burglum repeated incessantly: several of the emperor's court, making their way through the crowd, entreated me to come immediately to the palace, where her imperial majesty's apartment was on fire, by the carelessness of a maid of honour, who fell asleep while she was reading a romance. I got up in an instant; and orders being given to clear the way before me, and it being likewise a moonshine night, I made a shift to get to the palace without trampling on any of the people. I found they had already applied ladders to the walls of the apartment, and were well provided with buckets, but the water was at some distance. These buckets were about the size of large thimbles, and the poor people supplied me with them as fast as they could: but the flame was so violent that they did little good. I might easily have stifled it with my coat, which I unfortunately left behind me for haste, and came away only in my leathern jerkin. The case seemed wholly desperate and deplorable; and this magnificent palace would have infallibly been burnt down to the ground, if, by a presence of mind unusual to me, I had not suddenly thought

of an expedient.

I had, the evening before, drunk plentifully of a most delicious wine called glimigrim, (the Blefuscudians call it flunec, but ours is esteemed the better sort,) which is very diuretic. By the luckiest chance in the world, I had not discharged myself of any part of it. The heat I had contracted by coming very near the flames, and by labouring to quench them, made the wine begin to operate by urine; which I voided in such a quantity, and applied so well to the proper places, that in three minutes the fire was wholly extinguished, and the rest of that noble pile, which had cost so many ages in erecting, preserved from destruction.

It was now day-light, and I returned to my house without waiting to congratulate with the emperor: because, although I had done a very eminent piece of service, yet I could not tell how his majesty might resent the manner by which I had performed it: for, by the fundamental laws of the realm, it is capital in any person, of what quality soever, to make water within the precincts of the palace. But I was a little comforted by a message from his majesty, "that he would give orders to the grand justiciary for passing my pardon in form:" which, however, I could not obtain; and I was privately assured, "that the empress, conceiving the greatest abhorrence of what I had done, removed to the most distant side of the court, firmly resolved that those buildings should never be repaired for her use: and, in the presence of her chief confidents could not forbear vowing revenge.".

CHAPTER 6

As the common size of the natives is somewhat under six inches high, so there is an exact proportion in all other animals, as well as plants and trees: for instance, the tallest horses and oxen are between four and five inches in height, the sheep an inch and half, more or less: their geese about the bigness of a sparrow, and so the several gradations downwards till you come to the smallest, which to my sight, were almost invisible; but nature has adapted the eyes of the Lilliputians to all objects proper for their view: they see with great exactness, but at no great distance. And, to show the sharpness of their sight towards objects that are near, I have been much pleased with observing a cook pulling a lark, which was not so large as a common fly; and a young girl threading an invisible needle with invisible silk. Their tallest trees are about seven feet high: I mean some of those in the great royal park, the tops whereof I could but just reach with my fist clenched. The other vegetables are in the same proportion.

I shall say but little at present of their learning, which, for many ages, has flourished in all its branches among them: but their manner of writing is very peculiar, being neither

from the left to the right, like the Europeans, nor from the right to the left, like the Arabians, nor from up to down, like the Chinese, but aslant, from one corner of the paper to the other, like ladies in England.

They bury their dead with their heads directly downward, because they hold an opinion, that in eleven thousand moons they are all to rise again; in which period the earth (which they conceive to be flat) will turn upside down, and by this means they shall, at their resurrection, be found ready standing on their feet. The learned among them confess the absurdity of this doctrine; but the practice still continues, in compliance to the vulgar.

They look upon fraud as a greater crime than theft, and therefore seldom fail to punish it with death; for they allege, that care and vigilance, with a very common understanding, may preserve a man's goods from thieves, but honesty has no defence against superior cunning; and, since it is necessary that there should be a perpetual intercourse of buying and selling, and dealing upon credit, where fraud is permitted and connived at, or has no law to punish it, the honest dealer is always undone, and the knave gets the advantage. I remember, when I was once interceding with the emperor for a criminal who had wronged his master of a great sum of money, which he had received by order and ran away with; and happening to tell his majesty, by way of extenuation, that it was only a breach of trust, the emperor thought it monstrous in me to offer as a defence the greatest aggravation of the crime; and truly I had little to say in return, farther than the common

answer, that different nations had different customs; for, I confess, I was heartily ashamed.

Although we usually call reward and punishment the two hinges upon which all government turns, yet I could never observe this maxim to be put in practice by any nation except that of Lilliput. Whoever can there bring sufficient proof, that he has strictly observed the laws of his country for seventy-three moons, has a claim to certain privileges, according to his quality or condition of life, with a proportionable sum of money out of a fund appropriated for that use: he likewise acquires the title of snilpall, or legal, which is added to his name, but does not descend to his posterity. And these people thought it a prodigious defect of policy among us, when I told them that our laws were enforced only by penalties, without any mention of reward. It is upon this account that the image of Justice, in their courts of judicature, is formed with six eyes, two before, as many behind, and on each side one, to signify circumspection; with a bag of gold open in her right hand, and a sword sheathed in her left, to show she is more disposed to reward than to punish.

In choosing persons for all employments, they have more regard to good morals than to great abilities; for, since government is necessary to mankind, they believe, that the common size of human understanding is fitted to some station or other; and that Providence never intended to make the management of public affairs a mystery to be comprehended only by a few persons of sublime genius, of

which there seldom are three born in an age: but they suppose truth, justice, temperance, and the like, to be in every man's power; the practice of which virtues, assisted by experience and a good intention, would qualify any man for the service of his country, except where a course of study is required. But they thought the want of moral virtues was so far from being supplied by superior endowments of the mind, that employments could never be put into such dangerous hands as those of persons so qualified; and, at least, that the mistakes committed by ignorance, in a virtuous disposition, would never be of such fatal consequence to the public weal, as the practices of a man, whose inclinations led him to be corrupt, and who had great abilities to manage, to multiply, and defend his corruptions.

In like manner, the disbelief of a Divine Providence renders a man incapable of holding any public station; for, since kings avow themselves to be the deputies of Providence, the Lilliputians think nothing can be more absurd than for a prince to employ such men as disown the authority under which he acts.

In relating these and the following laws, I would only be understood to mean the original institutions, and not the most scandalous corruptions, into which these people are fallen by the degenerate nature of man. For, as to that infamous practice of acquiring great employments by dancing on the ropes, or badges of favour and distinction by leaping over sticks and creeping under them, the reader is to observe, that they were first introduced by the grandfather of the emperor

now reigning, and grew to the present height by the gradual increase of party and faction.

Ingratitude is among them a capital crime, as we read it to have been in some other countries: for they reason thus; that whoever makes ill returns to his benefactor, must needs be a common enemy to the rest of mankind, from whom he has received no obligation, and therefore such a man is not fit to live.

Their notions relating to the duties of parents and children differ extremely from ours. For, since the conjunction of male and female is founded upon the great law of nature, in order to propagate and continue the species, the Lilliputians will needs have it, that men and women are joined together, like other animals, by the motives of concupiscence; and that their tenderness towards their young proceeds from the like natural principle: for which reason they will never allow that a child is under any obligation to his father for begetting him, or to his mother for bringing him into the world; which, considering the miseries of human life, was neither a benefit in itself, nor intended so by his parents, whose thoughts, in their love encounters, were otherwise employed. Upon these, and the like reasonings, their opinion is, that parents are the last of all others to be trusted with the education of their own children; and therefore they have in every town public nurseries, where all parents, except cottagers and labourers, are obliged to send their infants of both sexes to be reared and educated, when they come to the age of twenty moons, at which time they are supposed to have some rudiments of

docility. These schools are of several kinds, suited to different qualities, and both sexes. They have certain professors well skilled in preparing children for such a condition of life as befits the rank of their parents, and their own capacities, as well as inclinations.

I have been a resident for nine months, and thirteen days. Having a head mechanically turned, and being likewise forced by necessity, I had made for myself a table and chair convenient enough, out of the largest trees in the royal park. Two hundred sempstresses were employed to make me shirts, and linen for my bed and table, all of the strongest and coarsest kind they could get; which, however, they were forced to quilt together in several folds, for the thickest was some degrees finer than lawn. Their linen is usually three inches wide, and three feet make a piece. The sempstresses took my measure as I lay on the ground, one standing at my neck, and another at my mid-leg, with a strong cord extended, that each held by the end, while a third measured the length of the cord with a rule of an inch long. Then they measured my right thumb, and desired no more; for by a mathematical computation, that twice round the thumb is once round the wrist, and so on to the neck and the waist, and by the help of my old shirt, which I displayed on the ground before them for a pattern, they fitted me exactly. Three hundred tailors were employed in the same manner to make me clothes; but they had another contrivance for taking my measure. I kneeled down, and they raised a ladder from the ground to my neck; upon this ladder one of them mounted, and let fall a plumb-

line from my collar to the floor, which just answered the length of my coat: but my waist and arms I measured myself. When my clothes were finished, which was done in my house, they looked like the patch-work made by the ladies in England.

I had three hundred cooks to dress my victuals, in little convenient huts built about my house, where they and their families lived, and prepared me two dishes a-piece. I took up twenty waiters in my hand, and placed them on the table: a hundred more attended below on the ground, some with dishes of meat, and some with barrels of wine and other liquors slung on their shoulders; all which the waiters above drew up, as I wanted, in a very ingenious manner, by certain cords, as we draw the bucket up a well in Europe. A dish of their meat was a good mouthful, and a barrel of their liquor a reasonable draught. Their mutton yields to ours, but their beef is excellent. I have had a sirloin so large, that I have been forced to make three bites of it; but this is rare. My servants were astonished to see me eat it, bones and all, as in our country we do the leg of a lark. Their geese and turkeys I usually ate at a mouthful, and I confess they far exceed ours. Of their smaller fowl I could take up twenty or thirty at the end of my knife.

One day his imperial majesty, being informed of my way of living, desired "that himself and his royal consort, with the young princes of the blood of both sexes, might have the happiness," as he was pleased to call it, "of dining with me." They came accordingly, and I placed them in chairs of state,

upon my table, just over against me, with their guards about them. Flimnap, the lord high treasurer, attended there likewise with his white staff; and I observed he often looked on me with a sour countenance, which I would not seem to regard, but ate more than usual, in honour to my dear country, as well as to fill the court with admiration. I have some private reasons to believe, that this visit from his majesty gave Flimnap an opportunity of doing me ill offices to his master. That minister had always been my secret enemy, though he outwardly caressed me more than was usual to the moroseness of his nature. He represented to the emperor "the low condition of his treasury; that he was forced to take up money at a great discount; that exchequer bills would not circulate under nine per cent. below par; that I had cost his majesty above a million and a half of sprugs" (their greatest gold coin, about the bigness of a spangle) "and, upon the whole, that it would be advisable in the emperor to take the first fair occasion of dismissing me."

I am here obliged to vindicate the reputation of an excellent lady, who was an innocent sufferer upon my account. The treasurer took a fancy to be jealous of his wife, from the malice of some evil tongues, who informed him that her grace had taken a violent affection for my person; and the court scandal ran for some time, that she once came privately to my lodging. This I solemnly declare to be a most infamous falsehood, without any grounds, further than that her grace was pleased to treat me with all innocent marks of freedom and friendship. I own she came often to my house, but always

publicly, nor ever without three more in the coach, who were usually her sister and young daughter, and some particular acquaintance; but this was common to many other ladies of the court. And I still appeal to my servants round, whether they at any time saw a coach at my door, without knowing what persons were in it. On those occasions, when a servant had given me notice, my custom was to go immediately to the door, and, after paying my respects, to take up the coach and two horses very carefully in my hands, and place them on a table, where I had fixed a movable rim quite round, of five inches high, to prevent accidents. And I have often had four coaches and horses at once on my table, full of company, while I sat in my chair, leaning my face towards them; and when I was engaged with one set, the coachmen would gently drive the others round my table. I have passed many an afternoon very agreeably in these conversations.

CHAPTER 7

Before I proceed to give an account of my leaving this kingdom, it may be proper to inform the reader of a private intrigue which had been for two months forming against me.

I had been hitherto, all my life, a stranger to courts, for which I was unqualified by the meanness of my condition. I had indeed heard and read enough of the dispositions of great princes and ministers, but never expected to have found such terrible effects of them, in so remote a country, governed, as I thought, by very different maxims from those in Europe.

When I was just preparing to pay my attendance on the emperor of Blefuscu, a considerable person at court (to whom I had been very serviceable, at a time when he lay under the highest displeasure of his imperial majesty) came to my house very privately at night, in a close chair, and, without sending his name, desired admittance. The chairmen were dismissed; I put the chair, with his lordship in it, into my coat-pocket: and, giving orders to a trusty servant, to say I was indisposed and gone to sleep, I fastened the door of my house, placed the chair on the table, according to my usual custom, and sat down by it. After the common salutations

were over, observing his lordship's countenance full of concern, and inquiring into the reason, he desired "I would hear him with patience, in a matter that highly concerned my honour and my life." His speech was to the following effect, for I took notes of it as soon as he left me:

"You are to know," said he, "that several committees of council have been lately called, in the most private manner, on your account; and it is but two days since his majesty came to a full resolution.

"You are very sensible that Skyresh Bolgolam has been your mortal enemy, almost ever since your arrival. His original reasons I know not; but his hatred is increased since your great success against Blefuscu, by which his glory as admiral is much obscured. This lord, in conjunction with Flimnap the high-treasurer, whose enmity against you is notorious on account of his lady, Limtoc the general, Lalcon the chamberlain, and Balmuff the grand justiciary, have prepared articles of impeachment against you, for treason and other capital crimes."

This preface made me so impatient, being conscious of my own merits and innocence, that I was going to interrupt him; when he entreated me to be silent, and thus proceeded:

"Out of gratitude for the favours you have done me, I procured information of the whole proceedings, and a copy of the articles; wherein I venture my head for your service.

Articles of Impeachment against the Man-Mountain

ARTICLE I.

Whereas, by a statute made in the reign of his imperial majesty Calin Deffar Plune, it is enacted, that, whoever shall make water within the precincts of the royal palace, shall be liable to the pains and penalties of high-treason; notwithstanding, the said Quinbus Flestrin, in open breach of the said law, under colour of extinguishing the fire kindled in the apartment of his majesty's most dear imperial consort, did maliciously, traitorously, and devilishly, by discharge of his urine, put out the said fire kindled in the said apartment, lying and being within the precincts of the said royal palace, against the statute in that case provided, etc. against the duty, etc.

ARTICLE II.

That the said Quinbus Flestrin, having brought the imperial fleet of Blefuscu into the royal port, and being afterwards commanded by his imperial majesty to seize all the other ships of the said empire of Blefuscu, and reduce that empire to a province, to be governed by a viceroy from hence, and to destroy and put to death, not only all the Big-

endian exiles, but likewise all the people of that empire who would not immediately forsake the Big-endian heresy, he, the said Flestrin, like a false traitor against his most auspicious, serene, imperial majesty, did petition to be excused from the said service, upon pretence of unwillingness to force the consciences, or destroy the liberties and lives of an innocent people.

ARTICLE III.

That, whereas certain ambassadors arrived from the Court of Blefuscu, to sue for peace in his majesty's court, he, the said Flestrin, did, like a false traitor, aid, abet, comfort, and divert, the said ambassadors, although he knew them to be servants to a prince who was lately an open enemy to his imperial majesty, and in an open war against his said majesty.

ARTICLE IV.

That the said Quinbus Flestrin, contrary to the duty of a faithful subject, is now preparing to make a voyage to the court and empire of Blefuscu, for which he has received only verbal license from his imperial majesty; and, under

colour of the said license, does falsely and traitorously intend to take the said voyage, and thereby to aid, comfort, and abet the emperor of Blefuscu, so lately an enemy, and in open war with his imperial majesty aforesaid.

"There are some other articles; but these are the most important, of which I have read you an abstract.

"In the several debates upon this impeachment, it must be confessed that his majesty gave many marks of his great lenity; often urging the services you had done him, and endeavouring to extenuate your crimes. The treasurer and admiral insisted that you should be put to the most painful and ignominious death, by setting fire to your house at night, and the general was to attend with twenty thousand men, armed with poisoned arrows, to shoot you on the face and hands. Some of your servants were to have private orders to strew a poisonous juice on your shirts and sheets, which would soon make you tear your own flesh, and die in the utmost torture. The general came into the same opinion; so that for a long time there was a majority against you; but his majesty resolving, if possible, to spare your life, at last brought off the chamberlain.

"Upon this incident, Reldresal, principal secretary for private affairs, who always approved himself your true friend, was commanded by the emperor to deliver his opinion, which he accordingly did; and therein justified the good thoughts you have of him. He allowed your crimes to be great, but that

still there was room for mercy, the most commendable virtue in a prince, and for which his majesty was so justly celebrated. He said, the friendship between you and him was so well known to the world, that perhaps the most honourable board might think him partial; however, in obedience to the command he had received, he would freely offer his sentiments. That if his majesty, in consideration of your services, and pursuant to his own merciful disposition, would please to spare your life, and only give orders to put out both your eyes, he humbly conceived, that by this expedient justice might in some measure be satisfied, and all the world would applaud the lenity of the emperor, as well as the fair and generous proceedings of those who have the honour to be his counsellors. That the loss of your eyes would be no impediment to your bodily strength, by which you might still be useful to his majesty; that blindness is an addition to courage, by concealing dangers from us; that the fear you had for your eyes, was the greatest difficulty in bringing over the enemy's fleet, and it would be sufficient for you to see by the eyes of the ministers, since the greatest princes do no more.

"This proposal was received with the utmost disapprobation by the whole board. Bolgolam, the admiral, could not preserve his temper, but, rising up in fury, said, he wondered how the secretary durst presume to give his opinion for preserving the life of a traitor; that the services you had performed were, by all true reasons of state, the great aggravation of your crimes; that you, who were able to bring over the enemy's fleet, might serve, upon the first discontent,

to carry it back.

"The treasurer was of the same opinion: he showed to what straits his majesty's revenue was reduced, by the charge of maintaining you, which would soon grow insupportable; that his sacred majesty and the council, who are your judges, were, in their own consciences, fully convinced of your guilt, which was a sufficient argument to condemn you to death, without the formal proofs required by the strict letter of the law.

"But his imperial majesty, fully determined against capital punishment, was graciously pleased to say, that since the council thought the loss of your eyes too easy a censure, some other way may be inflicted hereafter. And your friend the secretary, humbly desiring to be heard again, in answer to what the treasurer had objected, concerning the great charge his majesty was at in maintaining you, said, that his excellency, who had the sole disposal of the emperor's revenue, might easily provide against that evil, by gradually lessening your establishment; by which, for want of sufficient for you would grow weak and faint, and lose your appetite, and consequently, decay, and consume in a few months; neither would the stench of your carcass be then so dangerous, when it should become more than half diminished; and immediately upon your death five or six thousand of his majesty's subjects might, in two or three days, cut your flesh from your bones, take it away by cart-loads, and bury it in distant parts, to prevent infection, leaving the skeleton as a monument of admiration to posterity.

"Thus, by the great friendship of the secretary, the whole affair was compromised. It was strictly enjoined, that the project of starving you by degrees should be kept a secret; but the sentence of putting out your eyes was entered on the books; none dissenting, except Bolgolam the admiral, who, being a creature of the empress, was perpetually instigated by her majesty to insist upon your death, she having borne perpetual malice against you, on account of that infamous and illegal method you took to extinguish the fire in her apartment.

"In three days your friend the secretary will be directed to come to your house, and read before you the articles of impeachment; and then to signify the great lenity and favour of his majesty and council, whereby you are only condemned to the loss of your eyes, which his majesty does not question you will gratefully and humbly submit to; and twenty of his majesty's surgeons will attend, in order to see the operation well performed, by discharging very sharp-pointed arrows into the balls of your eyes, as you lie on the ground.

"I leave to your prudence what measures you will take; and to avoid suspicion, I must immediately return in as private a manner as I came."

His lordship did so; and I remained alone, under many doubts and perplexities of mind.

As to myself, I must confess, having never been designed for a courtier, either by my birth or education, I was so ill a judge of things, that I could not discover the lenity and favour of this sentence, but conceived it (perhaps erroneously) rather

to be rigorous than gentle. I sometimes thought of standing my trial, for, although I could not deny the facts alleged in the several articles, yet I hoped they would admit of some extenuation. But having in my life perused many state-trials, which I ever observed to terminate as the judges thought fit to direct, I durst not rely on so dangerous a decision, in so critical a juncture, and against such powerful enemies. Once I was strongly bent upon resistance, for, while I had liberty the whole strength of that empire could hardly subdue me, and I might easily with stones pelt the metropolis to pieces; but I soon rejected that project with horror, by remembering the oath I had made to the emperor, the favours I received from him, and the high title of nardac he conferred upon me. Neither had I so soon learned the gratitude of courtiers, to persuade myself, that his majesty's present seventies acquitted me of all past obligations.

But hurried on by the precipitancy of youth, and having his imperial majesty's license to pay my attendance upon the emperor of Blefuscu, I took this opportunity, before the three days were elapsed, to send a letter to my friend the secretary, signifying my resolution of setting out that morning for Blefuscu, pursuant to the leave I had got; and, without waiting for an answer, I went to that side of the island where our fleet lay. I seized a large man of war, tied a cable to the prow, and, lifting up the anchors, I stripped myself, put my clothes (together with my coverlet, which I carried under my arm) into the vessel, and, drawing it after me, between wading and swimming arrived at the royal port of Blefuscu, where the

people had long expected me: they lent me two guides to direct me to the capital city, which is of the same name. I held them in my hands, till I came within two hundred yards of the gate, and desired them "to signify my arrival to one of the secretaries, and let him know, I there waited his majesty's command."

I had an answer in about an hour, "that his majesty, attended by the royal family, and great officers of the court, was coming out to receive me." I advanced a hundred yards. The emperor and his train alighted from their horses, the empress and ladies from their coaches, and I did not perceive they were in any fright or concern. I lay on the ground to kiss his majesty's and the empress's hands. I told his majesty, "that I was come according to my promise, and with the license of the emperor my master, to have the honour of seeing so mighty a monarch, and to offer him any service in my power, consistent with my duty to my own prince;" not mentioning a word of my disgrace, because I had hitherto no regular information of it, and might suppose myself wholly ignorant of any such design; neither could I reasonably conceive that the emperor would discover the secret, while I was out of his power; wherein, however, it soon appeared I was deceived.

CHAPTER 8

Three days after my arrival, walking out of curiosity to the north-east coast of the island, I observed, about half a league off in the sea, somewhat that looked like a boat overturned. I pulled off my shoes and stockings, and, wailing two or three hundred yards, I found the object to approach nearer by force of the tide; and then plainly saw it to be a real boat, which I supposed might by some tempest have been driven from a ship. Whereupon, I returned immediately towards the city, and desired his imperial majesty to lend me twenty of the tallest vessels he had left, after the loss of his fleet, and three thousand seamen, under the command of his vice-admiral. This fleet sailed round, while I went back the shortest way to the coast, where I first discovered the boat. I found the tide had driven it still nearer. The seamen were all provided with cordage, which I had beforehand twisted to a sufficient strength. When the ships came up, I stripped myself, and waded till I came within a hundred yards off the boat, after which I was forced to swim till I got up to it. The seamen threw me the end of the cord, which I fastened to a hole in the fore-part of the boat, and the other end to a man of war; but I found all my labour to little purpose; for, being

out of my depth, I was not able to work. In this necessity I was forced to swim behind, and push the boat forward, as often as I could, with one of my hands; and the tide favouring me, I advanced so far that I could just hold up my chin and feel the ground. I rested two or three minutes, and then gave the boat another shove, and so on, till the sea was no higher than my arm-pits; and now, the most laborious part being over, I took out my other cables, which were stowed in one of the ships, and fastened them first to the boat, and then to nine of the vessels which attended me; the wind being favourable, the seamen towed, and I shoved, until we arrived within forty yards of the shore; and, waiting till the tide was out, I got dry to the boat, and by the assistance of two thousand men, with ropes and engines, I made a shift to turn it on its bottom, and found it was but little damaged.

I shall not trouble the reader with the difficulties I was under, by the help of certain paddles, which cost me ten days making, to get my boat to the royal port of Blefuscu, where a mighty concourse of people appeared upon my arrival, full of wonder at the sight of so prodigious a vessel. I told the emperor "that my good fortune had thrown this boat in my way, to carry me to some place whence I might return into my native country; and begged his majesty's orders for getting materials to fit it up, together with his license to depart;" which, after some kind expostulations, he was pleased to grant.

I did very much wonder, in all this time, not to have heard of any express relating to me from our emperor to the

court of Blefuscu. But I was afterward given privately to understand, that his imperial majesty, never imagining I had the least notice of his designs, believed I was only gone to Blefuscu in performance of my promise, according to the license he had given me, which was well known at our court, and would return in a few days, when the ceremony was ended. But he was at last in pain at my long absence; and after consulting with the treasurer and the rest of that cabal, a person of quality was dispatched with the copy of the articles against me. This envoy had instructions to represent to the monarch of Blefuscu, "the great lenity of his master, who was content to punish me no farther than with the loss of mine eyes; that I had fled from justice; and if I did not return in two hours, I should be deprived of my title of nardac, and declared a traitor." The envoy further added, "that in order to maintain the peace and amity between both empires, his master expected that his brother of Blefuscu would give orders to have me sent back to Lilliput, bound hand and foot, to be punished as a traitor."

The emperor of Blefuscu, having taken three days to consult, returned an answer consisting of many civilities and excuses. He said, "that as for sending me bound, his brother knew it was impossible; that, although I had deprived him of his fleet, yet he owed great obligations to me for many good offices I had done him in making the peace. That, however, both their majesties would soon be made easy; for I had found a prodigious vessel on the shore, able to carry me on the sea, which he had given orders to fit up, with my own

assistance and direction; and he hoped, in a few weeks, both empires would be freed from so insupportable an encumbrance."

With this answer the envoy returned to Lilliput; and the monarch of Blefuscu related to me all that had passed; offering me at the same time his gracious protection, if I would continue in his service; wherein, although I believed him sincere, yet I resolved never more to put any confidence in princes or ministers, where I could possibly avoid it; and therefore, with all due acknowledgments for his favourable intentions, I humbly begged to be excused. I told him, "that since fortune, whether good or evil, had thrown a vessel in my way, I was resolved to venture myself on the ocean, rather than be an occasion of difference between two such mighty monarchs." Neither did I find the emperor at all displeased; and I discovered, by a certain accident, that he was very glad of my resolution, and so were most of his ministers.

In about a month, when all was prepared, I sent to receive his majesty's commands, and to take my leave. The emperor and royal family came out of the palace; I lay down on my face to kiss his hand, which he very graciously gave me: so did the empress and young princes of the blood. His majesty presented me with fifty purses of two hundred sprugs a-piece, together with his picture at full length, which I put immediately into one of my gloves, to keep it from being hurt. The ceremonies at my departure were too many to trouble the reader with at this time.

I stored the boat with the carcases of a hundred oxen,

and three hundred sheep, with bread and drink proportionable, and as much meat ready dressed as four hundred cooks could provide. I took with me six cows and two bulls alive, with as many ewes and rams, intending to carry them into my own country, and propagate the breed. And to feed them on board, I had a good bundle of hay, and a bag of corn. I would gladly have taken a dozen of the natives, but this was a thing the emperor would by no means permit; and, besides a diligent search into my pockets, his majesty engaged my honour "not to carry away any of his subjects, although with their own consent and desire."

Having thus prepared all things as well as I was able, I set sail at six in the morning; and when I had gone about four-leagues to the northward, the wind being at south-east, at six in the evening I descried a small island, about half a league to the north-west. I advanced forward, and cast anchor on the lee-side of the island, which seemed to be uninhabited. I then took some refreshment, and went to my rest. I slept well, and as I conjectured at least six hours, for I found the day broke in two hours after I awaked. It was a clear night. I ate my breakfast before the sun was up; and heaving anchor, the wind being favourable, I steered the same course that I had done the day before, wherein I was directed by my pocket compass. My intention was to reach, if possible, one of those islands. which I had reason to believe lay to the north-east of Van Diemen's Land.

I discovered nothing all that day; but upon the next, about three in the afternoon, when I had by my computation

made twenty-four leagues from Blefuscu, I descried a sail steering to the south-east; my course was due east. I hailed her, but could get no answer; yet I found I gained upon her, for the wind slackened. I made all the sail I could, and in half an hour she spied me, then hung out her ancient, and discharged a gun. It is not easy to express the joy I was in, upon the unexpected hope of once more seeing my beloved country, and the dear pledges I left in it.

Gulliver's Travels

A VOYAGE TO BROBDINGNAG

CHAPTER 9

I again left my native country in two months after my return. We got lost in the sea because of many obstacles we had run into. Even the most experienced sailor couldn't tell the direction.

A boy on the top-mast discovered land. And then we came in full view of a great island, or continent; on the south side whereof was a small neck of land jutting out into the sea, and a creek too shallow to hold a ship of above one hundred tons. We cast anchor within a league of this creek, and our captain sent a dozen of his men well armed in the long-boat, with vessels for water, if any could be found. I desired his leave to go with them.

When we came to land we saw no river or spring, nor any sign of inhabitants. Our men therefore wandered on the shore to find out some fresh water near the sea, and I walked alone about a mile on the other side, where I observed the country all barren and rocky. I now began to be weary, and seeing nothing to entertain my curiosity, I returned gently down towards the creek; and the sea being full in my view, I saw our men already got into the boat, and rowing for life to the ship. I was going to holla after them, although it had been

to little purpose, when I observed a huge creature walking after them in the sea, as fast as he could: he waded not much deeper than his knees, and took prodigious strides: but our men had the start of him half a league, and, the sea thereabouts being full of sharp-pointed rocks, the monster was not able to overtake the boat. I ran as fast as I could, and then climbed up a steep hill, which gave me some prospect of the country. I found it fully cultivated; but that which first surprised me was the length of the grass, which, in those grounds that seemed to be kept for hay, was about twenty feet high.

I fell into a high road, for so I took it to be, though it served to the inhabitants only as a foot-path through a field of barley. Here I walked on for some time, but could see little on either side, it being now near harvest, and the corn rising at least forty feet. I was an hour walking to the end of this field, which was fenced in with a hedge of at least one hundred and twenty feet high, and the trees so lofty that I could make no computation of their altitude. There was a stile to pass from this field into the next. It had four steps, and a stone to cross over when you came to the uppermost. It was impossible for me to climb this stile, because every step was six-feet high, and the upper stone about twenty. I was endeavouring to find some gap in the hedge, when I discovered one of the inhabitants in the next field, advancing towards the stile, of the same size with him whom I saw in the sea pursuing our boat. He appeared as tall as an ordinary spire steeple, and took about ten yards at every stride, as near

as I could guess. I was struck with the utmost fear and astonishment, and ran to hide myself in the corn, whence I saw him at the top of the stile looking back into the next field on the right hand, and heard him call in a voice many degrees louder than a speaking-trumpet: but the noise was so high in the air, that at first I certainly thought it was thunder. Whereupon seven monsters, like himself, came towards him with reaping-hooks in their hands, each hook about the largeness of six scythes. These people were not so well clad as the first, whose servants or labourers they seemed to be; for, upon some words he spoke, they went to reap the corn in the field where I lay. I kept from them at as great a distance as I could, but was forced to move with extreme difficulty, for the stalks of the corn were sometimes not above a foot distant, so that I could hardly squeeze my body betwixt them. However, I made a shift to go forward, till I came to a part of the field where the corn had been laid by the rain and wind. Here it was impossible for me to advance a step; for the stalks were so interwoven, that I could not creep through, and the beards of the fallen ears so strong and pointed, that they pierced through my clothes into my flesh. At the same time I heard the reapers not a hundred yards behind me.

Being quite dispirited with toil, and wholly overcome by grief and dispair, I lay down between two ridges, and heartily wished I might there end my days. I bemoaned my desolate widow and fatherless children. I lamented my own folly and wilfulness, in attempting a second voyage, against the advice of all my friends and relations. In this terrible agitation of

mind, I could not forbear thinking of Lilliput, whose inhabitants looked upon me as the greatest prodigy that ever appeared in the world; where I was able to draw an imperial fleet in my hand, and perform those other actions, which will be recorded for ever in the chronicles of that empire, while posterity shall hardly believe them, although attested by millions. I reflected what a mortification it must prove to me, to appear as inconsiderable in this nation, as one single Lilliputian would be among us. But this I conceived was to be the least of my misfortunes; for, as human creatures are observed to be more savage and cruel in proportion to their bulk, what could I expect but to be a morsel in the mouth of the first among these enormous barbarians that should happen to seize me?

Scared and confounded as I was, I could not forbear going on with these reflections, when one of the reapers, approaching within ten yards of the ridge where I lay, made me apprehend that with the next step I should be squashed to death under his foot, or cut in two with his reaping-hook. And therefore, when he was again about to move, I screamed as loud as fear could make me: whereupon the huge creature trod short, and, looking round about under him for some time, at last espied me as I lay on the ground. He considered awhile, with the caution of one who endeavours to lay hold on a small dangerous animal in such a manner that it shall not be able either to scratch or bite him, as I myself have sometimes done with a weasel in England. At length he ventured to take me behind, by the middle, between his fore-

finger and thumb, and brought me within three yards of his eyes, that he might behold my shape more perfectly. I resolved not to struggle in the least as he held me in the air above sixty feet from the ground, although he grievously pinched my sides, for fear I should slip through his fingers. All I ventured was to raise mine eyes towards the sun, and place my hands together in a supplicating posture, and to speak some words in a humble melancholy tone, suitable to the condition I then was in: for I apprehended every moment that he would dash me against the ground, as we usually do any little hateful animal, which we have a mind to destroy. But my good star would have it, that he appeared pleased with my voice and gestures, and began to look upon me as a curiosity, much wondering to hear me pronounce articulate words, although he could not understand them. In the mean time I was not able to forbear groaning and shedding tears, and turning my head towards my sides; letting him know, as well as I could, how cruelly I was hurt by the pressure of his thumb and finger. He seemed to apprehend my meaning; for, lifting up the lappet of his coat, he put me gently into it, and immediately ran along with me to his master, who was a substantial farmer, and the same person I had first seen in the field.

The farmer having received such an account of me as his servant could give him, took a piece of a small straw, about the size of a walking-staff, and therewith lifted up the lappets of my coat; which it seems he thought to be some kind of covering that nature had given me. He blew my hairs aside to

take a better view of my face. He called his hinds about him, and asked them, as I afterwards learned, whether they had ever seen in the fields any little creature that resembled me. He then placed me softly on the ground upon all fours, but I got immediately up, and walked slowly backward and forward, to let those people see I had no intent to run away. They all sat down in a circle about me, the better to observe my motions. I pulled off my hat, and made a low bow towards the farmer. I fell on my knees, and lifted up my hands and eyes, and spoke several words as loud as I could: I took a purse of gold out of my pocket, and humbly presented it to him. He received it on the palm of his hand, then applied it close to his eye to see what it was, and afterwards turned it several times with the point of a pin, but could make nothing of it. Whereupon I made a sign that he should place his hand on the ground. I then took the purse, and, opening it, poured all the gold into his palm. There were six Spanish pieces of four pistoles each, beside twenty or thirty smaller coins. I saw him wet the tip of his little finger upon his tongue, and take up one of my largest pieces, and then another; but he seemed to be wholly ignorant what they were. He made me a sign to put them again into my purse, and the purse again into my pocket, which, after offering it to him several times, I thought it best to do.

The farmer, by this time, was convinced I must be a rational creature. He spoke often to me; but the sound of his voice pierced my ears like that of a water-mill, yet his words were articulate enough. I answered as loud as I could in

several languages, and he often laid his ear within two yards of me: but all in vain, for we were wholly unintelligible to each other. He then sent his servants to their work, and taking his handkerchief out of his pocket, he doubled and spread it on his left hand, which he placed flat on the ground with the palm upward, making me a sign to step into it, as I could easily do, for it was not above a foot in thickness. I thought it my part to obey, and, for fear of falling, laid myself at full length upon the handkerchief, with the remainder of which he lapped me up to the head for further security, and in this manner carried me home to his house. There he called his wife, and showed me to her; but she screamed and ran back, as women in England do at the sight of a toad or a spider. However, when she had a while seen my behaviour, and how well I observed the signs her husband made, she was soon reconciled, and by degrees grew extremely tender of me.

It was about twelve at noon, and a servant brought in dinner. It was only one substantial dish of meat, in a dish of about four-and-twenty feet diameter. The company were, the farmer and his wife, three children, and an old grandmother. When they were sat down, the farmer placed me at some distance from him on the table, which was thirty feet high from the floor. I was in a terrible fright, and kept as far as I could from the edge, for fear of falling.

The wife minced a bit of meat, then crumbled some bread on a trencher, and placed it before me. I made her a low bow, took out my knife and fork, and fell to eat, which gave them exceeding delight. The mistress sent her maid for a small

dram cup, which held about two gallons, and filled it with drink; I took up the vessel with much difficulty in both hands, and in a most respectful manner drank to her ladyship's health, expressing the words as loud as I could in English, which made the company laugh so heartily, that I was almost deafened with the noise. This liquor tasted like a small cider, and was not unpleasant. Then the master made me a sign to come to his trencher side; but as I walked on the table, being in great surprise all the time, as the indulgent reader will easily conceive and excuse, I happened to stumble against a crust, and fell flat on my face, but received no hurt. I got up immediately, and observing the good people to be in much concern, I took my hat, and waving it over my head, made three huzzas, to show I had got no mischief by my fall. But advancing forward towards my master, his youngest son, who sat next to him, an arch boy of about ten years old, took me up by the legs, and held me so high in the air, that I trembled every limb: but his father snatched me from him, and at the same time gave him such a box on the left ear, as would have felled an European troop of horse to the earth, ordering him to be taken from the table. But being afraid the boy might owe me a spite, and well remembering how mischievous all children among us naturally are to sparrows, rabbits, young kittens, and puppy dogs, I fell on my knees, and pointing to the boy, made my master to understand, as well as I could, that I desired his son might be pardoned. The father complied, and the lad took his seat again, whereupon I went to him, and kissed his hand, which my master took, and made

him stroke me gently with it.

In the midst of dinner, my mistress's favourite cat leaped into her lap. I heard a noise behind me like that of a dozen stocking-weavers at work; and turning my head, I found it proceeded from the purring of that animal, who seemed to be three times larger than an ox, as I computed by the view of her head, and one of her paws, while her mistress was feeding and stroking her. The fierceness of this creature's countenance altogether discomposed me; though I stood at the farther end of the table, above fifty feet off; and although my mistress held her fast, for fear she might give a spring, and seize me in her talons. But it happened there was no danger, for the cat took not the least notice of me when my master placed me within three yards of her. And as I have been always told, and found true by experience in my travels, that flying or discovering fear before a fierce animal, is a certain way to make it pursue or attack you, so I resolved, in this dangerous juncture, to show no manner of concern. I walked with intrepidity five or six times before the very head of the cat, and came within half a yard of her; whereupon she drew herself back, as if she were more afraid of me: I had less apprehension concerning the dogs, whereof three or four came into the room, as it is usual in farmers' houses; one of which was a mastiff, equal in bulk to four elephants, and another a greyhound, somewhat taller than the mastiff, but not so large.

When dinner was almost done, the nurse came in with a child of a year old in her arms, who immediately spied me,

and began a squall that you might have heard from London-Bridge to Chelsea, after the usual oratory of infants, to get me for a plaything. The mother, out of pure indulgence, took me up, and put me towards the child, who presently seized me by the middle, and got my head into his mouth, where I roared so loud that the urchin was frighted, and let me drop, and I should infallibly have broke my neck, if the mother had not held her apron under me. The nurse, to quiet her babe, made use of a rattle which was a kind of hollow vessel filled with great stones, and fastened by a cable to the child's waist: but all in vain; so that she was forced to apply the last remedy by giving it suck.

When dinner was done, my master went out to his labourers, and, as I could discover by his voice and gesture, gave his wife strict charge to take care of me. I was very much tired, and disposed to sleep, which my mistress perceiving, she put me on her own bed, and covered me with a clean white handkerchief, but larger and coarser than the mainsail of a man-of-war.

I slept about two hours, and dreamt I was at home with my wife and children, which aggravated my sorrows when I awaked, and found myself alone in a vast room, between two and three hundred feet wide, and above two hundred high, lying in a bed twenty yards wide. My mistress was gone about her household affairs, and had locked me in. The bed was eight yards from the floor. Some natural necessities required me to get down; I durst not presume to call; and if I had, it would have been in vain, with such a voice as mine, at so great

a distance from the room where I lay to the kitchen where the family kept. While I was under these circumstances, two rats crept up the curtains, and ran smelling backwards and forwards on the bed. One of them came up almost to my face, whereupon I rose in a fright, and drew out my hanger to defend myself. These horrible animals had the boldness to attack me on both sides, and one of them held his fore-feet at my collar; but I had the good fortune to rip up his belly before he could do me any mischief. He fell down at my feet; and the other, seeing the fate of his comrade, made his escape, but not without one good wound on the back, which I gave him as he fled, and made the blood run trickling from him. After this exploit, I walked gently to and fro on the bed, to recover my breath and loss of spirits. These creatures were of the size of a large mastiff, but infinitely more nimble and fierce; so that if I had taken off my belt before I went to sleep, I must have infallibly been torn to pieces and devoured. I measured the tail of the dead rat, and found it to be two yards long, wanting an inch; but it went against my stomach to drag the carcass off the bed, where it lay still bleeding; I observed it had yet some life, but with a strong slash across the neck, I thoroughly despatched it.

Soon after my mistress came into the room, who seeing me all bloody, ran and took me up in her hand. I pointed to the dead rat, smiling, and making other signs to show I was not hurt; whereat she was extremely rejoiced, calling the maid to take up the dead rat with a pair of tongs, and throw it out of the window. Then she set me on a table, where I showed

her my hanger all bloody, and wiping it on the lappet of my coat, returned it to the scabbard. I was pressed to do more than one thing which another could not do for me, and therefore endeavoured to make my mistress understand, that I desired to be set down on the floor; which after she had done, my bashfulness would not suffer me to express myself farther, than by pointing to the door, and bowing several times. The good woman, with much difficulty, at last perceived what I would be at, and taking me up again in her hand, walked into the garden, where she set me down. I went on one side about two hundred yards, and beckoning to her not to look or to follow me, I hid myself between two leaves of sorrel, and there discharged the necessities of nature.

CHAPTER 10

My mistress had a daughter of nine years old, a child of towardly parts for her age, very dexterous at her needle, and skilful in dressing her baby. Her mother and she contrived to fit up the baby's cradle for me against night: the cradle was put into a small drawer of a cabinet, and the drawer placed upon a hanging shelf for fear of the rats. This was my bed all the time I staid with those people, though made more convenient by degrees, as I began to learn their language and make my wants known. This young girl was so handy, that after I had once or twice pulled off my clothes before her, she was able to dress and undress me, though I never gave her that trouble when she would let me do either myself. She made me seven shirts, and some other linen, of as fine cloth as could be got, which indeed was coarser than sackcloth; and these she constantly washed for me with her own hands. She was likewise my school-mistress, to teach me the language: when I pointed to any thing, she told me the name of it in her own tongue, so that in a few days I was able to call for whatever I had a mind to. She was very good-natured, and not above forty feet high, being little for her age. She gave me the name of Grildrig, which the family took up, and afterwards

the whole kingdom. The word imports what the Latins call nanunculus, the Italians homunceletino, and the English mannikin. To her I chiefly owe my preservation in that country: we never parted while I was there; I called her my Glumdalclitch, or little nurse.

It now began to be known and talked of in the neighbourhood, that my master had found a strange animal in the field, about the bigness of a splacnuck, but exactly shaped in every part like a human creature; which it likewise imitated in all its actions; seemed to speak in a little language of its own, had already learned several words of theirs, went erect upon two legs, was tame and gentle, would come when it was called, do whatever it was bid, had the finest limbs in the world, and a complexion fairer than a nobleman's daughter of three years old. Another farmer, who lived hard by, and was a particular friend of my master, came on a visit on purpose to inquire into the truth of this story. I was immediately produced, and placed upon a table, where I walked as I was commanded, drew my hanger, put it up again, made my reverence to my master's guest, asked him in his own language how he did, and told him he was welcome, just as my little nurse had instructed me. This man, who was old and dim-sighted, put on his spectacles to behold me better; at which I could not forbear laughing very heartily, for his eyes appeared like the full moon shining into a chamber at two windows. Our people, who discovered the cause of my mirth, bore me company in laughing, at which the old fellow was fool enough to be angry and out of countenance. He had the character of

a great miser; and, to my misfortune, he well deserved it, by the cursed advice he gave my master, to show me as a sight upon a market-day in the next town, which was half an hour's riding, about two-and-twenty miles from our house. I guessed there was some mischief when I observed my master and his friend whispering together, sometimes pointing at me; and my fears made me fancy that I overheard and understood some of their words.

But the next morning Glumdalclitch, my little nurse, told me the whole matter, which she had cunningly picked out from her mother. The poor girl laid me on her bosom, and fell a weeping with shame and grief. She apprehended some mischief would happen to me from rude vulgar folks, who might squeeze me to death, or break one of my limbs by taking me in their hands. She had also observed how modest I was in my nature, how nicely I regarded my honour, and what an indignity I should conceive it, to be exposed for money as a public spectacle, to the meanest of the people. She said, her papa and mamma had promised that Grildrig should be hers; but now she found they meant to serve her as they did last year, when they pretended to give her a lamb, and yet, as soon as it was fat, sold it to a butcher. For my own part, I may truly affirm, that I was less concerned than my nurse. I had a strong hope, which never left me, that I should one day recover my liberty.

My master, pursuant to the advice of his friend, carried me in a box the next market-day to the neighbouring town, and took along with him his little daughter, my nurse, upon a

pillion behind him. The box was close on every side, with a little door for me to go in and out, and a few gimlet holes to let in air. The girl had been so careful as to put the quilt of her baby's bed into it, for me to lie down on. However, I was terribly shaken and discomposed in this journey, though it was but of half an hour: for the horse went about forty feet at every step and trotted so high, that the agitation was equal to the rising and falling of a ship in a great storm, but much more frequent. Our journey was somewhat farther than from London to St. Alban's. My master alighted at an inn which he used to frequent; and after consulting awhile with the inn-keeper, and making some necessary preparations, he hired the grultrud, or crier, to give notice through the town of a strange creature to be seen at the sign of the Green Eagle, not so big as a splacnuck (an animal in that country very finely shaped, about six feet long,) and in every part of the body resembling a human creature, could speak several words, and perform a hundred diverting tricks.

I was placed upon a table in the largest room of the inn, which might be near three hundred feet square. My little nurse stood on a low stool close to the table, to take care of me, and direct what I should do. My master, to avoid a crowd, would suffer only thirty people at a time to see me. I walked about on the table as the girl commanded; she asked me questions, as far as she knew my understanding of the language reached, and I answered them as loud as I could. I turned about several times to the company, paid my humble respects, said they were welcome, and used some other

speeches I had been taught. I took up a thimble filled with liquor, which Glumdalclitch had given me for a cup, and drank their health, I drew out my hanger, and flourished with it after the manner of fencers in England. My nurse gave me a part of a straw, which I exercised as a pike, having learnt the art in my youth.

I was that day shown to twelve sets of company, and as often forced to act over again the same fopperies, till I was half dead with weariness and vexation; for those who had seen me made such wonderful reports, that the people were ready to break down the doors to come in. My master, for his own interest, would not suffer any one to touch me except my nurse; and to prevent danger, benches were set round the table at such a distance as to put me out of every body's reach. However, an unlucky school-boy aimed a hazel nut directly at my head, which very narrowly missed me; otherwise it came with so much violence, that it would have infallibly knocked out my brains, for it was almost as large as a small pumpkin, but I had the satisfaction to see the young rogue well beaten, and turned out of the room.

My master gave public notice that he would show me again the next market-day; and in the meantime he prepared a convenient vehicle for me, which he had reason enough to do; for I was so tired with my first journey, and with entertaining company for eight hours together, that I could hardly stand upon my legs, or speak a word. It was at least three days before I recovered my strength; and that I might have no rest at home, all the neighbouring gentlemen from a hundred

miles round, hearing of my fame, came to see me at my master's own house. There could not be fewer than thirty persons with their wives and children; and my master demanded the rate of a full room whenever he showed me at home, although it were only to a single family; so that for some time I had but little ease every day of the week (except Wednesday, which is their Sabbath,) although I were not carried to the town.

My master, finding how profitable I was likely to be, resolved to carry me to the most considerable cities of the kingdom. Having therefore provided himself with all things necessary for a long journey, and settled his affairs at home, he took leave of his wife, and we set out for the metropolis, situate near the middle of that empire, and about three thousand miles distance from our house. My master made his daughter Glumdalclitch ride behind him. She carried me on her lap, in a box tied about her waist. The girl had lined it on all sides with the softest cloth she could get, well quilted underneath, furnished it with her baby's bed, provided me with linen and other necessaries, and made everything as convenient as she could. We had no other company but a boy of the house, who rode after us with the luggage.

My master's design was to show me in all the towns by the way, and to step out of the road for fifty or a hundred miles, to any village, or person of quality's house, where he might expect custom. We made easy journeys, of not above seven or eight score miles a-day; for Glumdalclitch, on purpose to spare me, complained she was tired with the

trotting of the horse. She often took me out of my box, at my own desire, to give me air, and show me the country, but always held me fast by a leading-string. We passed over five or six rivers, many degrees broader and deeper than the Nile or the Ganges: and there was hardly a rivulet so small as the Thames at London-bridge. We were ten weeks in our journey, and I was shown in eighteen large towns, besides many villages, and private families.

We arrived at the metropolis, called in their language Lorbrulgrud, or Pride of the Universe. My master took a lodging in the principal street of the city, not far from the royal palace, and put out bills in the usual form, containing an exact description of my person and parts. He hired a large room between three and four hundred feet wide. He provided a table sixty feet in diameter, upon which I was to act my part, and pallisadoed it round three feet from the edge, and as many high, to prevent my falling over. I was shown ten times a-day, to the wonder and satisfaction of all people. I could now speak the language tolerably well, and perfectly understood every word, that was spoken to me. Besides, I had learnt their alphabet, and could make a shift to explain a sentence here and there; for Glumdalclitch had been my instructor while we were at home, and at leisure hours during our journey. She carried a little book in her pocket, not much larger than a Sanson's Atlas; it was a common treatise for the use of young girls, giving a short account of their religion: out of this she taught me my letters, and interpreted the words.

CHAPTER 11

The frequent labours I underwent every day, made, in a few weeks, a very considerable change in my health: the more my master got by me, the more insatiable he grew. I had quite lost my stomach, and was almost reduced to a skeleton. The farmer observed it, and concluding I must soon die, resolved to make as good a hand of me as he could. While he was thus reasoning and resolving with himself, a sardral, or gentleman-usher, came from court, commanding my master to carry me immediately thither for the diversion of the queen and her ladies. Some of the latter had already been to see me, and reported strange things of my beauty, behaviour, and good sense. Her majesty, and those who attended her, were beyond measure delighted with my demeanour. I fell on my knees, and begged the honour of kissing her imperial foot; but this gracious princess held out her little finger towards me, after I was set on the table, which I embraced in both my arms, and put the tip of it with the utmost respect to my lip.

She made me some general questions about my country and my travels, which I answered as distinctly, and in as few words as I could. She asked, "whether I could be content to live at court?" I bowed down to the board of the table, and

humbly answered "that I was my master's slave: but, if I were at my own disposal, I should be proud to devote my life to her majesty's service." She then asked my master, "whether he was willing to sell me at a good price?" He, who apprehended I could not live a month, was ready enough to part with me, and demanded a thousand pieces of gold, which were ordered him on the spot, each piece being about the bigness of eight hundred moidores; but allowing for the proportion of all things between that country and Europe, and the high price of gold among them, was hardly so great a sum as a thousand guineas would be in England. I then said to the queen, "since I was now her majesty's most humble creature and vassal, I must beg the favour, that Glumdalclitch, who had always tended me with so much care and kindness, and understood to do it so well, might be admitted into her service, and continue to be my nurse and instructor."

Her majesty agreed to my petition, and easily got the farmer's consent, who was glad enough to have his daughter preferred at court, and the poor girl herself was not able to hide her joy. My late master withdrew, bidding me farewell, and saying he had left me in a good service; to which I replied not a word, only making him a slight bow.

She took me in her own hand, and carried me to the king, who was then retired to his cabinet. His majesty, a prince of much gravity and austere countenance, not well observing my shape at first view, asked the queen after a cold manner "how long it was since she grew fond of a splacnuck?" for such it seems he took me to be, as I lay upon my breast in her

majesty's right hand. But this princess, who has an infinite deal of wit and humour, set me gently on my feet upon the scrutoire, and commanded me to give his majesty an account of myself, which I did in a very few words: and Glumdalclitch who attended at the cabinet door, and could not endure I should be out of her sight, being admitted, confirmed all that had passed from my arrival at her father's house.

The king, although he be as learned a person as any in his dominions, had been educated in the study of philosophy, and particularly mathematics; yet when he observed my shape exactly, and saw me walk erect, before I began to speak, conceived I might be a piece of clock-work (which is in that country arrived to a very great perfection) contrived by some ingenious artist. But when he heard my voice, and found what I delivered to be regular and rational, he could not conceal his astonishment. He was by no means satisfied with the relation I gave him of the manner I came into his kingdom, but thought it a story concerted between Glumdalclitch and her father, who had taught me a set of words to make me sell at a better price. Upon this imagination, he put several other questions to me, and still received rational answers: no otherwise defective than by a foreign accent, and an imperfect knowledge in the language, with some rustic phrases which I had learned at the farmer's house, and did not suit the polite style of a court.

His majesty sent for three great scholars, who were then in their weekly waiting, according to the custom in that country. These gentlemen, after they had a while examined my

shape with much nicety, were of different opinions concerning me. They all agreed that I could not be produced according to the regular laws of nature, because I was not framed with a capacity of preserving my life, either by swiftness, or climbing of trees, or digging holes in the earth. They observed by my teeth, which they viewed with great exactness, that I was a carnivorous animal; yet most quadrupeds being an overmatch for me, and field mice, with some others, too nimble, they could not imagine how I should be able to support myself, unless I fed upon snails and other insects, which they offered, by many learned arguments, to evince that I could not possibly do. One of these virtuosi seemed to think that I might be an embryo, or abortive birth. But this opinion was rejected by the other two, who observed my limbs to be perfect and finished; and that I had lived several years, as it was manifest from my beard, the stumps whereof they plainly discovered through a magnifying glass. They would not allow me to be a dwarf, because my littleness was beyond all degrees of comparison; for the queen's favourite dwarf, the smallest ever known in that kingdom, was near thirty feet high. After much debate, they concluded unanimously, that I was only relplum scalcath, which is interpreted literally lusus naturae.

He desired the queen to order that a particular care should be taken of me; and was of opinion that Glumdalclitch should still continue in her office of tending me, because he observed we had a great affection for each other. A convenient apartment was provided for her at court:

she had a sort of governess appointed to take care of her education, a maid to dress her, and two other servants for menial offices; but the care of me was wholly appropriated to herself.

The queen commanded her own cabinet-maker to contrive a box, that might serve me for a bedchamber, after the model that Glumdalclitch and I should agree upon. This man was a most ingenious artist, and according to my direction, in three weeks finished for me a wooden chamber of sixteen feet square, and twelve high, with sash-windows, a door, and two closets, like a London bed-chamber. The board, that made the ceiling, was to be lifted up and down by two hinges, to put in a bed ready furnished by her majesty's upholsterer, which Glumdalclitch took out every day to air, made it with her own hands, and letting it down at night, locked up the roof over me. A nice workman, who was famous for little curiosities, undertook to make me two chairs, with backs and frames, of a substance not unlike ivory, and two tables, with a cabinet to put my things in. The room was quilted on all sides, as well as the floor and the ceiling, to prevent any accident from the carelessness of those who carried me, and to break the force of a jolt, when I went in a coach. I desired a lock for my door, to prevent rats and mice from coming in. The smith, after several attempts, made the smallest that ever was seen among them, for I have known a larger at the gate of a gentleman's house in England. I made a shift to keep the key in a pocket of my own, fearing Glumdalclitch might lose it. The queen likewise ordered the

thinnest silks that could be gotten, to make me clothes, not much thicker than an English blanket, very cumbersome till I was accustomed to them. They were after the fashion of the kingdom, partly resembling the Persian, and partly the Chinese, and are a very grave and decent habit.

The queen became so fond of my company, that she could not dine without me. I had a table placed upon the same at which her majesty ate, just at her left elbow, and a chair to sit on. Glumdalclitch stood on a stool on the floor near my table, to assist and take care of me. I had an entire set of silver dishes and plates, and other necessaries, which, in proportion to those of the queen, were not much bigger than what I have seen in a London toy-shop for the furniture of a baby-house: these my little nurse kept in her pocket in a silver box, and gave me at meals as I wanted them, always cleaning them herself. No person dined with the queen but the two princesses royal, the eldest sixteen years old, and the younger at that time thirteen and a month. Her majesty used to put a bit of meat upon one of my dishes, out of which I carved for myself, and her diversion was to see me eat in miniature: for the queen (who had indeed but a weak stomach) took up, at one mouthful, as much as a dozen English farmers could eat at a meal, which to me was for some time a very nauseous sight. She would craunch the wing of a lark, bones and all, between her teeth, although it were nine times as large as that of a full-grown turkey; and put a bit of bread into her mouth as big as two twelve-penny loaves. She drank out of a golden cup, above a hogshead at a draught. Her knives were twice as

long as a scythe, set straight upon the handle. The spoons, forks, and other instruments, were all in the same proportion. I remember when Glumdalclitch carried me, out of curiosity, to see some of the tables at court, where ten or a dozen of those enormous knives and forks were lifted up together, I thought I had never till then beheld so terrible a sight.

It is the custom, that every Wednesday (which, as I have observed, is their Sabbath) the king and queen, with the royal issue of both sexes, dine together in the apartment of his majesty, to whom I was now become a great favourite; and at these times, my little chair and table were placed at his left hand, before one of the salt-cellars. This prince took a pleasure in conversing with me, inquiring into the manners, religion, laws, government, and learning of Europe; wherein I gave him the best account I was able. His apprehension was so clear, and his judgment so exact, that he made very wise reflections and observations upon all I said. But I confess, that, after I had been a little too copious in talking of my own beloved country, of our trade and wars by sea and land, of our schisms in religion, and parties in the state; the prejudices of his education prevailed so far, that he could not forbear taking me up in his right hand, and stroking me gently with the other, after a hearty fit of laughing, asked me, "whether I was a whig or tory?" Then turning to his first minister, who waited behind him with a white staff, near as tall as the mainmast of the Royal Sovereign, he observed "how contemptible a thing was human grandeur, which could be mimicked by such diminutive insects as I: and yet," says he, "I

dare engage these creatures have their titles and distinctions of honour; they contrive little nests and burrows, that they call houses and cities; they make a figure in dress and equipage; they love, they fight, they dispute, they cheat, they betray!" And thus he continued on, while my colour came and went several times, with indignation, to hear our noble country, the mistress of arts and arms, the scourge of France, the arbitress of Europe, the seat of virtue, piety, honour, and truth, the pride and envy of the world, so contemptuously treated.

But as I was not in a condition to resent injuries, so upon mature thoughts I began to doubt whether I was injured or no. For, after having been accustomed several months to the sight and converse of this people, and observed every object upon which I cast mine eyes to be of proportionable magnitude, the horror I had at first conceived from their bulk and aspect was so far worn off, that if I had then beheld a company of English lords and ladies in their finery and birth-day clothes, acting their several parts in the most courtly manner of strutting, and bowing, and prating, to say the truth, I should have been strongly tempted to laugh as much at them as the king and his grandees did at me. Neither, indeed, could I forbear smiling at myself, when the queen used to place me upon her hand towards a looking-glass, by which both our persons appeared before me in full view together; and there could be nothing more ridiculous than the comparison; so that I really began to imagine myself dwindled many degrees below my usual size.

Nothing angered and mortified me so much as the queen's dwarf; who being of the lowest stature that was ever in that country (for I verily think he was not full thirty feet high), became so insolent at seeing a creature so much beneath him, that he would always affect to swagger and look big as he passed by me in the queen's antechamber, while I was standing on some table talking with the lords or ladies of the court, and he seldom failed of a smart word or two upon my littleness; against which I could only revenge myself by calling him brother, challenging him to wrestle, and such repartees as are usually in the mouths of court pages. One day, at dinner, this malicious little cub was so nettled with something I had said to him, that, raising himself upon the frame of her majesty's chair, he took me up by the middle, as I was sitting down, not thinking any harm, and let me drop into a large silver bowl of cream, and then ran away as fast as he could. I fell over head and ears, and, if I had not been a good swimmer, it might have gone very hard with me; for Glumdalclitch in that instant happened to be at the other end of the room, and the queen was in such a fright, that she wanted presence of mind to assist me. But my little nurse ran to my relief, and took me out, after I had swallowed above a quart of cream. I was put to bed: however, I received no other damage than the loss of a suit of clothes, which was utterly spoiled. The dwarf was soundly whipt, and as a farther punishment, forced to drink up the bowl of cream into which he had thrown me: neither was he ever restored to favour; for soon after the queen bestowed him on a lady of high quality,

so that I saw him no more, to my very great satisfaction; for I could not tell to what extremities such a malicious urchin might have carried his resentment.

He had before served me a scurvy trick, which set the queen a-laughing, although at the same time she was heartily vexed, and would have immediately cashiered him, if I had not been so generous as to intercede. Her majesty had taken a marrow-bone upon her plate, and, after knocking out the marrow, placed the bone again in the dish erect, as it stood before; the dwarf, watching his opportunity, while Glumdalclitch was gone to the side-board, mounted the stool that she stood on to take care of me at meals, took me up in both hands, and squeezing my legs together, wedged them into the marrow bone above my waist, where I stuck for some time, and made a very ridiculous figure. I believe it was near a minute before any one knew what was become of me; for I thought it below me to cry out. But, as princes seldom get their meat hot, my legs were not scalded, only my stockings and breeches in a sad condition. The dwarf, at my entreaty, had no other punishment than a sound whipping.

CHAPTER 12

The kingdom is a peninsula, terminated to the north-east by a ridge of mountains thirty miles high, which are altogether impassable, by reason of the volcanoes upon the tops: neither do the most learned know what sort of mortals inhabit beyond those mountains, or whether they be inhabited at all. On the three other sides, it is bounded by the ocean. There is not one seaport in the whole kingdom: and those parts of the coasts into which the rivers issue, are so full of pointed rocks, and the sea generally so rough, that there is no venturing with the smallest of their boats; so that these people are wholly excluded from any commerce with the rest of the world. But the large rivers are full of vessels, and abound with excellent fish; for they seldom get any from the sea, because the sea fish are of the same size with those in Europe, and consequently not worth catching; whereby it is manifest, that nature, in the production of plants and animals of so extraordinary a bulk, is wholly confined to this continent. However, now and then they take a whale that happens to be dashed against the rocks, which the common people feed on heartily. These whales I have known so large, that a man could hardly carry one upon his shoulders; and sometimes, for

curiosity, they are brought in hampers to Lorbrulgrud; I saw one of them in a dish at the king's table, which passed for a rarity, but I did not observe he was fond of it; for I think, indeed, the bigness disgusted him, although I have seen one somewhat larger in Greenland.

The king's palace is no regular edifice, but a heap of buildings, about seven miles round: the chief rooms are generally two hundred and forty feet high, and broad and long in proportion. A coach was allowed to Glumdalclitch and me, wherein her governess frequently took her out to see the town, or go among the shops; and I was always of the party, carried in my box; although the girl, at my own desire, would often take me out, and hold me in her hand, that I might more conveniently view the houses and the people, as we passed along the streets. I reckoned our coach to be about a square of Westminster-hall, but not altogether so high: however, I cannot be very exact.

Besides the large box in which I was usually carried, the queen ordered a smaller one to be made for me, of about twelve feet square, and ten high, for the convenience of travelling; because the other was somewhat too large for Glumdalclitch's lap, and cumbersome in the coach; it was made by the same artist, whom I directed in the whole contrivance. This travelling-closet was an exact square, with a window in the middle of three of the squares, and each window was latticed with iron wire on the outside, to prevent accidents in long journeys. On the fourth side, which had no window, two strong staples were fixed, through which the

person that carried me, when I had a mind to be on horseback, put a leathern belt, and buckled it about his waist. This was always the office of some grave trusty servant, in whom I could confide, whether I attended the king and queen in their progresses, or were disposed to see the gardens, or pay a visit to some great lady or minister of state in the court, when Glumdalclitch happened to be out of order; for I soon began to be known and esteemed among the greatest officers, I suppose more upon account of their majesties' favour, than any merit of my own. In journeys, when I was weary of the coach, a servant on horseback would buckle on my box, and place it upon a cushion before him; and there I had a full prospect of the country on three sides, from my three windows. I had, in this closet, a field-bed and a hammock, hung from the ceiling, two chairs and a table, neatly screwed to the floor, to prevent being tossed about by the agitation of the horse or the coach.

Whenever I had a mind to see the town, it was always in my travelling-closet; which Glumdalclitch held in her lap in a kind of open sedan, after the fashion of the country, borne by four men, and attended by two others in the queen's livery. The people, who had often heard of me, were very curious to crowd about the sedan, and the girl was complaisant enough to make the bearers stop, and to take me in her hand, that I might be more conveniently seen.

I was very desirous to see the chief temple, and particularly the tower belonging to it, which is reckoned the highest in the kingdom. Accordingly one day my nurse carried

me thither, but I may truly say I came back disappointed; for the height is not above three thousand feet, reckoning from the ground to the highest pinnacle top; which, allowing for the difference between the size of those people and us in Europe, is no great matter for admiration, nor at all equal in proportion (if I rightly remember) to Salisbury steeple. But, not to detract from a nation, to which, during my life, I shall acknowledge myself extremely obliged, it must be allowed, that whatever this famous tower wants in height, is amply made up in beauty and strength: for the walls are near a hundred feet thick, built of hewn stone, whereof each is about forty feet square, and adorned on all sides with statues of gods and emperors, cut in marble, larger than the life, placed in their several niches. I measured a little finger which had fallen down from one of these statues, and lay unperceived among some rubbish, and found it exactly four feet and an inch in length. Glumdalclitch wrapped it up in her handkerchief, and carried it home in her pocket, to keep among other trinkets, of which the girl was very fond, as children at her age usually are.

The king's kitchen is indeed a noble building, vaulted at top, and about six hundred feet high. The great oven is not so wide, by ten paces, as the cupola at St. Paul's: for I measured the latter on purpose, after my return. But if I should describe the kitchen grate, the prodigious pots and kettles, the joints of meat turning on the spits, with many other particulars, perhaps I should be hardly believed; at least a severe critic would be apt to think I enlarged a little, as

travellers are often suspected to do. To avoid which censure I fear I have run too much into the other extreme; and that if this treatise should happen to be translated into the language of Brobdingnag (which is the general name of that kingdom,) and transmitted thither, the king and his people would have reason to complain that I had done them an injury, by a false and diminutive representation.

His majesty seldom keeps above six hundred horses in his stables: they are generally from fifty-four to sixty feet high. But, when he goes abroad on solemn days, he is attended, for state, by a military guard of five hundred horse, which, indeed, I thought was the most splendid sight that could be ever beheld, till I saw part of his army in battalia, whereof I shall find another occasion to speak.

CHAPTER 13

I should have lived happy enough in that country, if my littleness had not exposed me to several ridiculous and troublesome accidents; some of which I shall venture to relate. Glumdalclitch often carried me into the gardens of the court in my smaller box, and would sometimes take me out of it, and hold me in her hand, or set me down to walk. I remember, before the dwarf left the queen, he followed us one day into those gardens, and my nurse having set me down, he and I being close together, near some dwarf apple trees, I must needs show my wit, by a silly allusion between him and the trees, which happens to hold in their language as it does in ours. Whereupon, the malicious rogue, watching his opportunity, when I was walking under one of them, shook it directly over my head, by which a dozen apples, each of them near as large as a Bristol barrel, came tumbling about my ears; one of them hit me on the back as I chanced to stoop, and knocked me down flat on my face; but I received no other hurt, and the dwarf was pardoned at my desire, because I had given the provocation.

Another day, Glumdalclitch left me on a smooth grass-plot to divert myself, while she walked at some distance with

her governess. In the meantime, there suddenly fell such a violent shower of hail, that I was immediately by the force of it, struck to the ground: and when I was down, the hailstones gave me such cruel bangs all over the body, as if I had been pelted with tennis-balls; however, I made a shift to creep on all fours, and shelter myself, by lying flat on my face, on the lee-side of a border of lemon-thyme, but so bruised from head to foot, that I could not go abroad in ten days. Neither is this at all to be wondered at, because nature, in that country, observing the same proportion through all her operations, a hailstone is near eighteen hundred times as large as one in Europe.

But a more dangerous accident happened to me in the same garden, when my little nurse, believing she had put me in a secure place (which I often entreated her to do, that I might enjoy my own thoughts,) and having left my box at home, to avoid the trouble of carrying it, went to another part of the garden with her governess and some ladies of her acquaintance. While she was absent, and out of hearing, a small white spaniel that belonged to one of the chief gardeners, having got by accident into the garden, happened to range near the place where I lay: the dog, following the scent, came directly up, and taking me in his mouth, ran straight to his master wagging his tail, and set me gently on the ground. By good fortune he had been so well taught, that I was carried between his teeth without the least hurt, or even tearing my clothes. But the poor gardener, who knew me well, and had a great kindness for me, was in a terrible fright:

he gently took me up in both his hands, and asked me how I did? but I was so amazed and out of breath, that I could not speak a word. In a few minutes I came to myself, and he carried me safe to my little nurse, who, by this time, had returned to the place where she left me, and was in cruel agonies when I did not appear, nor answer when she called. She severely reprimanded the gardener on account of his dog.

This accident absolutely determined Glumdalclitch never to trust me abroad for the future out of her sight. I had been long afraid of this resolution, and therefore concealed from her some little unlucky adventures, that happened in those times when I was left by myself. Once a kite, hovering over the garden, made a stoop at me, and if I had not resolutely drawn my hanger, and run under a thick espalier, he would have certainly carried me away in his talons. Another time, walking to the top of a fresh mole-hill, I fell to my neck in the hole, through which that animal had cast up the earth, and coined some lie, not worth remembering, to excuse myself for spoiling my clothes. I likewise broke my right shin against the shell of a snail, which I happened to stumble over, as I was walking alone and thinking on poor England.

I cannot tell whether I were more pleased or mortified to observe, in those solitary walks, that the smaller birds did not appear to be at all afraid of me, but would hop about within a yard's distance, looking for worms and other food, with as much indifference and security as if no creature at all were near them. I remember, a thrush had the confidence to snatch out of my hand, with his bill, a of cake that Glumdalclitch

had just given me for my breakfast. When I attempted to catch any of these birds, they would boldly turn against me, endeavouring to peck my fingers, which I durst not venture within their reach; and then they would hop back unconcerned, to hunt for worms or snails, as they did before. But one day, I took a thick cudgel, and threw it with all my strength so luckily, at a linnet, that I knocked him down, and seizing him by the neck with both my hands, ran with him in triumph to my nurse. However, the bird, who had only been stunned, recovering himself gave me so many boxes with his wings, on both sides of my head and body, though I held him at arm's-length, and was out of the reach of his claws, that I was twenty times thinking to let him go. But I was soon relieved by one of our servants, who wrung off the bird's neck, and I had him next day for dinner, by the queen's command. This linnet, as near as I can remember, seemed to be somewhat larger than an English swan.

The maids of honour often invited Glumdalclitch to their apartments, and desired she would bring me along with her, on purpose to have the pleasure of seeing and touching me. They would often strip me naked from top to toe, and lay me at full length in their bosoms; wherewith I was much disgusted because, to say the truth, a very offensive smell came from their skins; which I do not mention, or intend, to the disadvantage of those excellent ladies, for whom I have all manner of respect; but I conceive that my sense was more acute in proportion to my littleness, and that those illustrious persons were no more disagreeable to their lovers, or to each

other, than people of the same quality are with us in England. And, after all, I found their natural smell was much more supportable, than when they used perfumes, under which I immediately swooned away. I cannot forget, that an intimate friend of mine in Lilliput, took the freedom in a warm day, when I had used a good deal of exercise, to complain of a strong smell about me, although I am as little faulty that way, as most of my sex: but I suppose his faculty of smelling was as nice with regard to me, as mine was to that of this people. Upon this point, I cannot forbear doing justice to the queen my mistress, and Glumdalclitch my nurse, whose persons were as sweet as those of any lady in England.

The queen, who often used to hear me talk of my sea-voyages, and took all occasions to divert me when I was melancholy, asked me whether I understood how to handle a sail or an oar, and whether a little exercise of rowing might not be convenient for my health? I answered, that I understood both very well: for although my proper employment had been to be surgeon or doctor to the ship, yet often, upon a pinch, I was forced to work like a common mariner. But I could not see how this could be done in their country, where the smallest wherry was equal to a first-rate man of war among us; and such a boat as I could manage would never live in any of their rivers. Her majesty said, if I would contrive a boat, her own joiner should make it, and she would provide a place for me to sail in. The fellow was an ingenious workman, and by my instructions, in ten days, finished a pleasure-boat with all its tackling, able conveniently

to hold eight Europeans. When it was finished, the queen was so delighted, that she ran with it in her lap to the king, who ordered it to be put into a cistern full of water, with me in it, by way of trial, where I could not manage my two sculls, or little oars, for want of room. But the queen had before contrived another project. She ordered the joiner to make a wooden trough of three hundred feet long, fifty broad, and eight deep; which, being well pitched, to prevent leaking, was placed on the floor, along the wall, in an outer room of the palace. It had a cock near the bottom to let out the water, when it began to grow stale; and two servants could easily fill it in half an hour. Here I often used to row for my own diversion, as well as that of the queen and her ladies, who thought themselves well entertained with my skill and agility. Sometimes I would put up my sail, and then my business was only to steer, while the ladies gave me a gale with their fans; and, when they were weary, some of their pages would blow my sail forward with their breath, while I showed my art by steering starboard or larboard as I pleased. When I had done, Glumdalclitch always carried back my boat into her closet, and hung it on a nail to dry.

Another time, one of the servants, whose office it was to fill my trough every third day with fresh water, was so careless as to let a huge frog (not perceiving it) slip out of his pail. The frog lay concealed till I was put into my boat, but then, seeing a resting-place, climbed up, and made it lean so much on one side, that I was forced to balance it with all my weight on the other, to prevent overturning. When the frog was got

in, it hopped at once half the length of the boat, and then over my head, backward and forward, daubing my face and clothes with its odious slime. The largeness of its features made it appear the most deformed animal that can be conceived. However, I desired Glumdalclitch to let me deal with it alone. I banged it a good while with one of my sculls, and at last forced it to leap out of the boat.

But the greatest danger I ever underwent in that kingdom, was from a monkey, who belonged to one of the clerks of the kitchen. Glumdalclitch had locked me up in her closet, while she went somewhere upon business, or a visit. The weather being very warm, the closet-window was left open, as well as the windows and the door of my bigger box, in which I usually lived, because of its largeness and conveniency. As I sat quietly meditating at my table, I heard something bounce in at the closet-window, and skip about from one side to the other: whereat, although I was much alarmed, yet I ventured to look out, but not stirring from my seat; and then I saw this frolicsome animal frisking and leaping up and down, till at last he came to my box, which he seemed to view with great pleasure and curiosity, peeping in at the door and every window. I retreated to the farther corner of my room; or box; but the monkey looking in at every side, put me in such a fright, that I wanted presence of mind to conceal myself under the bed, as I might easily have done. After some time spent in peeping, grinning, and chattering, he at last espied me; and reaching one of his paws in at the door, as a cat does when she plays with a mouse, although I often

shifted place to avoid him, he at length seized the lappet of my coat (which being made of that country silk, was very thick and strong), and dragged me out. He took me up in his right fore-foot and held me as a nurse does a child she is going to suckle, just as I have seen the same sort of creature do with a kitten in Europe; and when I offered to struggle he squeezed me so hard, that I thought it more prudent to submit. I have good reason to believe, that he took me for a young one of his own species, by his often stroking my face very gently with his other paw. In these diversions he was interrupted by a noise at the closet door, as if somebody were opening it: whereupon he suddenly leaped up to the window at which he had come in, and thence upon the leads and gutters, walking upon three legs, and holding me in the fourth, till he clambered up to a roof that was next to ours.

I heard Glumdalclitch give a shriek at the moment he was carrying me out. The poor girl was almost distracted: that quarter of the palace was all in an uproar; the servants ran for ladders; the monkey was seen by hundreds in the court, sitting upon the ridge of a building, holding me like a baby in one of his forepaws, and feeding me with the other, by cramming into my mouth some victuals he had squeezed out of the bag on one side of his chaps, and patting me when I would not eat; whereat many of the rabble below could not forbear laughing; neither do I think they justly ought to be blamed, for, without question, the sight was ridiculous enough to every body but myself. Some of the people threw up stones, hoping to drive the monkey down; but this was strictly

forbidden, or else, very probably, my brains had been dashed out.

The ladders were now applied, and mounted by several men; which the monkey observing, and finding himself almost encompassed, not being able to make speed enough with his three legs, let me drop on a ridge tile, and made his escape. Here I sat for some time, five hundred yards from the ground, expecting every moment to be blown down by the wind, or to fall by my own giddiness, and come tumbling over and over from the ridge to the eaves; but an honest lad, one of my nurse's footmen, climbed up, and putting me into his breeches pocket, brought me down safe.

I was almost choked with the filthy stuff the monkey had crammed down my throat: but my dear little nurse picked it out of my mouth with a small needle, and then I fell a-vomiting, which gave me great relief. Yet I was so weak and bruised in the sides with the squeezes given me by this odious animal, that I was forced to keep my bed a fortnight. The king, queen, and all the court, sent every day to inquire after my health; and her majesty made me several visits during my sickness. The monkey was killed, and an order made, that no such animal should be kept about the palace.

I was every day furnishing the court with some ridiculous story: and Glumdalclitch, although she loved me to excess, yet was arch enough to inform the queen, whenever I committed any folly that she thought would be diverting to her majesty. The girl, who had been out of order, was carried by her governess to take the air about an hour's distance, or thirty

miles from town. They alighted out of the coach near a small foot-path in a field, and Glumdalclitch setting down my travelling box, I went out of it to walk. There was a cow-dung in the path, and I must need try my activity by attempting to leap over it. I took a run, but unfortunately jumped short, and found myself just in the middle up to my knees. I waded through with some difficulty, and one of the footmen wiped me as clean as he could with his handkerchief, for I was filthily bemired; and my nurse confined me to my box, till we returned home; where the queen was soon informed of what had passed, and the footmen spread it about the court: so that all the mirth for some days was at my expense.

CHAPTER 14

I used to attend the king's levee once or twice a week, and had often seen him under the barber's hand, which indeed was at first very terrible to behold; for the razor was almost twice as long as an ordinary scythe. His majesty, according to the custom of the country, was only shaved twice a-week. I once prevailed on the barber to give me some of the suds or lather, out of which I picked forty or fifty of the strongest stumps of hair. I then took a piece of fine wood, and cut it like the back of a comb, making several holes in it at equal distances with as small a needle as I could get from Glumdalclitch. I fixed in the stumps so artificially, scraping and sloping them with my knife toward the points, that I made a very tolerable comb; which was a seasonable supply, my own being so much broken in the teeth, that it was almost useless: neither did I know any artist in that country so nice and exact, as would undertake to make me another.

And this puts me in mind of an amusement, wherein I spent many of my leisure hours. I desired the queen's woman to save for me the combings of her majesty's hair, whereof in time I got a good quantity; and consulting with my friend the cabinet-maker, who had received general orders to do little

jobs for me, I directed him to make two chair-frames, no larger than those I had in my box, and to bore little holes with a fine awl, round those parts where I designed the backs and seats; through these holes I wove the strongest hairs I could pick out, just after the manner of cane chairs in England. When they were finished, I made a present of them to her majesty; who kept them in her cabinet, and used to show them for curiosities, as indeed they were the wonder of every one that beheld them. The queen would have me sit upon one of these chairs, but I absolutely refused to obey her, protesting I would rather die than place a dishonourable part of my body on those precious hairs, that once adorned her majesty's head. Of these hairs (as I had always a mechanical genius) I likewise made a neat little purse, about five feet long, with her majesty's name deciphered in gold letters, which I gave to Glumdalclitch, by the queen's consent. To say the truth, it was more for show than use, being not of strength to bear the weight of the larger coins, and therefore she kept nothing in it but some little toys that girls are fond of.

The king, who delighted in music, had frequent concerts at court, to which I was sometimes carried, and set in my box on a table to hear them: but the noise was so great that I could hardly distinguish the tunes. I am confident that all the drums and trumpets of a royal army, beating and sounding together just at your ears, could not equal it. My practice was to have my box removed from the place where the performers sat, as far as I could, then to shut the doors and windows of it, and draw the window curtains; after which I found their

music not disagreeable.

I had learned in my youth to play a little upon the spinet. Glumdalclitch kept one in her chamber, and a master attended twice a-week to teach her: I called it a spinet, because it somewhat resembled that instrument, and was played upon in the same manner. A fancy came into my head, that I would entertain the king and queen with an English tune upon this instrument. But this appeared extremely difficult: for the spinet was near sixty feet long, each key being almost a foot wide, so that with my arms extended I could not reach to above five keys, and to press them down required a good smart stroke with my fist, which would be too great a labour, and to no purpose. The method I contrived was this: I prepared two round sticks, about the bigness of common cudgels; they were thicker at one end than the other, and I covered the thicker ends with pieces of a mouse's skin, that by rapping on them I might neither damage the tops of the keys nor interrupt the sound. Before the spinet a bench was placed, about four feet below the keys, and I was put upon the bench. I ran sideling upon it, that way and this, as fast as I could, banging the proper keys with my two sticks, and made a shift to play a jig, to the great satisfaction of both their majesties; but it was the most violent exercise I ever underwent; and yet I could not strike above sixteen keys, nor consequently play the bass and treble together, as other artists do; which was a great disadvantage to my performance.

The king, who, as I before observed, was a prince of excellent understanding, would frequently order that I should

be brought in my box, and set upon the table in his closet: he would then command me to bring one of my chairs out of the box, and sit down within three yards distance upon the top of the cabinet, which brought me almost to a level with his face. In this manner I had several conversations with him. I one day took the freedom to tell his majesty, "that the contempt he discovered towards Europe, and the rest of the world, did not seem answerable to those excellent qualities of mind that he was master of; that reason did not extend itself with the bulk of the body; on the contrary, we observed in our country, that the tallest persons were usually the least provided with it; that among other animals, bees and ants had the reputation of more industry, art, and sagacity, than many of the larger kinds; and that, as inconsiderable as he took me to be, I hoped I might live to do his majesty some signal service." The king heard me with attention, and began to conceive a much better opinion of me than he had ever before. He desired "I would give him as exact an account of the government of England as I possibly could; because, as fond as princes commonly are of their own customs (for so he conjectured of other monarchs, by my former discourses), he should be glad to hear of any thing that might deserve imitation."

I began my discourse by informing his majesty, that our dominions consisted of two islands, which composed three mighty kingdoms, under one sovereign, beside our plantations in America. I dwelt long upon the fertility of our soil, and the temperature of our climate. I then spoke at large upon the

constitution of an English parliament; partly made up of an illustrious body called the House of Peers; persons of the noblest blood, and of the most ancient and ample patrimonies. I described that extraordinary care always taken of their education in arts and arms, to qualify them for being counsellors both to the king and kingdom; to have a share in the legislature; to be members of the highest court of judicature, whence there can be no appeal; and to be champions always ready for the defence of their prince and country, by their valour, conduct, and fidelity. That these were the ornament and bulwark of the kingdom, worthy followers of their most renowned ancestors, whose honour had been the reward of their virtue, from which their posterity were never once known to degenerate. To these were joined several holy persons, as part of that assembly, under the title of bishops, whose peculiar business is to take care of religion, and of those who instruct the people therein. These were searched and sought out through the whole nation, by the prince and his wisest counsellors, among such of the priesthood as were most deservedly distinguished by the sanctity of their lives, and the depth of their erudition; who were indeed the spiritual fathers of the clergy and the people.

That the other part of the parliament consisted of an assembly called the House of Commons, who were all principal gentlemen, freely picked and culled out by the people themselves, for their great abilities and love of their country, to represent the wisdom of the whole nation. And that these two bodies made up the most august assembly in

Europe; to whom, in conjunction with the prince, the whole legislature is committed.

I then descended to the courts of justice; over which the judges, those venerable sages and interpreters of the law, presided, for determining the disputed rights and properties of men, as well as for the punishment of vice and protection of innocence. I mentioned the prudent management of our treasury; the valour and achievements of our forces, by sea and land. I computed the number of our people, by reckoning how many millions there might be of each religious sect, or political party among us. I did not omit even our sports and pastimes, or any other particular which I thought might redound to the honour of my country. And I finished all with a brief historical account of affairs and events in England for about a hundred years past.

This conversation was not ended under five audiences, each of several hours; and the king heard the whole with great attention, frequently taking notes of what I spoke, as well as memorandums of what questions he intended to ask me.

He then desired to know, "What arts were practised in electing those whom I called commoners: whether a stranger, with a strong purse, might not influence the vulgar voters to choose him before their own landlord, or the most considerable gentleman in the neighbourhood? How it came to pass, that people were so violently bent upon getting into this assembly, which I allowed to be a great trouble and expense, often to the ruin of their families, without any salary or pension? because this appeared such an exalted strain of

virtue and public spirit, that his majesty seemed to doubt it might possibly not be always sincere." And he desired to know, "Whether such zealous gentlemen could have any views of refunding themselves for the charges and trouble they were at by sacrificing the public good to the designs of a weak and vicious prince, in conjunction with a corrupted ministry?" He multiplied his questions, and sifted me thoroughly upon every part of this head, proposing numberless inquiries and objections, which I think it not prudent or convenient to repeat.

Upon what I said in relation to our courts of justice, his majesty desired to be satisfied in several points: and this I was the better able to do, having been formerly almost ruined by a long suit in chancery, which was decreed for me with costs. He asked, "What time was usually spent in determining between right and wrong, and what degree of expense? Whether advocates and orators had liberty to plead in causes manifestly known to be unjust, vexatious, or oppressive? Whether party, in religion or politics, were observed to be of any weight in the scale of justice? Whether those pleading orators were persons educated in the general knowledge of equity, or only in provincial, national, and other local customs? Whether they or their judges had any part in penning those laws, which they assumed the liberty of interpreting, and glossing upon at their pleasure? Whether they had ever, at different times, pleaded for and against the same cause, and cited precedents to prove contrary opinions? Whether they were a rich or a poor corporation? Whether

they received any pecuniary reward for pleading, or delivering their opinions? And particularly, whether they were ever admitted as members in the lower senate?"

He fell next upon the management of our treasury; and said, "he thought my memory had failed me, because I computed our taxes at about five or six millions a-year, and when I came to mention the issues, he found they sometimes amounted to more than double; for the notes he had taken were very particular in this point, because he hoped, as he told me, that the knowledge of our conduct might be useful to him, and he could not be deceived in his calculations. But, if what I told him were true, he was still at a loss how a kingdom could run out of its estate, like a private person." He asked me, "who were our creditors; and where we found money to pay them?" He wondered to hear me talk of such chargeable and expensive wars; "that certainly we must be a quarrelsome people, or live among very bad neighbours, and that our generals must needs be richer than our kings." He asked, what business we had out of our own islands, unless upon the score of trade, or treaty, or to defend the coasts with our fleet?" Above all, he was amazed to hear me talk of a mercenary standing army, in the midst of peace, and among a free people. He said, "if we were governed by our own consent, in the persons of our representatives, he could not imagine of whom we were afraid, or against whom we were to fight; and would hear my opinion, whether a private man's house might not be better defended by himself, his children, and family, than by half-a-dozen rascals, picked up at a

venture in the streets for small wages, who might get a hundred times more by cutting their throats?"

He laughed at my "odd kind of arithmetic," as he was pleased to call it, "in reckoning the numbers of our people, by a computation drawn from the several sects among us, in religion and politics." He said, "he knew no reason why those, who entertain opinions prejudicial to the public, should be obliged to change, or should not be obliged to conceal them. And as it was tyranny in any government to require the first, so it was weakness not to enforce the second: for a man may be allowed to keep poisons in his closet, but not to vend them about for cordials."

He observed, "that among the diversions of our nobility and gentry, I had mentioned gaming: he desired to know at what age this entertainment was usually taken up, and when it was laid down; how much of their time it employed; whether it ever went so high as to affect their fortunes; whether mean, vicious people, by their dexterity in that art, might not arrive at great riches, and sometimes keep our very nobles in dependence, as well as habituate them to vile companions, wholly take them from the improvement of their minds, and force them, by the losses they received, to learn and practise that infamous dexterity upon others?"

He was perfectly astonished with the historical account gave him of our affairs during the last century; protesting "it was only a heap of conspiracies, rebellions, murders, massacres, revolutions, banishments, the very worst effects that avarice, faction, hypocrisy, perfidiousness, cruelty, rage,

madness, hatred, envy, lust, malice, and ambition, could produce."

His majesty, in another audience, was at the pains to recapitulate the sum of all I had spoken; compared the questions he made with the answers I had given; then taking me into his hands, and stroking me gently, delivered himself in these words, which I shall never forget, nor the manner he spoke them in: "My little friend Grildrig, you have made a most admirable panegyric upon your country; you have clearly proved, that ignorance, idleness, and vice, are the proper ingredients for qualifying a legislator; that laws are best explained, interpreted, and applied, by those whose interest and abilities lie in perverting, confounding, and eluding them. I observe among you some lines of an institution, which, in its original, might have been tolerable, but these half erased, and the rest wholly blurred and blotted by corruptions. It does not appear, from all you have said, how any one perfection is required toward the procurement of any one station among you; much less, that men are ennobled on account of their virtue; that priests are advanced for their piety or learning; soldiers, for their conduct or valour; judges, for their integrity; senators, for the love of their country; or counsellors for their wisdom. As for yourself," continued the king, "who have spent the greatest part of your life in travelling, I am well disposed to hope you may hitherto have escaped many vices of your country. But by what I have gathered from your own relation, and the answers I have with much pains wrung and extorted from you, I cannot but

conclude the bulk of your natives to be the most pernicious race of little odious vermin that nature ever suffered to crawl upon the surface of the earth."

CHAPTER 15

To confirm what I have now said, and further to show the miserable effects of a confined education, I shall here insert a passage, which will hardly obtain belief. In hopes to ingratiate myself further into his majesty's favour, I told him of "an invention, discovered between three and four hundred years ago, to make a certain powder, into a heap of which, the smallest spark of fire falling, would kindle the whole in a moment, although it were as big as a mountain, and make it all fly up in the air together, with a noise and agitation greater than thunder. That a proper quantity of this powder rammed into a hollow tube of brass or iron, according to its bigness, would drive a ball of iron or lead, with such violence and speed, as nothing was able to sustain its force. That the largest balls thus discharged, would not only destroy whole ranks of an army at once, but batter the strongest walls to the ground, sink down ships, with a thousand men in each, to the bottom of the sea, and when linked together by a chain, would cut through masts and rigging, divide hundreds of bodies in the middle, and lay all waste before them. That we often put this powder into large hollow balls of iron, and discharged them by an engine into some city we were besieging, which would

rip up the pavements, tear the houses to pieces, burst and throw splinters on every side, dashing out the brains of all who came near. That I knew the ingredients very well, which were cheap and common; I understood the manner of compounding them, and could direct his workmen how to make those tubes, of a size proportionable to all other things in his majesty's kingdom, and the largest need not be above a hundred feet long; twenty or thirty of which tubes, charged with the proper quantity of powder and balls, would batter down the walls of the strongest town in his dominions in a few hours, or destroy the whole metropolis, if ever it should pretend to dispute his absolute commands." This I humbly offered to his majesty, as a small tribute of acknowledgment, in turn for so many marks that I had received, of his royal favour and protection.

The king was struck with horror at the description I had given of those terrible engines, and the proposal I had made. "He was amazed, how so impotent and grovelling an insect as I" (these were his expressions) "could entertain such inhuman ideas, and in so familiar a manner, as to appear wholly unmoved at all the scenes of blood and desolation which I had painted as the common effects of those destructive machines; whereof," he said, "some evil genius, enemy to mankind, must have been the first contriver. As for himself, he protested, that although few things delighted him so much as new discoveries in art or in nature, yet he would rather lose half his kingdom, than be privy to such a secret; which he commanded me, as I valued any life, never to mention any more."

A strange effect of narrow principles and views! that a prince possessed of every quality which procures veneration, love, and esteem; of strong parts, great wisdom, and profound learning, endowed with admirable talents, and almost adored by his subjects, should, from a nice, unnecessary scruple, whereof in Europe we can have no conception, let slip an opportunity put into his hands that would have made him absolute master of the lives, the liberties, and the fortunes of his people! Neither do I say this, with the least intention to detract from the many virtues of that excellent king, whose character, I am sensible, will, on this account, be very much lessened in the opinion of an English reader: but I take this defect among them to have risen from their ignorance, by not having hitherto reduced politics into a science, as the more acute wits of Europe have done.

For, I remember very well, in a discourse one day with the king, when I happened to say, "there were several thousand books among us written upon the art of government," it gave him (directly contrary to my intention) a very mean opinion of our understandings. He professed both to abominate and despise all mystery, refinement, and intrigue, either in a prince or a minister. He could not tell what I meant by secrets of state, where an enemy, or some rival nation, were not in the case. He confined the knowledge of governing within very narrow bounds, to common sense and reason, to justice and lenity, to the speedy determination of civil and criminal causes; with some other obvious topics, which are not worth considering. And he gave it for his

opinion, "that whoever could make two ears of corn, or two blades of grass, to grow upon a spot of ground where only one grew before, would deserve better of mankind, and do more essential service to his country, than the whole race of politicians put together."

They have had the art of printing, as well as the Chinese, time out of mind: but their libraries are not very large; for that of the king, which is reckoned the largest, does not amount to above a thousand volumes, placed in a gallery of twelve hundred feet long, whence I had liberty to borrow what books I pleased. The queen's joiner had contrived in one of Glumdalclitch's rooms, a kind of wooden machine five-and-twenty feet high, formed like a standing ladder; the steps were each fifty feet long. It was indeed a moveable pair of stairs, the lowest end placed at ten feet distance from the wall of the chamber. The book I had a mind to read, was put up leaning against the wall: I first mounted to the upper step of the ladder, and turning my face towards the book, began at the top of the page, and so walking to the right and left about eight or ten paces, according to the length of the lines, till I had gotten a little below the level of mine eyes, and then descending gradually till I came to the bottom: after which I mounted again, and began the other page in the same manner, and so turned over the leaf, which I could easily do with both my hands, for it was as thick and stiff as a pasteboard, and in the largest folios not above eighteen or twenty feet long.

Their style is clear, masculine, and smooth, but not florid; for they avoid nothing more than multiplying unnecessary

words, or using various expressions. I have perused many of their books, especially those in history and morality. Among the rest, I was much diverted with a little old treatise, which always lay in Glumdalclitch's bed chamber, and belonged to her governess, a grave elderly gentlewoman, who dealt in writings of morality and devotion. The book treats of the weakness of human kind, and is in little esteem, except among the women and the vulgar.

However, I was curious to see what an author of that country could say upon such a subject. This writer went through all the usual topics of European moralists, showing "how diminutive, contemptible, and helpless an animal was man in his own nature; how unable to defend himself from inclemencies of the air, or the fury of wild beasts: how much he was excelled by one creature in strength, by another in speed, by a third in foresight, by a fourth in industry."

He added, "that nature was degenerated in these latter declining ages of the world, and could now produce only small abortive births, in comparison of those in ancient times." He said "it was very reasonable to think, not only that the species of men were originally much larger, but also that there must have been giants in former ages; which, as it is asserted by history and tradition, so it has been confirmed by huge bones and skulls, casually dug up in several parts of the kingdom, far exceeding the common dwindled race of men in our days." He argued, "that the very laws of nature absolutely required we should have been made, in the beginning of a size more large and robust; not so liable to destruction from every

little accident, of a tile falling from a house, or a stone cast from the hand of a boy, or being drowned in a little brook." From this way of reasoning, the author drew several moral applications, useful in the conduct of life, but needless here to repeat. For my own part, I could not avoid reflecting how universally this talent was spread, of drawing lectures in morality, or indeed rather matter of discontent and repining, from the quarrels we raise with nature. And I believe, upon a strict inquiry, those quarrels might be shown as ill-grounded among us as they are among that people.

As to their military affairs, they boast that the king's army consists of a hundred and seventy-six thousand foot, and thirty-two thousand horse: if that may be called an army, which is made up of tradesmen in the several cities, and farmers in the country, whose commanders are only the nobility and gentry, without pay or reward. They are indeed perfect enough in their exercises, and under very good discipline, wherein I saw no great merit; for how should it be otherwise, where every farmer is under the command of his own landlord, and every citizen under that of the principal men in his own city, chosen after the manner of Venice, by ballot?

I have often seen the militia of Lorbrulgrud drawn out to exercise, in a great field near the city of twenty miles square. They were in all not above twenty-five thousand foot, and six thousand horse; but it was impossible for me to compute their number, considering the space of ground they took up. A cavalier, mounted on a large steed, might be about ninety

feet high. I have seen this whole body of horse, upon a word of command, draw their swords at once, and brandish them in the air. Imagination can figure nothing so grand, so surprising, and so astonishing! it looked as if ten thousand flashes of lightning were darting at the same time from every quarter of the sky.

I was curious to know how this prince, to whose dominions there is no access from any other country, came to think of armies, or to teach his people the practice of military discipline. But I was soon informed, both by conversation and reading their histories; for, in the course of many ages, they have been troubled with the same disease to which the whole race of mankind is subject; the nobility often contending for power, the people for liberty, and the king for absolute dominion. All which, however happily tempered by the laws of that kingdom, have been sometimes violated by each of the three parties, and have more than once occasioned civil wars; the last whereof was happily put an end to by this prince's grand-father, in a general composition; and the militia, then settled with common consent, has been ever since kept in the strictest duty.

CHAPTER 16

I had always a strong impulse that I should some time recover my liberty, though it was impossible to conjecture by what means, or to form any project with the least hope of succeeding. The ship in which I sailed, was the first ever known to be driven within sight of that coast, and the king had given strict orders, that if at any time another appeared, it should be taken ashore, and with all its crew and passengers brought in a tumbril to Lorbrulgrud. He was strongly bent to get me a woman of my own size, by whom I might propagate the breed: but I think I should rather have died than undergone the disgrace of leaving a posterity to be kept in cages, like tame canary-birds, and perhaps, in time, sold about the kingdom, to persons of quality, for curiosities. I was indeed treated with much kindness: I was the favourite of a great king and queen, and the delight of the whole court; but it was upon such a foot as ill became the dignity of humankind. I could never forget those domestic pledges I had left behind me. I wanted to be among people, with whom I could converse upon even terms, and walk about the streets and fields without being afraid of being trod to death like a frog or a young puppy. But my deliverance came sooner than

I expected, and in a manner not very common; the whole story and circumstances of which I shall faithfully relate.

I had now been two years in this country; and about the beginning of the third, Glumdalclitch and I attended the king and queen, in a progress to the south coast of the kingdom. I was carried, as usual, in my travelling-box, which as I have already described, was a very convenient closet, of twelve feet wide. And I had ordered a hammock to be fixed, by silken ropes from the four corners at the top, to break the jolts, when a servant carried me before him on horseback, as I sometimes desired; and would often sleep in my hammock, while we were upon the road. On the roof of my closet, not directly over the middle of the hammock, I ordered the joiner to cut out a hole of a foot square, to give me air in hot weather, as I slept; which hole I shut at pleasure with a board that drew backward and forward through a groove.

When we came to our journey's end, the king thought proper to pass a few days at a palace he has near Flanflasnic, a city within eighteen English miles of the seaside. Glumdalclitch and I were much fatigued: I had gotten a small cold, but the poor girl was so ill as to be confined to her chamber. I longed to see the ocean, which must be the only scene of my escape, if ever it should happen. I pretended to be worse than I really was, and desired leave to take the fresh air of the sea, with a page, whom I was very fond of, and who had sometimes been trusted with me. I shall never forget with what unwillingness Glumdalclitch consented, nor the strict charge she gave the page to be careful of me, bursting at the

same time into a flood of tears, as if she had some forboding of what was to happen.

The boy took me out in my box, about half an hours walk from the palace, towards the rocks on the sea-shore. I ordered him to set me down, and lifting up one of my sashes, cast many a wistful melancholy look towards the sea. I found myself not very well, and told the page that I had a mind to take a nap in my hammock, which I hoped would do me good. I got in, and the boy shut the window close down, to keep out the cold. I soon fell asleep, and all I can conjecture is, while I slept, the page, thinking no danger could happen, went among the rocks to look for birds' eggs, having before observed him from my window searching about, and picking up one or two in the clefts.

After a while, I found myself suddenly awaked with a violent pull upon the ring, which was fastened at the top of my box for the conveniency of carriage. I felt my box raised very high in the air, and then borne forward with prodigious speed. The first jolt had like to have shaken me out of my hammock, but afterward the motion was easy enough. I called out several times, as loud as I could raise my voice, but all to no purpose. I looked towards my windows, and could see nothing but the clouds and sky. I heard a noise just over my head, like the clapping of wings, and then began to perceive the woful condition I was in; that some eagle had got the ring of my box in his beak, with an intent to let it fall on a rock, like a tortoise in a shell, and then pick out my body, and devour it: for the sagacity and smell of this bird enables him

to discover his quarry at a great distance, though better concealed than I could be within a two-inch board.

In a little time, I observed the noise and flutter of wings to increase very fast, and my box was tossed up and down, like a sign in a windy day. I heard several bangs or buffets, as I thought given to the eagle (for such I am certain it must have been that held the ring of my box in his beak), and then, all on a sudden, felt myself falling perpendicularly down, for above a minute, but with such incredible swiftness, that I almost lost my breath. My fall was stopped by a terrible squash, that sounded louder to my ears than the cataract of Niagara; after which, I was quite in the dark for another minute, and then my box began to rise so high, that I could see light from the tops of the windows. I now perceived I was fallen into the sea. My box, by the weight of my body, the goods that were in, and the broad plates of iron fixed for strength at the four corners of the top and bottom, floated about five feet deep in water. I did then, and do now suppose, that the eagle which flew away with my box was pursued by two or three others, and forced to let me drop, while he defended himself against the rest, who hoped to share in the prey. The plates of iron fastened at the bottom of the box (for those were the strongest) preserved the balance while it fell, and hindered it from being broken on the surface of the water. Every joint of it was well grooved; and the door did not move on hinges, but up and down like a sash, which kept my closet so tight that very little water came in. I got with much difficulty out of my hammock, having first ventured to

draw back the slip-board on the roof already mentioned, contrived on purpose to let in air, for want of which I found myself almost stifled.

How often did I then wish myself with my dear Glumdalclitch, from whom one single hour had so far divided me! And I may say with truth, that in the midst of my own misfortunes I could not forbear lamenting my poor nurse, the grief she would suffer for my loss, the displeasure of the queen, and the ruin of her fortune. Perhaps many travellers have not been under greater difficulties and distress than I was at this juncture, expecting every moment to see my box dashed to pieces, or at least overset by the first violent blast, or rising wave. A breach in one single pane of glass would have been immediate death: nor could any thing have preserved the windows, but the strong lattice wires placed on the outside, against accidents in travelling. I saw the water ooze in at several crannies, although the leaks were not considerable, and I endeavoured to stop them as well as I could. I was not able to lift up the roof of my closet, which otherwise I certainly should have done, and sat on the top of it; where I might at least preserve myself some hours longer, than by being shut up (as I may call it) in the hold. Or if I escaped these dangers for a day or two, what could I expect but a miserable death of cold and hunger? I was four hours under these circumstances, expecting, and indeed wishing, every moment to be my last.

Being in this disconsolate state, I heard, or at least thought I heard, some kind of grating noise on that side of

my box where the staples were fixed; and soon after I began to fancy that the box was pulled or towed along the sea; for I now and then felt a sort of tugging, which made the waves rise near the tops of my windows, leaving me almost in the dark. This gave me some faint hopes of relief, although I was not able to imagine how it could be brought about. I ventured to unscrew one of my chairs, which were always fastened to the floor; and having made a hard shift to screw it down again, directly under the slipping-board that I had lately opened, I mounted on the chair, and putting my mouth as near as I could to the hole, I called for help in a loud voice, and in all the languages I understood. I then fastened my handkerchief to a stick I usually carried, and thrusting it up the hole, waved it several times in the air, that if any boat or ship were near, the seamen might conjecture some unhappy mortal to be shut up in the box.

I found no effect from all I could do, but plainly perceived my closet to be moved along; and in the space of an hour, or better, that side of the box where the staples were, and had no windows, struck against something that was hard. I apprehended it to be a rock, and found myself tossed more than ever. I plainly heard a noise upon the cover of my closet, like that of a cable, and the grating of it as it passed through the ring. I then found myself hoisted up, by degrees, at least three feet higher than I was before. Whereupon I again thrust up my stick and handkerchief, calling for help till I was almost hoarse. In return to which, I heard a great shout repeated three times, giving me such transports of joy as are not to be

conceived but by those who feel them. I now heard a trampling over my head, and somebody calling through the hole with a loud voice, in the English tongue, "If there be any body below, let them speak." I answered, "I was an Englishman, drawn by ill fortune into the greatest calamity that ever any creature underwent, and begged, by all that was moving, to be delivered out of the dungeon I was in." The voice replied, "I was safe, for my box was fastened to their ship; and the carpenter should immediately come and saw a hole in the cover, large enough to pull me out." I answered, "that was needless, and would take up too much time; for there was no more to be done, but let one of the crew put his finger into the ring, and take the box out of the sea into the ship, and so into the captain's cabin." Some of them, upon hearing me talk so wildly, thought I was mad: others laughed; for indeed it never came into my head, that I was now got among people of my own stature and strength. The carpenter came, and in a few minutes sawed a passage about four feet square, then let down a small ladder, upon which I mounted, and thence was taken into the ship in a very weak condition.

The sailors were all in amazement, and asked me a thousand questions, which I had no inclination to answer. I was equally confounded at the sight of so many pigmies, for such I took them to be, after having so long accustomed mine eyes to the monstrous objects I had left. But the captain, observing I was ready to faint, took me into his cabin, gave me a cordial to comfort me, and made me turn in upon his own bed, advising me to take a little rest, of which I had great

need. Before I went to sleep, I gave him to understand that I had some valuable furniture in my box, too good to be lost: a fine hammock, a handsome field-bed, two chairs, a table, and a cabinet; that my closet was hung on all sides, or rather quilted, with silk and cotton; that if he would let one of the crew bring my closet into his cabin, I would open it there before him, and show him my goods. The captain, going upon deck, sent some of his men down into my closet, whence (as I afterwards found) they drew up all my goods, and stripped off the quilting; but the chairs, cabinet, and bedstead, being screwed to the floor, were much damaged by the ignorance of the seamen, who tore them up by force. Then they knocked off some of the boards for the use of the ship, and when they had got all they had a mind for, let the hull drop into the sea.

I slept some hours, but perpetually disturbed with dreams of the place I had left, and the dangers I had escaped. However, upon waking, I found myself much recovered. It was now about eight o'clock at night, and the captain ordered supper immediately, thinking I had already fasted too long. He entertained me with great kindness, observing me not to look wildly, or talk inconsistently: and, when we were left alone, desired I would give him a relation of my travels, and by what accident I came to be set adrift, in that monstrous wooden chest. He said "that about twelve o'clock at noon, as he was looking through his glass, he spied it at a distance, and thought it was a sail, which he had a mind to make, being not much out of his course, in hopes of buying some biscuit, his

own beginning to fall short. That upon coming nearer, and finding his error, he sent out his long-boat to discover what it was; that his men came back in a fright, swearing they had seen a swimming house. That he laughed at their folly, and went himself in the boat, ordering his men to take a strong cable along with them. That the weather being calm, he rowed round me several times, observed my windows and wire lattices that defended them. That he discovered two staples upon one side, which was all of boards, without any passage for light. He then commanded his men to row up to that side, and fastening a cable to one of the staples, ordered them to tow my chest, as they called it, toward the ship. When it was there, he gave directions to fasten another cable to the ring fixed in the cover, and to raise up my chest with pulleys, which all the sailors were not able to do above two or three feet." He said, "they saw my stick and handkerchief thrust out of the hole, and concluded that some unhappy man must be shut up in the cavity." I asked, "whether he or the crew had seen any prodigious birds in the air, about the time he first discovered me." To which he answered, that discoursing this matter with the sailors while I was asleep, one of them said, he had observed three eagles flying towards the north, but remarked nothing of their being larger than the usual size:" which I suppose must be imputed to the great height they were at; and he could not guess the reason of my question.

I then asked the captain, "how far he reckoned we might be from land?" He said, "by the best computation he could make, we were at least a hundred leagues." I assured him,

"that he must be mistaken by almost half, for I had not left the country whence I came above two hours before I dropped into the sea." Whereupon he began again to think that my brain was disturbed, of which he gave me a hint, and advised me to go to bed in a cabin he had provided. I assured him, "I was well refreshed with his good entertainment and company, and as much in my senses as ever I was in my life." He then grew serious, and desired to ask me freely, "whether I were not troubled in my mind by the consciousness of some enormous crime, for which I was punished, at the command of some prince, by exposing me in that chest; as great criminals, in other countries, have been forced to sea in a leaky vessel, without provisions: for although he should be sorry to have taken so ill a man into his ship, yet he would engage his word to set me safe ashore, in the first port where we arrived." He added, "that his suspicions were much increased by some very absurd speeches I had delivered at first to his sailors, and afterwards to himself, in relation to my closet or chest, as well as by my odd looks and behaviour while I was at supper."

I begged his patience to hear me tell my story, which I faithfully did, from the last time I left England, to the moment he first discovered me. And, as truth always forces its way into rational minds, so this honest worthy gentleman, who had some tincture of learning, and very good sense, was immediately convinced of my candour and veracity. But further to confirm all I had said, I entreated him to give order that my cabinet should be brought, of which I had the key in

my pocket; for he had already informed me how the seamen disposed of my closet. I opened it in his own presence, and showed him the small collection of rarities I made in the country from which I had been so strangely delivered. There was the comb I had contrived out of the stumps of the king's beard, and another of the same materials, but fixed into a paring of her majesty's thumb-nail, which served for the back. There was a collection of needles and pins, from a foot to half a yard long; four wasp stings, like joiner's tacks; some combings of the queen's hair; a gold ring, which one day she made me a present of, in a most obliging manner, taking it from her little finger, and throwing it over my head like a collar. I desired the captain would please to accept this ring in return for his civilities; which he absolutely refused. I showed him a corn that I had cut off with my own hand, from a maid of honour's toe; it was about the bigness of Kentish pippin, and grown so hard, that when I returned England, I got it hollowed into a cup, and set in silver. Lastly, I desired him to see the breeches I had then on, which were made of a mouse's skin.

I could force nothing on him but a footman's tooth, which I observed him to examine with great curiosity, and found he had a fancy for it. He received it with abundance of thanks, more than such a trifle could deserve. It was drawn by an unskilful surgeon, in a mistake, from one of Glumdalclitch's men, who was afflicted with the tooth-ache, but it was as sound as any in his head. I got it cleaned, and put it into my cabinet. It was about a foot long, and four inches in

diameter.

The captain was very well satisfied with this plain relation I had given him, and said, "he hoped, when we returned to England, I would oblige the world by putting it on paper, and making it public." My answer was, "that we were overstocked with books of travels: that nothing could now pass which was not extraordinary; wherein I doubted some authors less consulted truth, than their own vanity, or interest, or the diversion of ignorant readers; that my story could contain little beside common events, without those ornamental descriptions of strange plants, trees, birds, and other animals; or of the barbarous customs and idolatry of savage people, with which most writers abound. However, I thanked him for his good opinion, and promised to take the matter into my thoughts."

He said "he wondered at one thing very much, which was, to hear me speak so loud;" asking me "whether the king or queen of that country were thick of hearing?" I told him, "it was what I had been used to for above two years past, and that I admired as much at the voices of him and his men, who seemed to me only to whisper, and yet I could hear them well enough. But, when I spoke in that country, it was like a man talking in the streets, to another looking out from the top of a steeple, unless when I was placed on a table, or held in any person's hand." I told him, "I had likewise observed another thing, that, when I first got into the ship, and the sailors stood all about me, I thought they were the most little contemptible creatures I had ever beheld." For indeed, while I was in that

prince's country, I could never endure to look in a glass, after mine eyes had been accustomed to such prodigious objects, because the comparison gave me so despicable a conceit of myself. The captain said, "that while we were at supper, he observed me to look at every thing with a sort of wonder, and that I often seemed hardly able to contain my laughter, which he knew not well how to take, but imputed it to some disorder in my brain."

I answered, "it was very true; and I wondered how I could forbear, when I saw his dishes of the size of a silver three-pence, a leg of pork hardly a mouthful, a cup not so big as a nut-shell;" and so I went on, describing the rest of his household-stuff and provisions, after the same manner. For, although he queen had ordered a little equipage of all things necessary for me, while I was in her service, yet my ideas were wholly taken up with what I saw on every side of me, and I winked at my own littleness, as people do at their own faults. The captain understood my raillery very well, and merrily replied with the old English proverb, "that he doubted mine eyes were bigger than my belly, for he did not observe my stomach so good, although I had fasted all day;" and, continuing in his mirth, protested "he would have gladly given a hundred pounds, to have seen my closet in the eagle's bill, and afterwards in its fall from so great a height into the sea; which would certainly have been a most astonishing object, worthy to have the description of it transmitted to future ages:" and the comparison of Phaëton was so obvious, that he could not forbear applying it, although I did not much admire

the conceit.

The captain having been at Tonquin, was, in his return to England. I offered to leave my goods in security for payment of my freight: but the captain protested he would not receive one farthing. We took a kind leave of each other, and I made him promise he would come to see me at my house in Redriff. I hired a horse and guide for five shillings, which I borrowed of the captain.

As I was on the road, observing the littleness of the houses, the trees, the cattle, and the people, I began to think myself in Lilliput. I was afraid of trampling on every traveller I met, and often called aloud to have them stand out of the way, so that I had like to have gotten one or two broken heads for my impertinence.

When I came to my own house, for which I was forced to inquire, one of the servants opening the door, I bent down to go in, (like a goose under a gate,) for fear of striking my head. My wife run out to embrace me, but I stooped lower than her knees, thinking she could otherwise never be able to reach my mouth. My daughter kneeled to ask my blessing, but I could not see her till she arose, having been so long used to stand with my head and eyes erect to above sixty feet; and then I went to take her up with one hand by the waist. I looked down upon the servants, and one or two friends who were in the house, as if they had been pigmies and I a giant. I told my wife, "she had been too thrifty, for I found she had starved herself and her daughter to nothing." In short, I behaved myself so unaccountably, that they were all of the

captain's opinion when he first saw me, and concluded I had lost my wits. This I mention as an instance of the great power of habit and prejudice.

國家圖書館出版品預行編目資料

格列佛遊記（中英雙語典藏版）／強納森・史威夫
特(Jonathan Swift) 作；張惠凌譯；黃郁菱繪.-- 初版
-- 臺中市：晨星，2020.11　　面；　公分. --（愛藏
本；103）
中英雙語典藏版
譯自：Gulliver's Travels
ISBN 978-986-5529-80-2（精裝）

873.596　　　　　　　　　　　　　　109016261

愛藏本：103

格列佛遊記（中英雙語典藏版）
Gulliver's Travels

填寫線上回函，立刻享有
晨星網路書店50元購書金

作者｜強納森・史威夫特 (Jonathan Swift)
繪者｜黃郁菱
譯者｜張惠凌

責任編輯｜呂曉婕
封面設計｜鐘文君
文字編潤｜呂曉婕、謝宜真

負責人｜陳銘民
發行所｜晨星出版有限公司
　　　　行政院新聞局局版台業字第 2500 號
總經銷｜知己圖書股份有限公司
地址｜台北市 106 辛亥路一段 30 號 9 樓
　　　TEL：02-23672044／23672047　FAX：02-23635741
　　　台中市 407 工業 30 路 1 號
　　　TEL：04-23595819　FAX：04-23595493
E-mail｜service@morningstar.com.tw
晨星網路書店｜www.morningstar.com.tw
法律顧問｜陳思成律師
郵政劃撥｜15060393　知己圖書股份有限公司
讀者服務專線｜04-2359-5819#230

印刷｜上好印刷股份有限公司

出版日期｜2020 年 11 月 15 日
定價｜新台幣 260 元
ISBN 978-986-5529-80-2